THE
UNKILLABLES

J. Boyett

SALTIMBANQUE BOOKS

NEW YORK

The Unkillables

BY THE SAME AUTHOR

Brothel

Ricky

The Little Mermaid: A Horror Story

Ironheart

Stewart and Jean

The Victim (and Other Short Plays)

Poisoned (a play)

For Mary Sheridan.
For Pam Carter, Dawn Drinkwater, and Andy Shanks.

Acknowledgments

Many thanks to Kelly Kay Griffith and Rob Widdicombe for having read the manuscript and given valuable advice.

And thanks to you for reading! Please consider visiting me at www.jboyett.net and signing up for my mailing list.

The Unkillables

One

It was customary among the People to always keep a slave-woman like Gash-Eye. (Gash-Eye was what they called her—in her own tongue, in her girlhood, she'd been named Petal-Drift.) The People believed that, because Gash-Eye's race was closer to the earth and the dirt, she could see more clearly into the secret spaces as well as the spirit world. Gash-Eye believed that, too. It was definitely true that she could see better in this world than her captors could. At night, she could see a bat against the sky, where they could at most see a patch of black darker than the rest.

The name Gash-Eye came from the thick scar which ran down her forehead to her jutting brow, then resumed down her cheek below her eye. It was there to remind her that, if she didn't use her greater sight to serve her masters, she would be left with no sight at all. Every time the People took a new seer-captive, they named her Gash-Eye.

The threat of being blinded and left to die in the forest was one way the People held her in check. The other was by fathering upon her a child; if she disobeyed too egregiously, they told her, then her son would be killed, and his eye sockets, nostrils, mouth, and anus would be plugged with packed mud so that his spirit would be unable to escape, and would be forced to feed on itself throughout all the wheels of eternity. And sometimes they would invent still other fates to threaten him with, if inspiration struck.

It was her son that held her; many were the days that being blinded and left to die in the forest didn't sound so bad to Gash-Eye. Because her son held her, he was called the Jaw. The child fathered upon the Gash-Eye was always called the Jaw. This one had been fathered by Chert, one of the People's best hunters, a strong man who kept his own counsel. Since fathering the Jaw upon her, Chert had rarely spoken to Gash-Eye. He prided himself on his tracking abilities and didn't wish the aid of her eyesight; as for what she might see in the spirit world, he had no interest in that at all.

One night in spring Gash-Eye was sitting in the dark beyond the People's fires, keeping watch. The fires were over the top of the small hill, on the opposite slope. This was just after the weather had turned sweet, and she let her mind wander, her thoughts reminding her of her old name she'd not heard since the People had killed her band and captured her, years ago.

The People had been at this site for several moons. Usually they would have moved along by now, but this soft grassy hill surrounded by rich forest was such a fine spot that perhaps they would stay till someone or something more dangerous came and drove them off. On the slope of the hill were several boulders—Gash-Eye was looking down into the valley from behind one now—and higher up was the mouth of a cave where the People had kept warm through much of the winter.

Night had almost completely fallen, but there was a big bright moon. Gash-Eye saw movement in the distant trees below. She gave the signal, a sound that would be taken by the uninitiated for birdsong.

Instantly young Pebble was by her side. "What is it, Gash-Eye?" he whispered, enjoying the game of secrecy. It wasn't fair that Gash-Eye had to keep watch so quietly, always acting as if they were being tracked and hunted, when on the opposite slope of the hill the People were talking and singing softly at the fires.

They were quieter than usual, true, because about a quarter of the men were still recovering from the Mushroom of the Inner Eye, which sent the hunters on brief tours into the underworld; it was a way to make sure the underworld was calm, so that the animals they sent there would not become agitated and come back seeking vengeance for their deaths. After returning from the voyage, the hunters felt nauseous and lazy, which was why no more than a quarter ever took it at once.... Of course, when they wanted Gash-Eye to check on the state of things in the spirit realm they made her eat twice as much, since her whole purpose was to see into secret places, and they only ever gave her half as much time to recover. Such was her lot in life.

"Something moving," she whispered, in answer to Pebble's question. No matter how many years she spent with the People, she would never be able to pronounce their language correctly—the shape of her mouth wouldn't allow it. Meanwhile, she felt the sounds of her girlhood tongue slipping from her memory as years passed. Squinting into the trees, she said, "People."

Pebble turned his face uphill and gave a quick whistle; the talking and singing was cut short. Turning back to Gash-Eye, Pebble hissed, "How many?"

"I can't tell from up here."

Some of the lead hunters came racing from the other slope, Chert among them. They hid behind Gash-Eye's boulder. "What did she see?" asked Chert, not bothering to look at her.

"People," said Pebble. "She can't see how many."

"Where are they, Gash-Eye?" Even speaking directly to her, Chert didn't bother to look at her.

She pointed at the spot in the trees where she could still make out some movement. The others stared, and finally shook their heads.

"Too far," said one. "Too dark."

Chert slipped noiselessly down the hill to reconnoitre. Gash-Eye knew that he would be able to get close enough to see them, without them ever hearing. Gash-Eye felt little affection for Chert, but she did harbor a grudging respect. And the hatred she'd once borne him had been mitigated by the way he treated the Jaw. She was sure that past fathers of past Jaws had not cared enough even to spit on their spawn. But Chert protected the half-breed from many torments that would otherwise have been his birthright.

They sat watching. Gash-Eye looked closely, ready to let her masters know if she saw anything else worth reporting. She could make out Chert's progress down the hillside, though she doubted the others could. Soon he would disappear into the trees and hide himself as he crept closer to the band of strangers.

Suddenly Gash-Eye, Pebble, and the hunters gasped as a green light appeared in the stand of trees.

"I see the people!" said Pebble. All of them could see them now.

"Quiet," ordered one of the men, but then he himself said, "What is that?"

It was green and bright, like a pale green star come to earth. As they watched it grew brighter, much brighter.

Gash-Eye suddenly clasped her hands together tightly to keep from crying out. For an instant she'd glimpsed the shape of one of the strangers in the ominous illumination, his paleness, she'd caught a flash of the person's gait, and she was certain: they were her kind. She hadn't seen a living member of her species since the People had killed her band. In the years since, the People had killed a few more, but she'd only been allowed to see the corpses.

The next moment it struck her as strange that she should react so. In her girlhood, her band and theirs would probably have either avoided each other or fought. It was only her years spent with the People that now tricked her into a familial feeling about these strangers.

Someone else was approaching from behind. Gash-Eye held herself perfectly still; from the rhythm of his steps she knew who it was. Once he arrived, she heard the Jaw say, "What is it? Strangers?"

"None of your concern, half-breed," growled Spear, one of the hunters.

"How brave Spear is when my father is absent," said the Jaw.

"How brave the Jaw is, even in the presence of its mother."

"Quiet," ordered Stick, the eldest of the hunters, a man of nearly fifty summers. "Look at the green light. Try to think of what it might be, not new ways to insult each other."

"The one insult is more than enough to shame a purer man than the Jaw," said Spear. But his heart wasn't in it, and all the Jaw's attention was on the light, so that he seemed not even to hear the jibe.

They continued to stare at the distant glow, amazed. Then all of a sudden it winked out.

"What happened?" demanded Stick. "Gash-Eye, what happened?"

She was almost certain she had seen them toss something over the light, maybe a fur. "I couldn't make it out," she lied. Though it was mad, she couldn't help but see her old, long-murdered, half-forgotten family in these strangers' gestures and bulky, pale forms.

The hunters broke from behind the boulder, creeping downslope to meet Chert. To a member of the People, their dark-skinned lithe bodies would have been nearly invisible in the darkness, but Gash-Eye could still see them. "You stay here, Gash-Eye," ordered Spear. "See if anything more happens."

The Jaw was the last to leave. Before he did, she grabbed him by the wrist, wondering if he would consent to being restrained.

He did, reluctantly. Theirs was an unstable and fraught relationship. Sometimes he loved and pitied her. Sometimes the shame of being her son would overwhelm him and he would shun her even more assiduously than the rest of the band did. Now, as usual when he'd been included in the life of the People by his father's favor (because he had been allowed to partake in the ceremony of the Mushroom), the Jaw was reticent and shame-faced before his mother, as if he resented her as a reminder that he wasn't *really* a human, and was suffered to live like one only at his father's whim. "What is it?" he grunted.

"Your father has always protected you," she said. "Stay close to him tonight."

"What?" His light-brown, medium-sized brow, halfway between hers and his father's, twisted in confusion. "Why? What's going to happen tonight?"

"Go. Go back with the others. I don't want them to remember that we talked for long tonight."

"Why?" With his next words, his voice grew more anxious: "What are you going to do?"

Chert was upon them without their having heard his approach. He paused and looked them over; Gash-Eye thought he was going to question them, but instead he curtly said, "Come." Gash-Eye pretended to believe she was included in the summons, not just the Jaw, and as they walked around to the opposite slope Chert didn't bother to correct her.

They rejoined the rest of the People. Some were naked, but most wore skins to protect against the night's slight chill. The hunters were waiting for Chert near the mouth of the cave, the curious women and children ranked behind them. Gash-Eye waited, apart from either group. "What is the bright thing, Chert?" asked Stick.

"I don't know. A ball, that glows like a soft green moon. But they can control it. You saw how it grew brighter? I was creeping upon them just then. In that pale cool green fire I saw them take a dog whose neck had been broken. They dangled it over the green ball and put its head inside it, and as they did so it glowed brighter."

"What do you mean they put the dog's head inside the ball?" demanded Spear. "What does that mean?"

Rarely did Chert allow anyone to hear him sound as uncertain as he did now. "I don't know," he confessed. "There were people between me and the thing, and its opening was facing away from me. But it moved jerkily as they put the dog's head in. And there was a crunching sound, almost ... almost as if it were eating the head."

"Eating it!" sneered Spear.

"I said it was as if it were eating it, fool. I make no claim to know what it is or what exactly they're doing with it.... But I say we can take it from them. They're Big-Brows."

He said this without so much as a glance at Gash-Eye. But many of the People grinned her way and hissed their jeers at her.

Chert ignored this. It was only the women, children, and old men who hissed, anyway—the hunters, even Spear, kept their attention upon the question at hand.

Stick weighed the news. "If they're Big-Brows, the night will favor them," he said.

"Their magic light will help *us*," said Spear. "The Big-Brows are the ones who can see in the dark."

"What do we need with a magic green light, anyway?" asked Antler, calmly. "Can't we make a fire when we need light? The Big-Brows need the light, they have no fire." Antler's caution, care, and steadiness had won him a reputation for wisdom among some members of the clan.

Then there were those like Spear, who liked to accuse him of cowardice. "It's treasure!" he snarled. "Who knows what other powers it may have? Why let the dummies prance away with it, especially after they dare enter our territory? And we should take it now, before the Overhills get wind of it." The Overhills were what they called another local band, not Big-Brows but humans like the People. They weren't exactly friends, but they had sometimes exchanged meat, skins, weapons, women.

Ignoring Spear, Chert addressed himself to Antler: "It was no ordinary thing," he said. "It is special and valuable, and we should take it. When I saw it, I felt how I wanted it." In the People's tongue, there was a certain way to inflect the verb "to want" that made it signify "I plan to take," and Chert used that form now. He was strong enough a hunter that this assertion ended all debate.

"Well," Spear said. "Good. I will lead the raid down upon the Big-Brows." Jealous of Chert's prestige, Spear was eager to grab whatever glory he could.

Chert looked at Spear, but did not argue. Spear pretended not to pay attention to Chert, while checking his reaction out of the corners of his eyes. Once it was plain no one was going to fight him for the right to lead the raid, he continued: "I'll take Gash-Eye with me, to be our eyes. Bring the noose."

Immediately the thick knotted vines of the noose were slipped over Gash-Eye's head and neck, then tightened; someone had been holding it ready.

Emboldened, Spear flung his hand in a disdainful gesture at the Jaw, and said, "And take the half-breed, some of you, and hold him in the back! Hold him somewhere away from Chert."

Now Chert stepped toward Spear. "Why?" he said, voice as hard as his name yet suddenly quieter than ever. "Why should I not be trusted near the Jaw?"

The excited murmurs that had been building were hushed. Spear faltered. Casting his eyes about the group, he said, "You all know why."

But no one stepped forward to help him. Eyeing Spear coldly, Chert said, "I've always brought as much meat to the People as any man. Does Spear claim he's brought more than me?"

Spear kept quiet.

"Does Spear claim to have brought even as much as I have?"

Still Spear stayed silent, except that now his teeth could be heard grinding together.

Chert continued to watch him, waiting to see if Spear would dare challenge his right to say all he did. When Spear volunteered nothing, Chert said, "The Jaw stays with me. He and I will flank the Big-Brows on one side, Antler and Stick can lead the flank on the other. Spear may go in first."

There was some muttering at this. Plenty of heads more level than Spear's had noted Chert's unnatural attachment to the half-breed; for example, no Jaw before this one had ever been accorded the privilege of participating in the Ceremony of the Mushroom of the Inner Eye, but Chert often (but not always) demanded it for his son, as he had done today.

It didn't take sharp eyes or a keen nose to understand that such an attachment might destroy the Jaw's value as a hostage to hold over Gash-Eye. If Gash-Eye misbehaved, the Jaw would be easier to kill if he were separated from his father. But neither did one need a keen nose to smell that Spear had angered Chert past the point at which it would be safe to argue with him. Not on the subject of his son.

As far as Gash-Eye was concerned, things could not have gone better. For her son, at least. She was jerked back as someone tugged on her noose. She, Spear, and the hunter holding her noose began to slink down the hill. Though they made no sound, she knew that Chert, the Jaw, Antler, and Stick would be falling in behind them.

Spear crept alongside her a ways, long enough to hiss in her ear: "Remember your purpose! You're here to see their numbers, see where they are, and tell me with hand signs. *Quietly.* Don't try to plan anything else, dummy, or we'll roast your son and feed him to you. And don't think soft Chert will protect him, not against us all. And even if he *did* save the boy, remember, he won't stop us from leaving you empty-socketed in the forest, after we've had our fun first."

Even though Gash-Eye was supposed to be seeing on his behalf, Spear couldn't help himself from walking a few paces ahead of her. Gash-Eye shuddered behind him. Not because of the threat to take her eyes, but because of what he'd said about the Jaw. She didn't take his threat to cook her own son as hyperbole. The People had told her the tale of a former Gash-Eye who'd rebelled; they'd built a little enclosure, roasted her Jaw, and walled her up alone with him, offering her no other food but her son. She'd held out more than a week, drinking rainwater. Finally hunger had gotten the better of her, and when she did die it was from eating the meat after it had spoiled.

It wasn't worth the risk to save her fellow Big-Brows below. (In the language of her girlhood, they hadn't called themselves Big-Brows, of course—they'd called themselves the People, too. Every people Gash-Eye had ever heard of called themselves the People, in their own tongue.) She reminded herself that these were not her band, the band of her youth. They would speak a language she would not recognize; they would have strange ways. Her people, her true people, had been left smoking and hacked apart in a clearing, and animals and birds had long since stolen their bones.

No, she wouldn't be fooled by the fact that the bodies of the people below were shaped like hers. The only blood-tie she had left was her son, and she couldn't depend on Chert to defend him. No matter how well Chert might sometimes treat the Jaw, it was only sometimes, and the truth was that Chert was her enemy, and that the Jaw was not of the People. The People would kill him if she rebelled. So Gash-Eye would obediently lead Spear and the others to the band of Big-Brows. Once the killing started, she could close her strong eyes.

In the shadows among the trees she saw a shape moving. That was a person, she could tell.

She was about to signal to Spear, when the person stepped out from between the trees into a patch of moonlight.

Gash-Eye gasped. Even at this distance she could make out the features of his face. Spear looked at her sharply, then faced forward again. The figure ahead was lit so brightly in the moonshine, soon even Spear would see him.

Not since she was a child had Gash-Eye seen another of her own kind, alive. She hadn't realized how strongly she would be affected by the sight of one's pale face. Meanwhile, the Big-Brow hadn't noticed her and the others yet.

She tried to twist around and look over her shoulder, to assure herself that the Jaw was safe with Chert; but the man holding her noose jerked on it and growled close to her ear, much too soft for the still-distant Big-Brows to hear. Spear heard, though, and turned to glare at her in alarm, wondering what she was up to.

Gash-Eye knew from that glare that Spear was on the verge of silencing her forever—after all, there was bound to be a replacement for her in the band below—so she grabbed her chance before it was gone. "Run!" she screamed, not in the People's language that she'd spoken for sixteen years, but in her native tongue. Even as she cried out she wondered what madness had possessed her.

The hunter behind her yanked her noose and cut off her breath. But, although Gash-Eye had been so cowed over the years that her captors and even she had forgotten how strong she was, now desperation spurred her on, and she smacked the hunter in the temple, sending him stunned to the ground.

Spear gave away his position to the Big-Brows by turning on her with a cry of rage. Maybe she could have swatted him aside just as she'd done the man behind her, but she knew that if she struck Spear he would stop at nothing to kill the Jaw, not to mention her. She danced out of the way of his spear thrust and ran back uphill, shouting another warning as she went.

She was tackled by someone. With relief, she realized it was Stick and Antler, instead of Chert. Perhaps that was because Chert was busy jabbing his spearhead through the Jaw's throat; but Gash-Eye felt certain that his absence meant Chert was ushering the boy back uphill, keeping him away from Spear until tempers calmed.

Spear caught up an instant after Antler and Stick brought her down. While they held her, he kicked her furiously in the face and chest.

They were too busy beating her to pursue the Big-Brows, and Gash-Eye imagined they were hurriedly disappearing from the patch of forest below. She nearly grinned—but since her lips were the only things defending her teeth from Spear's rampage, she kept them sealed.

Two

Gash-Eye knelt in the middle of the circle, head bowed. She was naked—they had stripped off the skins she wore. Dawn had broken just as Spear was beating her, and the ensuing commotion had given day time enough to arrive. Three boys stood poised to beat her head with long sticks if she raised it, but by rolling her eyes all the way to the side, she was able to see the last blue sky of her life.

That was all right, that it would be her last. Her gamble had worked. They weren't going to kill the Jaw.

Not that Spear had given up trying. "It's the custom!" he was shouting again. "It's what the Jaw is for!"

"The reason we hold the Jaw under threat is to control Gash-Eye." Chert didn't deign to look directly at Spear, but addressed the circle at large. "It's too late to control Gash-Eye, she's already betrayed us. We're going to kill her for it. There's no point in killing the Jaw, too."

"The point is to punish her," said Spear.

"Punish her by killing her," said Chert. "The Jaw is a good hunter. Better than many. It makes no sense to kill him on your whim, Spear."

"I am not the one acting on a whim. We've always known that the custom is to kill the Jaw if the Gash-Eye rebels. That's why he's called the Jaw—because he's the way we can hold Gash-Eye. Don't worry, now that we know you can't face the necessity, we won't let you father the next Jaw...."

"I can face as much as you can and more," said Chert, and stepped close to him, looking into his eyes. Spear didn't step back. "I say he lives. My blood's in him. I know what I agreed

15

to when I fathered him, but now that he's here I've changed my mind. Do what you want with the Big-Brow mother, I don't give a damn about her. As for the Jaw, if you can manage some way to kill the Big-Brow blood in him while leaving mine be, then go ahead. But if you harm the part of him that is mine, then I'll kill you. It is Chert who says so, Spear."

Spear's face had gone dark with fury. "Consult the People!" he sputtered. "See what the other hunters say, you see if they don't agree that I'm right!"

"I don't care what the rest say." Chert turned his calm and defiant face to the onlookers. "What I say to Spear, I say to all. I have brought much meat to the People, and my word has strength."

The gathered People looked on, in disquiet. There were a lot of them, more than sixty individuals (not that anyone had ever counted)—so far as anyone knew, it was the biggest band of humans that had ever existed.

Spear and Chert stood together, looking out at the group. Chert stood half a head taller than him and was broader. His head was like a big rounded block. Spear's face was shaped like a triangle, the point of his chin and the long thin shaft of his body making his name a fitting one. When Spear had only just begun to grow hair on his face, he had challenged his father, and demanded he yield his place in the front ranks of the fire. That was a traditional right of the People, albeit a rarely-exercised one. The father could either yield, or refuse and fight a duel. Spear's father had chosen the duel, and the next day had been food for birds.

More than anyone else, Spear hated the unnatural interest Chert sometimes took in the Jaw, as if he were grooming him for manhood. Usually when young hunters were groomed it was so they could one day take their fathers' places by the fire. But the Jaw would not be able to do that the peaceful way, when Chert died, because he was not of the People, he was the Jaw. And even less conceivable was the idea of him challenging his father for the place, the way Spear had done—no Jaw would be granted that privilege due only to humans, and if the Jaw ever killed his father it would be considered plain murder. Whenever Chert did include his son in the group, even when the People went along more or less uncomplainingly, there was always a whiff of mockery to their cooperation. It was akin to the amusement far-future humans would feel at seeing chimps dressed in human clothes, except that the People honored animals and would never treat one with the same disdain they did the Jaw.

Stick raised his hands. "Peace, peace," he called. "Spear is right when he says that custom demands we kill the Jaw. But Chert is right when he says the Jaw has proved a mighty hunter. He is not an ordinary Jaw—perhaps because of his father's blood, perhaps because of his father's favor. So Stick says, let there be peace. Stick's advice is, let the Jaw live, if only in thanks for the meat Chert has brought us. Let the Jaw live among us as before, except for the days of rites and sacrifices, when he must keep apart as always. Meanwhile we will kill Gash-Eye. And when we find the next Gash-Eye, I say let Spear have the honor of fathering the Jaw upon her, and let us return to the old ways with that."

The tone of the murmuring that rustled through the onlookers was uncertain, but basically approving. Gash-Eye closed her eyes, at peace. They were going to kill her, send her into the darkness. Her passage there might be unpleasant, but all she need do was have patience.

Even Spear was almost ready to relinquish his hope of killing the Jaw. He said, "All right—but only on the condition that I be the one to take out her eyes and kill her in the forest." Traditionally, the man who'd fathered the Jaw was also the one who killed the Gash-Eye, if and when the time came.

But Chert gave no sign of resenting this impingement on his privileges. Looking at Spear with eyes half-lidded in contempt, he said, "As you wish."

So it was done. Now that Spear was mollified, no one else was likely to fight to have the Jaw killed. With her son's life secured, Gash-Eye had room to feel the first sharp needles of fear at what Spear had in store for her.

But all was not over yet. Her eyes still closed, she heard a voice say, "Don't touch her." Then she recognized the voice as the Jaw's. She opened her eyes.

Spear was jabbing his finger at the Jaw. "You be quiet!" he said. "You're lucky enough to be living through this. Don't press that luck!"

"That's right, boy," said Chert, turning toward his son, body tense.

Gash-Eye tried to catch his gaze, to appeal to him to stop, but he was glaring down at his clenched fists. "I won't let my mother buy my life with her own," he growled. He was in the grip of another of his strange ideas that no one else would understand. The Jaw sometimes had a dreamy air about him, that would have alienated the People even if he hadn't been a half-breed—or maybe it was because of his alienation from them that he would retreat into uselessly tracking the trails of his own mind. To look at his absent eyes sometimes, one would think he was looking into the hidden places, the way his Big-Brow mother could—as if there were another, mysterious world beyond this, that interested him more than this one—it was the kind of faraway gaze that offended those who were perfectly happy to live in the world around them.

"And what will you do about it?!" demanded Spear. "Stop us from killing her?! Stop us all?!"

"I cannot stop you all, though I could stop just you, Spear. I cannot stop you from killing her, that is. But I can stop you from buying my life with hers. If you tear out her eyes, if you kill her in the traditional way, or in any way, then I'll kill myself, Chert."

"Kill yourself!" said Chert.

"And I'll try to take Spear down to darkness with me."

"It is his big heavy brow that drags him down to the darkness under the earth!" jeered Spear.

Chert stepped forward and gripped the Jaw by his upper arm. The Jaw tried to shake him off, but Chert was strong.

"Shut up with that nonsense," he growled. "Kill yourself? You think I'll let you do such a thing?"

"I'll find a way, sooner or later, no matter how you try to stop me."

"Obey your father, half-breed," snarled Spear. "Only a human such as I has the right to defy his father. Not a creature such as you." Then he shrugged, and, turning to the rest of the People, cried, "Let the half-breed do as he likes. Or let Chert dissuade him, if he can. But we've already decided what's to be done with Gash-Eye. Nothing changes that."

"Listen to him, my son!" Gash-Eye thought she caught the Jaw flinching with embarrassment at her mangled pronunciation of the People's tongue, exaggerated in this moment of her distress; then lightning burst in her eyes as the back of Spear's hand walloped her across the face.

"Quiet, animal!" he shouted. "We can settle this without you!"

The Jaw took a step forward, but Chert's hand on his arm yanked him back. The frame he'd inherited from his mother would have made him the match of most of the People, but maybe not Chert. His father glared at him; then turned to Spear and stepped forward himself. "No one touches the Big-Brow, then."

A scandalized, resentful murmur rippled through the crowd. "Are you insane?" said Spear. "Gash-Eye betrayed us. She warned the prey! She lost us the magic glowing ball! Her betrayal might have gotten any of us killed! Yet now you want her and the Jaw to both go unpunished?"

"The Big-Brows might have gotten the better of you, Spear, that's true. But we other hunters had nothing to fear."

All could see how Spear had trouble swallowing that jibe, and the bile it called up.

"Why are we talking about it? We kill her, surely!" That was Maple, who'd edged halfway between the ranks of the women and the men. Ever since she'd begun to leave childhood behind, it had excited Maple to persuade the handsome young hunters to beat Gash-Eye.

"I don't see why," said Hoof, who had always disdained to indulge Maple's brutal whims. "Gash-Eye has led us to much game and the Jaw has brought us much meat. I will not dispute that her treachery deserves a beating, and perhaps even a marking or the loss of a toe or a finger. But death? Any of us would have done the same in her place."

"Quiet, Hoof!" said Spear.

"Yes," agreed Stick. "May your tongue be hereafter warded, Hoof, from speaking such evil as to say that one of the People might ever be in the place of a Gash-Eye or a Jaw."

Stick continued: "Chert. None of us would disrespect you. No man would impede you from walking where you will. But in this Spear is right. The People must send Gash-Eye back to the darkness. Your son speaks hotly, he will not follow through."

Chert looked at the Jaw and gauged the resolve in his face, then turned back to Stick. "No."

"Gash-Eye tried to lead us into the darkness. Now the dark spirits below are alerted. They await the food they were promised. We must send them Gash-Eye in our stead, else they will rise up and claim us."

"No. Find something else to send them."

"To hell with this," said Spear, and grabbed an axe from one of the nearby men. He raised it overhead, but before he could split Gash-Eye's skull Chert was beside him, arresting Spear's arm in his tight grip.

"I said no," repeated Chert, grim but still calm.

"There's a way things are done, damn you!"

For a reply, Chert tossed the man to the ground with one hand. Spear glared up at him, half-mad, baring his teeth, the axe still in his hand. The crowd tensed. Something bad was about to happen. The young men eyed each other, trying to see who would help Chert, who Spear, and how close the contest would be.

The band was minutes away from destroying itself, perhaps. The terror of that knowledge must have been what distracted them for so long from the invaders, till one of the small children cried, "Look!," pointing down the hill.

They looked. Instantly the quarrel between Chert and Spear was all but forgotten, even by Chert and Spear themselves. "Big-Brows!" someone said; but he said it with a rising, uncertain intonation.

Shuffling up the slope were two Big-Brows. But they were like no Big-Brows anyone had ever seen. Their skins were pitch-black, not like the healthy brown of the People's or the ruddy pink of most Big-Brows', and they gleamed with a strange oiliness. Their gait was halting and stilted. Their eyes were distant and red, feverish-looking; they seemed oblivious to the fact that they were wandering into a hostile camp in which they'd be badly outnumbered.

"They're sick," said Stick, sounding worried.

Some of the younger hunters edged out to meet the Big-Brows, uneasy but wanting to prove their mettle.

"Don't get near them, they're sick," Stick said.

The strange Big-Brows had nearly reached the People. One of the young men took another step toward them. Brandishing his spear, he said, "Have you come for death, weak giants?"

As if in reply the nearest Big-Brow grabbed the youth's spear and yanked it toward himself. The youth didn't think fast enough to let go of his weapon, and he tumbled toward the Big-Brow—moving fast all of a sudden, the Big-Brow grabbed him by the neck and pulled the youth's head to his slick drooling mouth and bit it. He seemed to bite impossibly hard; Gash-Eye was sure she'd heard the boy's skull crack.

Before any of the People could even start screaming, the other Big-Brow grabbed another youth, Pebble, by the arm. The panicking boy tried to jerk free, but shrieked as the Big-Brow clamped his jaws on his arm first.

Now there were screams. Hunters threw their spears into the Big-Brows. Many spears hit their targets, but then merely remained stuck in the invaders' bodies. Neither Big-Brow seemed troubled by them.

The first youth still dangled from the Big-Brow's mouth, neck clearly broken. Bits of skull broke loose and snapped up around the Big-Brow's lips as his teeth sank deeper and deeper into the youth's brain. The Big-Brow shook the lifeless body in his jaws.

Pebble's arm remained trapped in the invader's mouth. It didn't seem like his wounds should be mortal, not yet. But he had gone into a wild seizure, foaming at the mouth, and if one looked closely one could see veins of black crawling up the skin of his arm, originating at the bite.

All this happened in only a moment, the time it took Chert to race forward and try to rescue Pebble. First Chert struck the Big-Brow in the temple. But the Big-Brow didn't seem to notice, though the blow should have been enough to kill him; something about the oily squishiness of the Big-Brow's flesh made Chert feel, not exactly scared, but queasy. There was a spongy give to the Big-Brow's skull, as if it wasn't made of bone. Instead of directly attacking the Big-Brow again, Chert grabbed the youth around the ribs and tried to yank him from his tormentor's grip.

Chert was shocked when the now-blackened arm popped off easily, and he and the boy went sailing backwards, Chert landing hard on his back and then the boy landing on top of him, knocking the air out of his lungs. Chert forced himself to recover because the Big-Brow had let the mangled ruined arm drop from his maw and was coming for Chert again, his jaws nearly snapping on the hunter's face before Chert could roll out of reach and spring to his feet. The Big-Brow sprinted after him, head jutting forward, jaws snapping spasmodically. Only a spear hurled right through his neck toppled the Big-Brow before he could catch his prey.

Chert tried to catch his breath. The Big-Brow had attacked leading with his teeth, not his arms, he noted. Like an animal.

Screams were to be expected at a time like this, so Chert hadn't really been paying attention to them. Now he noticed that they had a certain quality—an extra edge of desperate terror—something more extreme and raggedy than the sad but familiar mourning of a boy fallen in the hunt or a fight.

Quickly he looked around to take stock of the situation. And found that he couldn't. The scene was incomprehensible.

The first Big-Brow was bright green now—his naked body seemed to glow with a green light, bright even in the daytime. Tossed aside was the body of his victim, the whole crown of his skull missing; from here it looked like the skull had been emptied. The Big-Brow raised its arms and roared, spears sticking through its torso and drabs of brain hanging from its lips. It leaped forward with astonishing speed at a hunter who'd gotten too close. The man was able to jab his spear into the Big-Brow, but that did nothing. The green Big-Brow grabbed him and pulled the top of his head into his mouth. Again there was that horrible crunch as the Big-Brow chomped down onto the crown of the man's skull. Panicking nerves jangled through the corpse and made it dance a floppy jig. This time Chert was sure he heard a slurping sound coming from the Big-Brow. As the monster sucked down its victim's brain, its body shone an even brighter green in the daytime sun.

Someone screamed his name and Chert looked to see what they were warning him of: before him, the Big-Brow who'd just been downed was rising to his feet again, even though the spear that was still stuck halfway through his neck had nearly beheaded him. Chert started to back away, but something grabbed his ankle.

He looked down at Pebble, the one-armed corpse he'd failed to rescue. That one arm was stretched out, its hand firm around Chert's ankle. The body was nearly completely black now; Chert could see the color change continuing swiftly. The arm pulled the rest of the body closer to Chert, along with that oily grinning head with its clattering, snapping jaws.

Chert stepped forward with his free foot and put it on Pebble's corpse's head while he tried to wrest the other foot loose. He was careful to keep his heel and toes and all parts of his foot free of the corpse's gnashing, hungry teeth. The head tried to thrash beneath him and nearly knocked him off-balance; but this creature seemed weaker than its now-green brethren (instinctively, Chert was already classing this new Pebble with the Big-Brow invaders), and he was finally able to shake free. Something told him that if those jaws had made contact with his flesh, the body would have rediscovered its strength quickly enough, along with a newfound speed to match that of the feeding Big-Brows.

Stones were flying—some of the People were hurling them at the monsters. Chert was lucky not to get hit by one himself.

He looked for his son and saw him hoisting Gash-Eye up, draping her arm over his shoulder. The Jaw and the girl Quarry were helping her toward the cave. Gash-Eye was bleeding from the temple—one of those stones had hit her, and she seemed woozy and off-balance. Damn that Big-Brow bitch! Why couldn't she retreat under her own power, instead of slowing down the Jaw that way?

Meanwhile the shining-green invader had another victim in its teeth—a woman; men were retreating, spears raised as they moved backwards, in their panic abandoning anyone outside their perimeter. The woman howled and shook just as Pebble's corpse had done. The green Big-Brow had only been able to grab her by the arm. He was trying to drag her resisting body closer so he could reach her head, and had almost succeeded when a spear meant for him slammed into her and knocked her out of his grip. With an angry roar he flung himself at the line of young men. They stabbed at him desperately with their spears, and shrieking women ran from behind the line and struck the Big-Brow with their knives, but the Big-Brow seemed not to notice as he nabbed one of the hunters and hugged the boy to him, chomping loudly through the skull to get to the brain.

Chert raced around the flank of the hunters' line—they were so keyed-up he felt that if he'd run straight at them, expecting them to part, they would have impaled him instead. The Jaw was still helping Gash-Eye to the cave. She seemed to be pleading with the Jaw about something, as he angrily dismissed whatever she was saying.

"Come on!" shouted Chert as he reached them; to Gash-Eye, he said, "Move on your own if you're coming with us, damn you!"

It wasn't like the screams had ever stopped. But they reached such a crescendo that all three of them turned to look behind. One-armed Pebble was completely black now, too, like the Big-Brows had been, and was eating the brain of his spasming sister Acorn. Others of their friends and families, the ones whose skulls hadn't been emptied, were already covered in those expanding webs of black lines and were rampaging among their yet-unbitten former fellows.

In a panic the surviving hunters were running up the hill. Chert, Gash-Eye, and the Jaw were between them and the mouth of the cave. Pebble, green now that he'd eaten a brain, launched himself at the runners from behind, tackling some of them. They in turn fell into the Jaw and his parents, knocking them down and landing atop them. The green hunter (it no longer felt right to call it "Pebble") snapped among the fallen until it had a man's head firmly in its jaws. With its remaining arm it grabbed at the air, trying to get hold of one of the people scrambling away.

Chert rose, hauling the Jaw up with him. He started to drag the Jaw toward the cave again, but jumped back when the green arm swiped near him. He saw that the other Big-Brow, bright green still, as well as some of Chert's former brethren, were running away from them and up the hill, pursuing the People to the cave. Looking down the slope, Chert saw nobody. He decided that away from those things was a good direction to run, and started pulling the Jaw after him.

"No!" the Jaw shouted, pulling back. "My mother!" But Chert was stronger, and forced his son to come with him.

Till they heard Gash-Eye howling something in her strange accent, even more incomprehensible now than ever, as if she were reverting to the language of her childhood. At that sound, the Jaw dug in his heels. "No!" he shouted again.

Chert realized that the Jaw was going to escape from him, or else delay them both so much that those things would notice them and come bounding down the hill. Soon there would be lots of them, too—it was plain to see how the evil black-web spirit and the green-glowing spirit were sweeping through and consuming the People. Chert spun the Jaw around by the shoulder and punched him as hard as he could in the face.

The Jaw tumbled onto his back, dazed eyes rolling in confusion. For good measure, Chert knelt and punched him once more. Now his son was more or less unconscious.

Chert hoisted the boy's huge weight across his shoulders. He rose, screaming with effort. If he'd stopped to wonder whether he would succeed, he might have failed.

Once upright, he continued down the hill, moving fast. He didn't turn around. If one of those corrupted things was pursuing them, he still wouldn't be able to run any faster than he already was, not without abandoning the Jaw.

The Jaw was stirring. Chert hurried, trying to reach the forest and its hiding places before the boy was able to fight him.

As Chert crashed into the trees, a horrible scream from Gash-Eye came twisting down the hill after them. The Jaw began to struggle in earnest; still Chert was able to hold him firm across his shoulders. "Let me go!" said the Jaw. "My mother!"

"She's dead," said Chert, and believed it. Something must have been moments from killing her. What else could a scream like that mean?

Three

Chert dodged the Jaw again, letting the boy fall into the brush behind him. He turned to see his son rising to his feet, determined to attack once more. Chert's stern face didn't betray his worry. If this kept up, he'd have to try to incapacitate the boy again with another blow to the head, and he didn't want to risk damaging him. More, he couldn't deny, at least privately, the risk that the Jaw might actually manage to kill him.

"Stop this," said Chert.

"You killed my mother," said the Jaw.

Chert wanted to point out that the boy's mother had been nothing but a Big-Brow slave and was more something shameful he should forget, than someone valuable he should avenge. But he was willing to bend so far as to set that aside. "I didn't kill your mother," he said instead. "I only stopped you from killing yourself."

"You stopped me from saving her," said the Jaw, and launched himself again.

Expertly Chert stepped aside, at the same time sticking his leg in the boy's way and grabbing and tossing him along. The Jaw went flying. Chert was freakishly strong, about even with his half-breed son (he didn't know it, but this strength came from a Big-Brow great-grandfather). Even so, he could feel age and the ravages of a hard life catching up with him, and he knew that the Jaw would be able to take him soon, if not today. That knowledge stirred in him the primeval rage between fathers and sons, and it was not entirely physical exertion that made him breathe hard as he fought down the urge to kill. "Stop this," he repeated. "You have my blood. I don't want to spill my own blood."

"You spilled my mother's."

The sheer stupidity was enough to make Chert want to beat the boy to death. "How?" he shouted. "How did I do that?" He turned and began marching back in the direction from which he'd carried the Jaw. Over his shoulder, he called, "Come on then, damn you. Come back to that cursed eruption of demons, since your idiotic Big-Brow blood doesn't have the sense to run from it."

The Jaw was on his feet again. Uncertainly, he watched his father walk away, before following him.

By the time they were nearing the edge of the forest, the Jaw was only a few steps behind. Chert did not deign to turn and look at him or give any sign that he feared another attack. They backtracked along the obvious trail of smashed and broken plants Chert had made in his wild flight.

They reached the edge of the woods. Not even Chert could quite control his heartbeat as he cautiously parted the branches to look up the slope. The Jaw drew up alongside him.

One of the original Big-Brows was still up there—his bright green had faded, and Chert guessed he would soon be black again. It was the brain-eating that made them glow green, he'd gathered. They got faster when they were very close to a brain, and they got much much faster once they'd eaten it. The other Big-Brow was nowhere to be seen. The rest of the bodies shuffling around up there were Chert's possessed brethren, formerly of the People, a couple of them green (one pale, one dark), the other four black. Chert knew others of the People had been turned, and he wondered with trepidation how close by they were, and listened for any person-sized creature shuffling through the underbrush.

Most of the creatures or demons or whatever they were had spears sticking from them, slowing them as their ends dragged along the ground, or else they had gaping black-oozing holes where spears had been jabbed into their flesh and had come out again. Most of the wounds seemed clearly mortal, and yet the dead walked. On some of them body parts dangled, limbs attached only by precarious strips of flesh. A woman named Thrush, or who had once been named Thrush, had had her right arm ripped off. They could see the black arm some distance away from her, pulling itself by its hand's fingers along the grass.

"How could we have saved Gash-Eye from those things?" whispered Chert. "You're mad if you think we could have. It's a miracle we saved ourselves."

The Jaw stubbornly refused to answer.

Chert knew that if the boy had had an argument against him, he would have voiced it, and that his silence amounted to tacit agreement. Still he craved to have it in words, so they could finish this conflict and get on with surviving. "What could we have done for her?" he insisted. "Show me a thing that can be killed, and I tell you I can kill it. But what would you have me do against creatures that grow stronger and stronger, the more they die?"

"You managed to rescue *me*," said the Jaw accusingly.

In disgust, Chert turned back to the creatures. They exercised upon him a weird fascination that let him forget his stupid son. He knew that they should leave this area, that there was no way to be sure the creatures in their unfed state were as clumsy as Chert thought, that they might be able to sneak up on him and the Jaw after all. He told himself that he was studying them, so as to be better prepared should he ever need to fight them again. But it was the horrible mystery of the things that drew his mind to them.

What were they? How could anyone defeat them? He felt for them a revulsion and hatred he had never felt for anything before; certainly not for the animals he hunted and to whom he always offered ritual thanks. There were plenty of creatures that Chert *wanted* to see removed from the world, animals like the big-fanged tigers who had been known to kill his friends and kinsmen; but this was the first time Chert had ever seen anything that he knew in his gut *should* be wiped off the earth, destroyed utterly, completely removed from the universe of clean spirits.

But what could possibly do it? What power could defeat the unkillable, the undead? Chert could imagine nothing from this world that could be up for the challenge.

A strange humming vibrated his bones and something made all his hairs stand on end.

There swooped overhead a monstrous bird, so fast and alien that even the mighty Chert and the Jaw squealed in fright and jumped further back into the bushes. The Jaw nearly ran, but held his ground when he realized his father was going nowhere. Chert stared up at the huge thing. It was not a bird after all, he realized, though he had no inkling what it might be instead; it had no wings to flap but glided smoothly through the air, plainly guided with intention and control; it had no head, either, and now seemed less like an animal than a huge impossibly regular and smooth stone, blinking stars embedded in its surface. Also on its surface were strange markings; Chert could not imagine how men could have formed them, but they definitely looked like made things.

The huge magic stone came to a halt over the hill. It floated, stationary—not even birds could do that. Beside him Chert heard the Jaw whimpering, and felt his own mind starting to buckle. *It's hovering like an insect,* he told himself. *Birds don't hover, but insects do.* Somehow, being able to find some precedent for the thing in the world he already knew, no matter how big a stretch that precedent was, helped him stave off madness.

He tore his eyes away from it long enough to look down at the Jaw and grip his shoulder. "It's just a thing," he insisted. The Jaw's eyes were wide, he was making barely audible gibbering noises. "It's just a thing, like anything else," he repeated.

Whatever Chert meant by those words, they seemed to work. The Jaw still looked terrified, but he managed to nod and silence himself.

They should have run. But Chert wanted to see what the floating stone would do.

With a blast of strange thunder, a line of red light instantaneously filled the space between the stone and the head of one of the living corpses, and the creature's head exploded. After toppling, its body continued to crawl weakly along the grass on its belly.

"A spear of fire!" gasped the Jaw in amazement.

"You're right, that's exactly what it is!" said Chert, excited to have an explanation for the phenomenon, even one that made no sense. "That's exactly what it is!" Smoke drifted up from the smoldering chunks of the corpse's head. Again the red spear appeared, this time connecting the floating stone with the head of another corpse, with identical results. As they watched, the stone dealt the same treatment to each of the undead. Despite the fact that five of the corpses had been their brethren an hour earlier, both Chert and the Jaw felt their chests swell with desperate grateful joy once all the heads had exploded.

The huge stone continued to float overhead. Happy as Chert might be for what it had done so far, he watched it with trepidation. It was an impossibly powerful thing, of a nature and an origin Chert couldn't begin to fathom. He would be relieved when it went on its way. Now that he knew there were such things in the world, both the undead and the impossible stone, Chert felt he would never be at ease again.

For a long time they watched the stone hover there and do nothing. Finally Chert's reason began to reawaken. "We must go," he said to the Jaw. "Boy, we must go. This is dangerous ground now."

The Jaw blinked, as if he'd been in a trance. He nodded.

They turned their backs on the stone, and the hillside where their people had been destroyed, and took the first steps of their new, lonely wandering. It would be dangerous, to be only two hunters with no band, with nothing but the skins they wore. The Jaw, as a half-breed, was especially likely to be killed, whether they came across people like the People or Big-Brows. Every few paces they looked back to snatch patchy glimpses of the floating stone through the trees of the forest.

They moved swiftly. Before long, they had recovered themselves enough that they were not leaving obvious trails.

Although in mourning for his People, Chert was a pragmatic man, and he was already looking to the future. Perhaps these mad spirits were only passing through, but in case they were planning to make a new home here he and the Jaw would move far away. They were strong hunters and would find a band willing to take them in. Grief was fine, and they would find a place for it, but for the most part life would be normal.

So far away was Chert in his own musings, that it was the Jaw who raised a hand to signal they should stop and crouched in the brush. Chert followed suit. There was some animal nearby, rattling through the vegetation. Chert tried not to show how shaken he was at not having heard the noise himself, first. He guessed the animal to be sick and disoriented, from the commotion it made. He doubted any human alone would be foolhardy enough to make so much noise, unless it were a child, and whatever this was sounded too big to be a child.

Of course, it might be one of those undead things.

The Jaw began to creep toward the sounds to investigate. Chert grabbed his shoulder to hold him back, but the Jaw shook off his hand. Seeing that his son wouldn't be dissuaded, Chert crept along after him.

They were already almost upon the new mysterious thing when they saw a flash of bright white tramping through the trees. Both Chert and the Jaw froze again. There were such things as white birds and animals, but this was a sort of white they'd never seen before, a glittery, shiny white. Chert was infuriated to see yet another alien intrusion into his world.

From the way the thing moved it was soon plain that it was a human, or some spirit disguised as a human. Chert wondered if it were sick, it seemed so clumsy and confused—not clumsy and oblivious, the way the undead had been, when there were no brains nearby for them to eat.

Chert was about to signal to the boy that they should slink away, hopefully without being noticed by the new thing, when the Jaw suddenly stood and thrust the intervening branches aside, roaring a challenge into the woman's face.

For it was a woman, albeit a tall one, taller than them. They could tell from the shape of her body underneath the strange white hides she wore. And by her pale face, seen through a sheet of dull ice, transparent and impossibly solid here in the spring sunshine. Surrounding the rest of her head was some sort of hollow white stone, different from the stone that floated but also impossibly smooth and regular. Through the ice she gaped at them in terror.

Chert didn't care if she was terrified. He'd had enough monsters, of any variety. Grabbing a stone from the ground, he sprang up and past the Jaw and with a hunting cry slammed the stone into her face hard enough to smash the ice.

Except it didn't smash. Though the woman went flying onto her back, the ice wasn't even cracked. Chert was certain the round white stone that covered her head would bear no marks, either. With wonder, he realized that it was a sort of protective garb. But how long must it take to hollow out a round stone? And wouldn't it make your neck tired?

She tried to scramble away, blinking at them in a panic as she thrashed back through the underbrush. They blinked too, at the gleaming reflection of the sunlight from where it hit her white hide from between the tree leaves. She was making noises, babbling something in an unknown tongue.

To hell with the stone on her head—if she could be scared, she could be killed. It would feel good to kill something, after their earlier futile battle with the undead. Still holding the stone, Chert stepped forward, preparing to find out if the white hide she wore also had magical protective properties.

The Jaw stopped him with a hand to his chest. "Listen!" he said, staring at the woman, face strained in concentration. "Listen to what she's saying!"

Exasperated, Chert wanted to say that she was talking in no language he understood, then get back to the business of beating her to death with the rock and his feet. But he paused, willing to briefly humor the Jaw. He even listened closely, certain though he was that it would do no good, and after a

33

moment was surprised to realize that he could understand a few words.

"Me friend is," she was saying. She spoke, not the tongue of the People, but that of the other band which habitually passed through a swath of territory over the range of hills, that the People called the Overhills. The People had had dealings enough with them that most had learned their language's basics. Chert was far from fluent, but even he could tell how it was being butchered by this new monster. "Me is," she said again, followed by a string of words they couldn't understand. Then, "Me is fight no-die."

That was easy enough to understand. "What are the no-dies?" demanded Chert. "Where do they come from?"

The monster just blinked at them. She shook her head and said, "No is understanding, not. Hard is the language."

The effort of translating from her travesty of a tongue he only knew imperfectly in the first place was exasperating to Chert. The Jaw was less put out. As the monster got back to her feet, eyeing them cautiously, he said, in the Overhill tongue, "How do you fight them?"

"Head destroy," she said. "In the distance, to destroy from. Fire with. Small, tight, strong fire."

The phrase "small, tight, strong fire" would have been meaningless, if they hadn't seen the red lances emanating from the smooth floating stone. "But the bodies live on," said Chert, in Overhill, thinking of the crawling arm and the corpse that had continued to drag itself along. "Even after the head is gone, the body lives."

Her eyes clouded as she deciphered his speech; once she understood, she shook her head and said, "Not long times that it lives, after head."

That was good news, if true. The Jaw spoke: "Give us the small tight strong fire."

Chert reflected that it was his son who was asking the most important questions, not himself. He felt a mixture of pride, and anger at being bested.

The monster was nodding enthusiastically. But what she said was, "Is danger. Must learn. Is the time for to teach."

The Jaw looked at Chert. The anger at his father seemed to have been forgotten in the midst of a newfound, dark enthusiasm. "That makes sense," he said in the People's tongue. "A new weapon should mean new skills."

Chert nodded slowly. It would be good to have access to the fire weapon, in case they met more of the undead things; and it would be handy magic to have, when they were trying to persuade a strange band to take them in. But he wasn't particularly happy with the notion of following this new monster someplace and spending months with her while she trained them.

Which was exactly what she seemed to have in mind. "Came," she said, stepping back in the direction she'd come from and waving them to follow. "Came." She was trying to tell them to come. "From this place, away is the safer." Chert wasn't sure he was going to obey, but the Jaw moved after her with no hesitation. Biting down on his irritation, Chert fell into step as well.

Out of habit, Chert and the Jaw moved so as not to leave too obvious a trail. But it was wasted effort, because the monster crashed so messily through the woods that it was almost as if they were following a bear, or a huge stumbling baby. Chert stared at her stone head-garb and her impossible hide, and thought about the hard unmelting ice protecting her face, and wondered how a creature so stupid could have come across such powerful tools.

He said to the Jaw, "Do you think it's wise to follow this monster?"

"She looks human to me. She looks like one of you, only with the color of a Big-Brow."

Chert's mouth puckered in annoyance to hear his son refer to humans as "you," thus perversely identifying himself with his Big-Brow blood. "Human or spirit or monster or witch, I see no reason why we should so casually follow her."

The Jaw scowled at him. "What do you mean? We're following so as to learn to use the strong tight fire. So we can kill those things that will not die."

The monster peered at them over her shoulder, probably anxiously wondering what they were talking about in their foreign tongue. Chert pretended not to notice her curiosity. "I say we would be better served by getting far away from here. Why should we risk our lives trying to kill the undead?"

"Because they killed our People. Because they killed my mother. Are you a coward?"

Chert refrained from pointing out that by rights Gash-Eye should have been executed anyway. And falling prey to those monsters was a better fate than what Spear had planned for her. "We're hunters," he said. "What can we do with those things after we kill them? Eat them? I wouldn't eat them."

"No, we're not going to eat them. We're going to destroy them so they can never harm us again."

"A better way to keep them from harming us would be to go far away. In all my rangings and wanderings, in all my life, I've never seen things like what we fought today. My days are more than half done, and I see no reason to expect I will ever see them again."

The Jaw glared straight ahead. Although he kept walking, Chert guessed that his silence meant he had no ready answer.

The monster turned to look nervously over her shoulder again. In Overhill, she said, "If questions is existing, me is can be answerer." Chert pretended not to have heard her; even the Jaw was too deep in sullen thought to acknowledge her offer.

Chert pressed, now while the boy was weakened by doubt. "Your heart is swollen and enflamed," he said. "I know. I understand. You look through bloody water. But trust me. We should work to preserve while there is something to preserve."

"What is there to preserve? Everyone's dead."

"You are my son and I am your father. There's something to preserve. We should not be following this monster to new dangers. We should escape her, and find a band."

The Jaw didn't reply.

Chert said, "This monster who's leading us is somehow linked to the undead creatures we couldn't defeat today. I don't know what the link is, and I don't care about solving the mystery. I want no more of any of it."

Still the Jaw said nothing. Then, just when Chert was on the verge of insisting they bolt, he spoke: "I want to see what she's going to show us."

From his tone, Chert understood it would be no good arguing any more right now. For a moment he considered running away by himself and leaving his stupid half-breed son to his fate; but he knew he wasn't going to do that.

So for a little while they would follow this monster. It wouldn't be the first foolish thing Chert had ever done. And he had to admit that he was not without curiosity as to the fire weapon; and was even curious as to the nature of these new monsters and magical artifacts that had invaded his world, though never finding out what they were would be a small price to pay for never seeing any of them again.

He would consent to follow the monster alongside the Jaw. But as soon as he could get his son away from her he would do it, even if it meant once more beating the Jaw senseless so that he could be carried. And if it meant killing the monster in the white skins, he wouldn't think twice.

Four

It was Quarry who had half-dragged Gash-Eye to safety in the cave—Gash-Eye hadn't quite been dead weight, but she'd been so stunned she was hardly able to walk. If it hadn't been for Quarry, those unkillable things would have gotten her—the rest of the People would have left her out on the hillside.

At first, most of the survivors had sat in the gloom of the cave and howled their grief, men, women, and children. But that didn't last long before Spear and those hunters closest to him went among them, slapping the noisy ones into silence. When Spear saw Gash-Eye he slapped her too, though she hadn't made a sound. She didn't seem to notice.

But Quarry did. Even if she'd been a boy, she would have been too small and weak and young to challenge Spear. (She was small for her age, even though she had begun the bleeding three moon-cycles ago, and had already been initiated into eating the Mushroom of the Inner Eye.) But once Spear's attention was elsewhere, she persuaded Gash-Eye to get up and move deeper back into the gloom, where she was less likely to be noticed. Then she let her slump once more in a daze upon the floor.

While Gash-Eye was still stunned, Quarry ventured to the front of the cave and overheard Spear saying to one of his friends, "At least those monsters got rid of the half-breed for us." He meant only that, since the Jaw wasn't here with them now, he must have died in the unkillables' onslaught. But Quarry misunderstood, and thought Spear had seen the Jaw killed with his own eyes.

Quarry made her way back to Gash-Eye and tried to tend to her. When Gash-Eye came to herself she gasped, "The Jaw! We have to go back!"

Quarry squeezed her big hand. "No, Gash-Eye. He died."

For a moment Quarry thought Gash-Eye was going to break her hand, her grip tightened so. The girl rode it out, betraying no discomfort.

"Are you sure?" choked Gash-Eye. "Did you see it? See it happen?"

Quarry had not. But she remembered the bitter satisfaction with which Spear had uttered the fact, as if even in the midst of such carnage he were able to find pleasure in the Jaw's destruction. If Quarry left Gash-Eye with any doubt, Gash-Eye would go asking the other People about her son, and Spear would be inspired to give her a lush, sumptuous, cruel account of all his gory suffering. So Quarry said, "Yes. I saw. I'm so sorry, Gash-Eye. But he died quickly, and with no pain. And he died really— he wasn't changed into one of those black-and-green things."

Gash-Eye's eyes squeezed shut and she slumped back again. If the muscles around her eyes hadn't been so agonizingly tight, Quarry wouldn't have thought she was conscious.

The People had started putting on the extra, heavier skins that had been left inside the cave mouth as winter had receded. A large supply of firewood had been left there, too. Even this little ways in, the cool unclean breeze coming up from the bowels of the earth lowered the temperature.

Quarry wore a fat, thick bearskin that had been a gift from her mother. Though her mother had been dead a year, and was no longer there to stick up for her, the People had let her keep the gift.

The hunters were trying to hold a council, despite the world having ended. "I am the oldest," said Stick, "and I have never seen or heard of anything like what we have witnessed today. So I will not bother to ask whether anyone else has."

There were a few tentative protests from those who pointed out that it was not so uncommon to see the dead walk the earth, but Spear cut short such objections with contempt: "Yes, many of us have seen wraiths, spirits rising up as steam from their new home under the ground. But who could compare that with the full-bodied horrors we faced today?"

"I agree with Spear," said Stick. "I myself have seen spirits who have returned, many, many times. Sometimes in dreams, sometimes at twilight. But they always waited to return till after they had already died." It was hard to see Stick's expression in the dimness, but by his voice they could tell that he was re-seeing the dreadful sights of the day. "Besides, all those apparitions were the people I had known, albeit returned in a different form. But these things today … these black and green monstrosities that the Big-Brows transformed our people to … I don't know why, but I feel that the blackened, newly unkillable friends who attacked us today were more dead than any ghost I ever saw, no matter how entrenched in those bodies they were."

"Stick is right," said another, Granite. "My brother would never have tried to kill us that way. Whatever demon inhabited his form after that Big-Brow bit him, it wasn't my brother."

"The Big-Brows," said Spear, "the Big-Brows! Yes, let's talk about the Big-Brows!"

Gash-Eye, who could see in this dimness far better than the others, saw Spear coming her way, squinting at the People as he went, looking for her. She could have escaped, but didn't bother.

Spear found her. He grabbed her by the forearm and shook her. "Here's the one that led them to us!"

"Why should you think that, Spear?" said Stick. He sounded disdainful of Spear's stupid accusation, but Gash-Eye knew better than to expect that disdain to translate into aid if Spear decided to beat her to death. But, again, she didn't care. She was supposed to be dead, anyway—that had been her plan.

Spear spun around to answer Stick's question, but didn't let go of Gash-Eye's arm. "They were Big-Brows, weren't they?!"

"I imagine they were Big-Brows who'd been changed into monsters, and who were just as much taken by surprise as we were."

"They appeared after Gash-Eye sent a signal to that group of Big-Brows in the forest, didn't they? None of us speak her Big-Brow tongue—who knows what she said? Whatever it was, didn't it summon those monsters that nearly killed us all? Wasn't the trick with the green light just a lure, to bring us in close?"

Muttered words bubbled up in the darkness. The shattered survivors of the People would be only too happy to blame Gash-Eye for the whole thing. *Fine,* she thought. *Let them tear me apart, and stop lollygagging.*

"That's crazy!" said Quarry. Spear jumped, not having noticed her there in the darkness. "There's no reason to think Gash-Eye was any more responsible than any of us!"

But there was suspicion even in wise old Stick's voice as he said, "I don't know—Gash-Eye was also the one to point out the Big-Brows with the green light in the first place, wasn't she?"

"Because that's her job. We make her do that."

Gash-Eye tried to stir herself, to muster the will to tell Quarry not to bother about her. She felt like she was nearly able to, but was annoyed at the necessity—it would be so much easier if everyone would simply allow her to rest there till she died, or else kill her.

"Keep your mouth shut, girl," warned Spear. "Or you'll share in what she's getting."

Quarry's voice trembled, but she spoke up anyway: "You know good and well she had nothing to do with those unkillables. You've always hated her, and you're using the unkillables as an excuse to put her to death now!"

Spear walloped the girl's head hard with his fist. She fell back, stunned. "I've got time to do you both," said Spear, sounding satisfied with the prospect, as if it made up for the destruction of their band.

But as he was about to bring his fist clubbing down on the girl again, Gash-Eye thrust herself up from the rock floor and shoved him hard in the chest, sending him flying backward. Now that she was fully awake again, her strength was a match for Spear's. She grabbed Quarry and tore off deeper into the cave, following the rocky slope downward, the girl in her arms. Already Spear was howling in outrage.

The cave opened out and grew bigger as one went deeper in and down. Gash-Eye stopped and held still. The mouth of the cave was so distant, this was near the limit of where she could see anything. But if she were nearly blind here, then the People would be completely so, giving her an advantage over Spear and the rest of them. And now that the room had opened out, there was more space for Gash-Eye and Quarry to hide, if the People did come groping after them. Gash-Eye held Quarry close, not wanting her to stray and get lost, keeping her hand clamped over the girl's mouth even though she was sure Quarry was clever enough not to make noise.

"Big-Brow!" shrieked Spear. Terrible echoes bounced and rebounded through the cave. "You bitch! I'll eat you and that little girl both!"

"Stop it, Spear!" scolded Stick. "Leave them! If they want to skulk in the dark, let them! If Gash-Eye comes back, we'll kill her for having warned her fellow Big-Brows. But everyone knows Quarry's right, there's no way Gash-Eye is behind the unkillables, and merely warning off that band of Big-Brows is not cause enough to risk our lives hunting her. As for Quarry, I say she shall not be hurt."

Stick's admonition wasn't enough to quiet Spear all at once. "I'll kill her!" he raged. "I'll cut open her belly and suck out her guts! You hear me, Gash-Eye? Come out and face me, you freak!"

Suddenly Gash-Eye became aware of something moving in the darkness. It was between her and Spear—she had dashed past it. She stared at the shape, squinting, until she was sure. Perhaps her rush past had awakened it. The People would not be able to see it.

That is, the People would not be able to see it, yet. It was shuffling their way, and would be upon them soon.

"I hear you, Spear," she said. Her loud words reverberated through the cavern so that it was impossible to pinpoint where she was, though she could make out Spear cocking his head and trying to do just that. "Would you like to kill me before or after I tell you about the unkillable that I see in here with us?"

43

No one spoke.

"It's headed your way," she added.

Still, no one answered. In the stillness all could now hear the scraping of its soles against the rock floor.

Though it took her a moment to be certain, Gash-Eye saw that now, in fact, it was turning back down toward her and Quarry.

Spear answered: "You're lying, Big-Brow. You're trying to frighten us."

"If that's true you have nothing to fear, and can come after me with no worries that you'll bump into something else."

Spear didn't move. From the People came keening and sobbing, and hushed warding chants. The unkillable turned again, and shuffled once more toward them.

"You led us here on purpose!" cried Spear.

"Stop being a fool, Spear!" said Stick. "Gash-Eye. We know you're not in league with these things. That's just Spear's prattle. Tell us where it is, that we may defend ourselves." There was bustling commotion. To the others, Stick said, "Where will you go, outside?! There are still a dozen of those things out there!" Again to Gash-Eye, Stick said, "Tell us where it is, Gash-Eye. Be our eyes. Fulfill your purpose, and all will be forgotten regarding your warning to your fellow Big-Brows, last night."

While Stick had been speaking, Gash-Eye had taken her hand from Quarry's mouth and, too quiet for anyone else to hear, whispered, "Stay here. Stay silent. You will not be able to see me, but I will be able to see you, and I will return to fetch you. But you must be silent."

Now, as Stick waited for her reply, as they all listened to the bare black feet scattering pebbles, Gash-Eye took a few careful steps, leaning over to pick up two stones about the size of skulls. She gripped them tightly in her palms and crept forward. Even for her the thing was hard to see—she could see it only as a blotch of darker shadow. It was moving so slowly. Gash-Eye wondered if that was because it was weak with hunger. If so, she wondered if it would speed up once it had food at hand.

The panicked refugees toward the front of the cave were getting noisier and noisier. It had not occurred to them that their commotion might be attracting the unkillable, not even to Stick, who shouted, "Gash-Eye, don't let that thing drive us back outside to its fellows! Tell us where it is!" Even he was edging backward.

Their clamor disguised whatever slight sounds Gash-Eye might be making as she snuck up behind the creature. She held her arms outstretched, still gripping the stones, ignoring the strain in her muscles. She was unlikely to get more than one chance to kill this thing. From what she'd seen of the others of its kind, she might have no chance at all.

Now she was only two paces behind it, staring at the back of its head. The creature paused, as if it were listening, and Gash-Eye wondered if she'd made a sound. For an instant she imagined she saw, not the back of the thing's head, but its face there in the shadows before her. Although moments ago she'd been ready to welcome death, now that she faced it in the form of this awful monster she was terrified. One last time she gauged the distance between them.

As hard as she could, she clapped the two stones together. Resistance jolted her arms as the creature's skull came between the stones—she'd calculated well.

Gash-Eye struck hard enough to kill any creature she'd ever encountered before. But she was shocked to find that the head of this thing actually popped with a squirting sound—as if its skull had been weak and rotten. Chunks of wet brain and shards of bone splattered back into her face. Instinctively she sealed her lips, and, dropping the stones, rubbed her face clean on the backs of her forearms.

Meanwhile the unkillable thing dropped to its knees before her, then onto its belly. It continued to crawl forward till Gash-Eye set her feet on its calf and held it in place. Its arms tried weakly to twist around and take hold of her, but they couldn't reach. Gash-Eye wasn't very scared of the thing anymore. Now that its head was smashed like an old brown fruit, it had no more mouth to bite her with.

The People didn't know whether to be hopeful at the crashing sound, or more terrified than ever. "Gash-Eye?" called Stick. "Gash-Eye, is that you? What was that noise?" In the darkness she could make out Spear, head still cocked, straining to pick up some clue of what was happening.

"I am here, Stick," she said. Her voice, rougher and thicker than the People's, reverberated eerily. "I am here, all you People, with you in the dark. The unkillable thing that would have murdered you lies defeated under my foot."

Relief mixed with uncertainty could be heard in the People's murmurings, and in Stick's voice: "We thank you, Gash-Eye.... If it's true that you've saved us from one of those things, all will be forgiven...."

"You took me for a purpose," she continued, cutting him off; "you had a purpose for me, when you took me all those years ago. It was that I might see into the dark places. The dark places of the earth, when the sun goes down, and also the dark places of the universe. You could use me as a tool in your rites, to see into the future and into the other hidden places of the world.

"But now we are in the world you knew no longer. No more will you merely peer into the darkness. Now you will live here, in my realm, with me. There will be no more light and if you wish to see you must do it with my eyes.

"Leave this cave if you wish to face what awaits you there. I can see the outside as clearly as I saw that unkillable which was hidden from you all, and I say that if you go out there you will face the black and green non-death of your brethren. I see it: a scene of unkillable monsters, roving the forest, covering the hill like ants on a pile." Hopefully no one would crawl forth and peek out the mouth of the cave, in case she was wrong. "We must move even deeper down into this cave if you want to be safe."

She turned her back on her stunned captors and went to where she'd left Quarry. The girl was huddled and trembling, blind in the darkness. She whimpered when Gash-Eye touched her, then relaxed as she realized who it was. Gash-Eye gathered her up into her strong arms, picked her up and held her.

"Is this true, Gash-Eye?" ventured Stick, fearfully. When she didn't deign to answer, he said, "Must we really stay here always, and never see the sun?"

"For a while. I will tell you when we may safely leave." If she could draw them away from the light and into the places where only she could see, then they would need her, and she would be safe and would be able to keep the girl safe too.

Quarry was weeping, almost soundlessly; Gash-Eye gently shushed and caressed her. Then she thought of something. Turning back toward Stick, she said, "And my name is not Gash-Eye. It's Petal-Drift."

Five

They didn't travel very long before the monster, or the woman, insisted they rest. Chert wanted to put more distance between themselves and the catastrophe, but the monster, who'd managed to convey that her name was Veela, assured them it was safe. "No no-die," she kept repeating. "No no-die, for far." Well, Chert supposed, maybe she really did have some way of knowing.

She kept picking up objects and saying something, then holding the rock or stick or whatever it was expectantly toward Chert and the Jaw. It didn't take long to figure out she wanted them to teach her the words for things, and they switched from Overhill to the People's tongue. If they were going to teach her a language, it might as well be their own. Veela seemed confused at first, then exasperated when she realized they were teaching her a whole new tongue, instead of building on the one she'd already started. But there wasn't much she could do about it.

It got even more confusing for her when they switched back to Overhill, wanting to question her without having to teach her a whole language first. "Give us the strong tight fire," said the Jaw. "Give it to us, so we can go back and kill the no-dies." Chert also was eager to learn the secret of the strong tight fire, albeit not so he could rush back to fight the undead.

Veela nodded enthusiastically, but what she said was, "Time, takes many. For try, try, try. Difficult."

Fine. Chert and the Jaw could understand that it would take time to learn a strange new weapon. But that was all the more reason to start practicing, and they were frustrated at her refusal to produce it.

She managed to explain that she wanted to be able to talk to them better before training them for her people's weapons. So they went back to repeating to her the words for things. She retained them surprisingly well, and soon was picking up words for actions and colors, too. Her sentences were still jumbles of the couple hundred words she'd learned, but the hunters could tell it wouldn't be long before she was able to have a basic conversation. Even so, they didn't want to wait to start learning. The Jaw, especially.

He said to her, "I want to kill the no-dies." It was the thousandth time he'd said it.

She nodded enthusiastically. "Need the help," she said. "Help we need, to kill the no-dies. No-die, all. Must needs kill all no-dies."

The Jaw nodded. That was fine with him.

But Veela pressed the point, as if he'd not understood completely; "*All,*" she repeated.

They stayed at that resting spot all the next day. For some reason she wanted to stay in the area—when they tried to figure out exactly why, she either didn't have the fluency or the desire to explain. Chert was suspicious and impatient and several times muttered to the Jaw that they should be on their way, with or without the pretty monster, but the Jaw refused and Chert didn't want to try to physically pull him away.

She learned the language fast. Chert wondered if she had magical help. She had a small something, shaped like a nut pierced with tiny regular holes, with a shiny surface like impossibly smooth stone, almost like ice except that, like the protective sheet that had been over her face, which she'd raised, it didn't melt. Perhaps it really was a nut, from some unimaginable tree. Or it could be something completely different. Chert was getting used to the idea that there were things in the world so completely beyond his understanding that he couldn't even define the boundaries of his incomprehension.

Anyway, there was a tiny man living inside the nut. Sometimes Veela would hold it up to her mouth and speak through the holes to the little man inside it, and he would respond in his strange high-pitched buzzing voice. He sounded remarkably at ease and confident, considering that Veela had him trapped in a nut and was hundreds of times bigger than him. Perhaps the nut was of such strong material that he didn't fear she'd be able to break into it.

And then again, maybe he had some mysterious value, despite his size. At times Veela listened to him closely and with great attention, and Chert remembered old Pine, from his boyhood, who'd had a withered arm and no teeth left, but who'd been kept alive because of his great wisdom and counsel. Perhaps the tiny man was like that.

And maybe he even had some more direct power, some form of magic, for example. There were times when Chert distinctly felt that she'd asked the little man for something, and he'd refused, and she'd been helplessly frustrated by his refusal.

One such time was after the Jaw had pressed her for the secret of the strong tight fire. She'd avoided giving him a straight answer, but soon afterward had consulted the miniature man in the nut. They'd had what sounded like an argument, and afterward Veela had looked unhappy, though her body language was strange and hard to read. The Jaw had asked again for the strong tight fire, and this time she said, "Waiting is being needed." Impressively, she was able to say this in the People's tongue already, even though they'd only met her this morning.

Chert said to the Jaw, "That tiny man inside the nut won't let her give us the fire." Veela cocked her ear at the two of them, frustrated not to be able to understand what they said.

The Jaw turned to Chert with contempt. "What do you mean? How could that tiny man possibly stop her from doing anything?"

"I have no idea. I've given up trying to understand things. But I'm telling you, that's what he said."

The Jaw remained dubious, but was too uncertain to argue.

"What are the no-dies?" the Jaw kept asking.

Veela said a word in her own language that neither of them understood. After much pantomiming and retching noises, she communicated to them its meaning: "Disease?" said the Jaw.

Veela repeated the word twice to memorize it, and said, "No-dies, disease. Type of disease. Bite of a no-die grants you disease. Must kill no-die. All things of world will be no-die."

That last bit didn't quite make sense, though it did sound ominous. They went back and forth a while, rehashing the sentence, Veela repeating the phrase with variations, till by chance they taught her the word "or." Then she said, "Must kill no-dies, or all things of world will be no-die."

"That's ridiculous," said Chert. "No disease spreads to every person of the world. There are no spirits that hungry."

"No-die spirit, hungry," insisted Veela. "Very, very hungry."

"Where does the spirit come from?" asked Chert. "Why have we never heard of it before?"

Veela pretended not to know. Being civilized, she was better at lying than anyone Chert and the Jaw had ever met, so they believed in her ignorance.

"In any case," said Chert, "you can't kill a spirit. If men could kill spirits, they would have long since killed all the disease spirits and no one would ever get sick. What we must do is learn the proper rites to appease this no-die spirit, so that it will look for its prey elsewhere."

Their next project was to teach Veela what the word "appease" meant. Once she'd learned it, and grasped the sense of what Chert had said, she grew excited, shaking her head and waving her arms and saying, "No, no, no! No appease! Kill all no-die spirit. Or world is be no-die people, no-die wolf, no-die squirrel, no-die bird...."

"She means all people and all animals everywhere will become undead," said the Jaw.

"No spirit could ever be that hungry!" repeated Chert, exasperated. "How could a spirit be big enough to eat the world?! For that, it would have to be as big as the world. If it was as big as the world, it would fill all of it, and have no one place to call its home. And who ever heard of a spirit without a home? Where would it take its sacrifice?"

"But what if this particular spirit *is* that hungry?"

"Then there's no use worrying about it, because you can't kill a spirit."

The Jaw fell silent. He was unhappy, but Chert's points were unanswerable.

But Veela wouldn't let it go. "Must help kill no-die," she said. "Must help. Stranger here, us. Have weapons. Need help, but."

"'Us'?" said the Jaw. "There are more of you?"

She looked blankly at the Jaw. From the way her eyes then went to the stone nut, Chert understood that she was wondering why they were surprised, when she'd assumed they knew she meant the little man in the nut. She must believe the little trapped man had some powerful magic indeed, if she thought he could help destroy those hordes of undead. "Must help," she repeated.

"Why use us? Why not use the flying stone, with its strong tight fire?" asked Chert.

Veela got the gist of what he said, though she seemed confused by the phrase "flying stone." She said, "Weapon, tired becomes."

So the spirit that guided or inhabited the strong tight fire was too fickle to explode all the undead heads at once, but required multiple sacrifices and exhortations. Or else it really did grow tired. That would be even more worrisome, especially if Veela proved correct about the nature of the spirit of the undead sickness—how could a spirit that quickly and easily grew tired fight an infinitely gluttonous and infinitely larger one?

"But why do you need *us*?" demanded the Jaw. "What can we do, compared to you? You're the one with the strong tight fire."

Veela struggled to respond. It was a linguistic struggle but also a diplomatic one, since she didn't want to come out and say that she lacked faith in her partner Dak's ability to monitor the zombies as well as he claimed he could. For example, she knew the ship's rinky-dink sensors couldn't penetrate the planet surface to see what might be going on in the cave networks.

On top of that, she and Dak were clearly prone to error, since they'd let a zombie mouse stow away on their ship, coming all the way back with them through time. And that mouse had apparently bitten a member of Population Group B (the people Chert and the Jaw knew as Overhills), after she'd already chosen their language as the one to start studying. The plague had wiped that whole group out in an hour. And while zapping them all in the heads with lasers, Dak had failed to notice that a band of Neanderthals had come across a stray zombie. They'd beheaded it and started using its head as a fucking lamp, till one of them got himself bitten. A lot of people had died because Dak had been preoccupied—not that the perimeter wall he was busy with wasn't important. There were plenty of drones on the ship—if they could access them Veela was certain they could locate and destroy every zombie on the planet, but they were locked up in a special hold and Dak couldn't decipher the lock, so he was stuck using only the ship's on-board laser.

"Need friends, know land," she said, wishing she knew the word for "environment." Although these people probably didn't have a concept of "environment" that matched well with hers—the closest might be something like "world." She said, "Need friends, know land. Need friends, know tongues." Even though all the other people in this immediate area were apparently dead or zombified, Veela wanted to be able to communicate with those outside the perimeter in case some zombies had escaped, regardless of how impossible Dak claimed that would be.

Also, she wanted to be able to communicate with people beyond the perimeter because hopefully they would survive all this, and would one day go out and interact with those folks. It wasn't as if she and Dak could go back where they'd come from. And remembering the Jaw's scream and Chert's blow from the rock, she decided she'd prefer not to be alone next time she had to go through the getting-to-know-you process.

"If we can't use the strong tight fire," pressed Chert, "how can we fight the no-dies?"

"Need help, talk to other people. Explain no-dies, other people."

"And what if we run across no-dies before running across other people who need explaining?"

"Head." After some pantomiming, they guessed she was trying to indicate the word "remove." They taught it to her, and she said, "Remove head. After, no-die body die. No-die body live not with head, short time. After, no-die body die."

Chert grew angry. "You want us to walk up to those things and take their heads off with axes? Instead of trying to persuade the spirit of the strong tight fire to fight harder? How powerful do you think we are?"

Veela was desperate. She was nearly crying. "Need help. Need help."

"Then ask for it from the powerful spirit of the strong tight fire. Ask for it from your magic man in his little nut. My son and I are not even medicine men. If we try to fight these things with only our stones and our arms, we'll die."

"But I want to fight them, Father," said the Jaw.

Chert was drawn up short for a speechless moment. Never before had the Jaw called him "Father" like that. Of course he knew it was an attempt to soften him and make him more amenable to Veela's pleas. Understanding the ploy didn't make it entirely ineffective. Nevertheless, Chert said to the Jaw, "I tell you that if we fight those things in that way we will be killed, or else become like them. I'm sorry, my son. But the truth is a stone that cannot be broken."

"Need help," Veela kept repeating. She actually was crying now. At first Chert thought something was wrong with her; then he realized she was trying to hold back her tears, which struck him as an odd thing to do. "Need help. Or whole world no-die will be. Whole world no-die."

"We should agree," insisted the Jaw. "Even if we don't end up destroying all the undead, at least we might learn more about the strong tight fire. That may prove valuable, yes?"

Very well—they could agree, and maybe glean some knowledge from this monster, who might be nothing but a very strange woman, after all. Anyway, Chert could tell he wasn't going to be able to pry the Jaw away just yet. It was not only the lust for vengeance that held him, Chert sensed, but another kind of lust, too. Well, if it did turn out this Veela was simply a woman, they would be able to take her with them by force, no matter how desperately she wanted to stay near this cursed ground and commit suicide by throwing rocks at those undead. Best to wait, though, till they had been better able to gauge her powers.

Veela was greatly relieved when they told her they'd stay with her and lend their strength to the fight against the undead, so much so that Chert wondered if she had an exaggerated notion of their prowess. Privately, she herself felt that the benefit they brought was mainly psychological. It felt good to have any allies in this impossible fight, in this alien time. And hopefully she really would be able to learn something of value from them.

In fact, it was not long before exactly that happened, although she was not to appreciate the significance of the datum for quite some time.

It was while they were tramping along again through the forest, before nightfall. The woman followed Chert and the Jaw. She hadn't wanted to move at all, but Chert had insisted that they put some distance between them and the site of the no-die attack. Chert wondered if she had any idea where she was at all—she just seemed so stupid.

They passed a patch of purple-capped Mushrooms of the Inner Eye, and the Jaw pointed them out to Chert. "I want to eat one," he said.

"We don't have time," said Chert.

"The journey is never long, for those who are left behind." (Time passed differently when one traveled through the underworld, and the voyager could sometimes feel that many days had gone by.) "And I want to see if my mother is there below."

Chert tried to keep his shoulders from sagging. "Why?" he asked. "What good will that do?"

"I just want to see if she's there."

"Whether you see her or not, it won't mean anything. You aren't a shaman. You don't know how to ask the spirits which visions are true and which are not. And there's no shaman here for us to tell what we saw."

"I want to see."

Veela watched the scene with obvious incomprehension. She began moving toward the patch of Mushrooms of the Inner Eye.

Chert thought she was going to try to eat one. He stopped arguing with the Jaw long enough to grab her arm, prompting her to squeal in fright. The childish, dangerously noisy reaction did not exactly augment Chert's respect for the woman. "Those are for the People, only," he snarled.

Veela bowed her head repeatedly and shrunk in her shoulders, trying to indicate submission. She hadn't intended to eat the mushroom—she'd been interested in the patch because she'd guessed that this fungus had some kind of ritual significance for her new buddies.

Chert turned back to the Jaw. Between his son's stubbornness and the monster woman's nosiness, he had trouble keeping his temper. "Without the shaman to guide you, you will understand nothing of what you see," he said, forcing his voice to remain calm. "And you will create danger for me and the woman. We will have to guard you while your spirit voyages out from its body. Even if it only takes a short time, that will not be safe for us."

That turned out to be the right argument; the notion that he would be a burden was an affront to the Jaw's pride, if nothing else. With a frown he turned his back on the mushroom patch and walked away.

Chert followed his son. While their backs were turned, Veela reached for one of the mushrooms.

But Chert spun around and grabbed her arm, held his face close to hers, and growled. Veela again put on her cowed, submissive face, which wasn't hard to do. Okay, so the guy definitely did not want her eating that shroom—she could take a hint. Meanwhile she made a mental note of just how much sharper than hers his senses were. Pretty impressive, how he'd known what she was up to while she was still behind him.

He kept a sharp eye on her after that, till they were well away from the mushroom patch. For now, Veela only tried to discreetly memorize the distinctive purple design on the cap of the fungus. It might be interesting to analyze whatever it was these guys were tripping on, even if it was probably nothing more than a garden-variety psychedelic.

Six

Eventually dusk was presaged in the sky. Veela indicated they all should go to sleep. The Jaw offered to stand the first watch. At first Veela didn't understand what he meant; once they'd explained it, she shook her head and held up the nut. Chert and the Jaw figured out she was saying the little man in the nut would stand guard.

"How will *he* be able to keep watch?" demanded Chert, pointing scornfully at the nut. "Even if you let him out, he must be smaller than a bug. It would take him a day and a night to walk a circuit around our sleeping bodies."

"And sealed inside the nut, he can only see straight ahead, through the side that the tiny holes are on," said the Jaw, frowning in confusion. "What if something approaches from the side with no holes?"

It took Veela some time to understand what they were saying, and when she did she laughed and assured them that, no, they would be safe enough with only the man in the nut watching. Annoyed by her foolishness, Chert and the Jaw agreed that the Jaw would take the first watch, and Chert the second. Chert grimly told himself that if this Veela thought they weren't going to wake her up for the third watch, she had a surprise in store. He decided he would surreptitiously stay awake himself, during her turn. If he saw her nod off, then he would know she was worse than useless, and he would kill her.

Despite all the uncertainties the day had left him with, Chert fell asleep soon after lying down. He'd hoped for dreamlessness, but at least there were no visions terrible enough to wake him. He woke easily when the Jaw shook him to take his turn. Out of the corner of his eye he watched his son lie down and almost immediately fall asleep. Chert had not always paid much attention to the Jaw. For his first three years the child had been mostly in the company of Gash-Eye, in whom Chert had had no interest once he'd finished the honor of ceremonially cutting her face and fathering the boy upon her. And later, as the boy had grown, even if he had not been a half-breed, it would not have been Chert's way to wish the child to fawn at his heels, and far less to fawn at his. But over the winters, Chert had developed an unorthodox interest in his son. He knew the boy hated him sometimes. But he didn't always hate him, because he appreciated how Chert included him in the band, instead of leaving him to be the mere slave he'd been destined to be. Now that they'd been thrown together this way, Chert was surprised to find there was something pleasant about the easy familiarity that was developing between them. Even considering the circumstances.

Chert looked into the dark forest and listened. He was willing to admit that he wished they'd had Gash-Eye with them now, with her freakish Big-Brow eyesight. Also, it would have been good for the Jaw. It was natural that he should miss her. The Jaws were always left alone with their Gash-Eye mothers more than the People's children were with theirs; fostering a closer, more loving bond between mother and child made the Jaw a more effective hostage.

The nut screamed—it wailed like a spirit being murdered. Chert jumped so high he nearly fell over, then stared at the thing in shock. Surely the little man who lived inside it must have been killed by the noise.

The Jaw was on his feet, staring wild-eyed. Veela leaped up and grabbed the nut; it stopped screaming with an abruptness even more shocking than the noise had been. She said something to Chert in her own language and then, seeing his incomprehension, remembered herself and said, "No-die, you see?"

Mouth gaping stupidly, Chert shook his head.

Now the little man in the nut was talking to Veela, sounding unfazed. Veela spoke to him in their language. Chert and the Jaw stood and stared at them during their exchange. Veela was upset about something—as she and the little man talked, she got angrier and angrier, while Chert and the Jaw could tell from the little man's calm tone that he retained the upper hand.

At last she flung down the nut, and picked up the Jaw's spear. Chert snatched it away from her. She said, "Must fight. Come, no-die comes."

"Then use your strong tight fire, damn you."

"Tired, the fire is," she said bitterly, and glared down at the nut.

"Well, I'm tired too. Too tired to fight a band of things that don't die. Now just tell me where the no-dies are so the Jaw and I can slip past them...."

He trailed off, because he could see by the approaching green glow where the undead were.

One of them, at least. He hoped that was all there was. It was still too distant to make out clearly through the trees.

"Green is," said Veela. "Means eated. Means strong."

"Then get your damn strong tight fire."

"No can. But together. Together, fight. Together, survive."

The thing came closer. Chert realized it was not a reanimated person, but a deer. It stumbled through the trees clumsily, but it definitely knew they were there and was closing in. If it had been an undead in a human body Chert would have tried to persuade the Jaw to run away, but he figured a deer, even an undead one, would be able to catch up with them.

He looked over his shoulder and saw the Jaw had his spear ready, looking grim and prepared. "The woman says we have to destroy the head," Chert reminded him. "So that's what we'll do and we'll hope she's right." *And then we'll leave her behind and go our own way, if this is all the help she is,* he silently added. The Jaw nodded at him, then turned his eyes back to the glowing green deer.

The dead animal made more noise thrashing through the underbrush than it ever had done in life. Once there were not too many trees blocking the way between it and them, Chert saw his son's spear go flying past his shoulder and into the thing's neck.

The spear didn't stop the thing. But it gave it pause. The deer reared back and made an unearthly noise, a kind of wrathful bleat. There was a whistle inside the sound, as the air expelled by the deer was partially blocked by the spear handle lodged in its throat.

The deer began advancing again right away, its head cocked at a funny angle because of the spear. Again it bleated, with that eerie whistle.

The Jaw sprang past Chert, at the deer. The deer snapped at him but missed. The Jaw grabbed the spear and tried to use it as a handle to swing the animal's head around and smash it into a tree. But the deer reared up on its hind legs and swung itself back and forth, throwing the Jaw and sending him flying head-first into a tree, instead. For the second time that day, the youth was knocked out.

Chert darted forward and slipped his own spear between the thing's ribs. When it tried to come down onto its front feet again, the spear held him propped up for a few moments. The thing waved its feet and screamed in rage at being immobilized. As Chert retreated from it, he took a quick swipe with his axe at the sinews of its left hip.

Chert knew his spear wasn't going to stand up to the weight of that thrashing animal, so as soon as he saw he'd succeeded in delaying it he rushed for the Jaw. Sure enough, as he was hefting his son onto his sore shoulders for the second time since morning, the spear snapped and the animal came crashing down. He was no longer naïve enough to hope that damage to the undead's organs would have any effect, but as he glanced back it looked to him like he'd managed to do some damage to the hip.

"Chert!" screamed Veela. "Chert!"

Without looking at her he tore off through the night with his son on his back. He was leaving their weapons behind; as far as he was concerned, that meant they were providing the woman with more help than they owed or she deserved. He hoped whatever other undead creatures might be out tonight would also have a helpful green glow, so he could avoid them. As for Veela, he thought he'd taken the measure of her unimaginably pathetic tracking abilities. It was safe to say she'd never find them again, unless that little man had some magic that could help her.

Behind him he heard the woman screaming something unintelligible. He ignored her—he had enough to worry about, hauling the Jaw's weight through the forest in the dark, and had no idea Veela was trying to warn him they wouldn't be able to get far.

Seven

Veela spent a couple minutes trying to smash the deer's skull with a rock. Because the animal had no arms and hands to grip her with, she was able to hang on desperately to its neck as it tried to twist its head around and snap at her with its small mouth.

"Dak!" she kept saying. It was hard to keep from screaming, but she knew the communicator would be able to pick up her voice even if she whispered, and she was afraid being loud would attract more zombies. Not that there was much point in keeping her voice down, what with all the thrashing she and the deer were doing, as she kept trying to bash it. "Dak, you have to shoot this fucking thing!"

"We have to conserve our energy," he replied blithely from the communicator. "It isn't like there are any power stations where we can refuel."

Veela jerked her head back an instant before the glowing deer could bite her in the face. "But this thing is going to kill me!"

"Don't worry, I'm monitoring your progress; you're doing better than you think you are. If things get too hairy, I'll step in. But we are going to eventually have to live in this world without the technological advantages we're accustomed to."

That was true. And while it didn't feel to Veela like she was doing very well against the zombie deer, she supposed she was too close to the situation to be an objective judge. For a while she continued to keep her arm locked around the deer's neck and bang it ineffectually in the head with her rock. This zombie's motor skills had been particularly impaired during its transformation; still, it would have bucked her off easily, if not for the damage Chert had done to its hip. She was getting exhausted, and knew that her arms would soon slip loose from the deer; at which point, either the deer would manage to inflict only a superficial bite and she'd turn into a zombie herself, or else the deer would eat her brain. *"Dak!"* she wailed, in despair.

"Oh, all right," he snapped. "Stand back."

"I'm scared to let go."

"Veela, which is it? Do you want me to shoot it, or do you want to kill it yourself? Right now you're too close to the head for me to safely hit it."

"Okay. On three." Veela counted to three, then hesitated, unable to make herself let go. Then she was scared that Dak was about to shoot anyway and would hit her with the laser. With a whimper she let go and was flung back into the trees.

The impact knocked the air out of her. She should have planned her retreat better, she realized. The zombie deer turned its head to her and bleated in rage.

Just when Veela was wondering if Dak had experienced some kind of instrument failure, the pale green light emanating from the deer was superseded by the blinding red bolt sizzling down from the sky. With the spots popping in front of her eyes it was hard for Veela to be sure, but the laser seemed to have passed through the deer's right hip, slowing it down by inflicting more joint damage, but coming nowhere near the brain. The deer's back right leg collapsed, but with its two front legs it pulled itself her way, blank eyes fixed upon her face. Veela was frozen. Had the son of a bitch decided two laser blasts would be too great a drain on their dwindling energy supplies? The deer kept coming. She couldn't look away from it. That was her death, that glowing green deer.

There was another blinding red blast. Only now did she find herself able to scamper a few feet away. As her eyesight returned she stared at the gently writhing corpse, unable to yet make out its form in detail because of the laser's after-image but still seeing that green glow. But it was no longer an approaching glow, and after a few seconds she realized it was fading.

She became aware that Dak was hailing her. "Veela? Veela? Are you all right? I know you're all right, I can see you on the sensors. Answer me."

Veela shook herself. Her vision had recovered enough that she could see a smoky charred ruin where the deer's head had been. Its body stirred only lightly. She tried to get to her feet, but was too shaky and exhausted, so she crawled to the communicator. "Thanks a lot," she said.

"You're welcome," said Dak, then, surprised, said, "Wait, was that sarcasm? I just saved your life!"

"You waited long enough."

"I explained to you why."

"Yeah, well." Veela took the communicator and leaned against a tree. She looked out into the darkness of this world that was so beautiful, and yet entirely barren of all the things she had once used in her day-to-day life—and was infected, now, with the pestilence that had destroyed her own world. Or helped to destroy it—she and Dak had certainly done their part. She nearly gave in to the desire to weepingly give up. But she reminded herself that they had about forty-five thousand years in which to avert the very final catastrophe, as long as they could kill these fucking zombies first. Holding the communicator in her palm more as a reminder of home than as a practical tool, she nevertheless used it to say to Dak, "I'm going to go back to sleep now. Please keep watch."

"Of course I will," he said, then added, "I'll have the computer do it, that is."

It was useless, trying to sleep in this forest. It was filled with living things, and every time one of them made any sound her eyes snapped open. She hoped Dak was keeping an eye out for, say, regular bears, as well as the zombie variety. Even the breezes made her anxious. Never, in her life before, had she tried to sleep in an environment that was not artificially regulated. Strictly speaking, she'd never even been in such an environment; there had always been weather satellites, perimeter barriers, landscape design, and so on, even when she had gone outside beyond the sight of any building, which had been rare. Somehow, she'd been able to sleep when those two guys had been with her, especially the young one, whose name seemed to be "Jaw" (the older one's name seemed to be a subcategory of rock—Veela had a feeling these people would have about a billion more ways to describe varieties of rock than anyone in her century). Maybe she wouldn't have been able to sleep around just the older guy— but, foolish though it might be, for some reason she trusted the younger one.

When the world began to be illuminated by the tree-hidden dawn, she sat up. As soon as Dak saw her movement through the sensor attached to the communicator, he scolded her: "Did you sleep at all? I need you to be alert."

"It's hard to sleep down here. Anyway, it sounds like *you're* still awake."

"Yes, but I had the ship put me into a deep REM for four hours, so I'm relatively well-rested." Veela silently observed that it must be nice, staying with the ship. "Well, since you're up, let's get started."

First he wanted her to fill him in on everything from her exchange with the Cro-Magnon and the Neanderthal that she hadn't had a chance to translate for him yesterday. He couldn't understand the necessity of delay while she hastened to get away from the blackened corpse of the zombie deer, and then as she began to fill him in he was annoyed that she hadn't gotten more information.

"I do have to learn their whole language, you know," she said.

"But I was right about learning a Cro-Magnon language, wasn't I?"

"It wasn't the one those two speak."

"But I was right about learning *a* Cro-Magnon language."

This had been a bone of contention between them. There had been three human groups within the perimeter Dak had lain down: the Cro-Magnons Dak and Veela called Group B, who spoke the Overhill language; the so-called "People," who were Group A; and Group C, the Neanderthals that Gash-Eye had spotted and warned off the night before last. One spy-bug drone apiece had been dropped among all three populations—those were all that Dak had had available, until he could access that locked hold where the others were kept. While they were still in orbit, Veela had run quick linguistic analyses on all of them and had determined the Neanderthal language would be the easiest to learn, because it was most similar to her and Dak's language. Moreover, she figured that with their greater physical strength, the Neanderthals would have made formidable allies. Plus, everyone from Veela's century who'd ever so much as read an article on paleogenetics knew that Neanderthals had had freakishly good eyesight. Having less faith than Dak in the infallibility of their sensors, she thought that might come in handy.

Dak had been surprisingly chauvinistic about the whole thing: "I don't think you should be wasting time learning to speak like a *Neanderthal*, when there are more advanced humans nearby."

"The Neanderthals are just as intelligent."

"They went extinct, didn't they?"

"We're going to go extinct too, remember? In fact, the way things are going to turn out, the Neanderthals will have spent more time on the planet than we will."

Dak finally brought her around by postulating that their thicker skulls would make it harder to actually get at their brains, meaning that if Veela happened to be near them instead of Cro-Magnons during a zombie attack, she was less likely to wind up surrounded by empty-headed corpses than by huge, zombified Neanderthals. And now that the Neanderthals had all been killed or zombified, she had to admit it was a good thing she'd gone along with him. Of course, she couldn't help but once more point out, the Cro-Magnons whose language she'd begun learning had also all been either killed or zombified.

"Ah, yes, but at least that language was in the same family as the one we need," said Dak.

She thought about those spy-bug drones that had collected linguistic data until their batteries had run down—now they lay inert somewhere on the forest floor, inconspicuous little brown permaplast pellets, indestructible and useless. Veela had been appalled at how quickly they'd run down. Never before had she been exposed to real power loss—even during the apocalypse in her own time, there had been plenty of raw electricity zapping around. But Dak said the solar conversion apparatus was under the aegis of stuff the ship's computer had locked him out of, like that hold filled with weapons and drones. In Veela's experience, even when a solar panel did break down, you could always just plug your whatsit into the nearest freeport. Obviously, there were none of those here, and they had to rely on a few dozen portable power packs, and whatever was left in the ship's power core. Veela had no idea how much power that amounted to, and so just had to take Dak's word for everything.

Veela wanted to hear about what Dak had been doing to contain the zombie crisis. Since she was the one down here on the planet surface, she felt a certain entitlement to know something about the conditions.

Dak confirmed that he'd thrown up a perimeter wall around the zombie contagion, using the cranes, lasers, robot arms, and other equipment that could be extended directly from the ship's hull. "Are you certain you got it up in time?" asked Veela. "You're sure no zombies got across first?"

"Reasonably sure."

Great.

Dak told her that absolutely all humans within the perimeter had been killed or zombified, except her, the Cro-Magnon, and the Neanderthal, whose features, the computer had decided, were actually those of a half-Neanderthal. "It might explain why he was with the Cro-Magnon group, if he's related to them," said Dak.

The more they talked, the less impressed she got. Not to mention pissed off. She knew that zombification could sweep through a population like wildfire, but she still didn't understand how Dak could have lapsed so badly in his monitoring as to let all those people die or be zombified.

"I told you, Veela," he said more than once. "I couldn't keep an eye on those populations and secure the perimeter, all at the same time."

Veela didn't see why not, but figured it would be counterproductive to keep saying so. Maybe setting up the perimeter wall was more involved than she thought. Anyway, Dak was probably upset about it, too, despite his almost cavalier tone—this was probably just how he dealt with negative emotion.

Still, it sure seemed to her that he'd done a bad job. It was hard to see how he could have done less to contain the plague even if he'd wanted it to spread.

There hadn't been all that many humans in the area to begin with, so it followed that there weren't all that many once-human zombies. That was a bit comforting. And the animals, so far, were doing a good job of keep away from the shuffling, smelly, uncoordinated undead hunters. A formerly human zombie was vastly less likely to hear an animal's brainsong than a human's, anyway. But the zombies did bite them sometimes, as Veela had seen with her deer. It was only a matter of time before every creature within the perimeter had either had its brain slurped out or been turned into a zombie. It would be impossible for anything trapped in there with them to survive.

They were lucky the things were vulnerable at all. A bodybuilder or a weightlifter—anyway, somebody a lot stronger than Veela—might be able to break through the skull and burst the transformed brain inside with their bare hands; the average full-grown man could probably do it with a rock. In order to immediately grow strong enough to bite through a healthy skull, the zombified jaw's bones and muscles cannibalized mass and nutrients from the nearest available source, the rest of the head. As a result the zombie skull was comparable in strength to, say, a fairly thin wooden bowl.

"Pretty lucky," Veela had remarked to Dak, days ago, back when they were still in transit back to Earth. "If the zombie venom strengthened the skull as much as it does the teeth, those fucking things would be invulnerable."

"Yes," Dak had said absently, as if tasting something unpleasant. "That's a design flaw that the gengineers really should have fixed." Veela had been simultaneously impressed and repulsed by the cold-blooded scientific remove from which he was able to view the matter.

Now, back in the forest, she said, "Um, so, listen … about my being down here, with these zombies … maybe you could come pick me up? Along with the two guys?"

"You want me to bring the two primitives aboard the ship?" He sounded startled. "After they just abandoned you to the deer?"

Veela could see how it might sound weird. But she said, "At least until we're sure all the zombies have been destroyed. It's not exactly safe for them down here, either."

"Yes, of course, point taken…. Well, I'm not entirely sure how appropriate their presence would be aboard the ship, but at the moment the point is moot. While building the wall, I had no drones available, you know, and so had to use not only the extendible cranes but any controllable ship's protuberance, meaning portions of the landing apparatus had to be pressed into service. Obviously, the apparatus wasn't designed for such work, and it sustained a bit of damage. Meaning that, at the moment, I'm unable to land."

Veela felt suddenly chilly. "You can't land?" she repeated, in a small voice.

"No need to worry, the damage will be quite easy to repair, I'm sure, once I have a spare moment to figure it out. Right now I'm preoccupied with my plan to destroy the zombies."

Well, Veela supposed, it was probably all right—after all, if the damage were irreparable, then Dak should have been the one freaking out. It wasn't like the ship was going to float around up there indefinitely, and it wasn't like there was an infinite supply of food aboard.

She dropped the subject, and asked, "How high is the perimeter wall?"

"Three and a half meters."

Another shock. "Dak," she said, after a silent moment. "I don't think that's going to be high enough."

"Have you spotted some four-meter-tall zombies I should know about?"

Veela had a vision of a horde of zombies somehow figuring out there might be fresh brains on the other side of that wall, and climbing atop one another's squirming bodies to get to them. Of course, there weren't enough humanoid zombies in the area to create a horde, but it could just as easily be a horde composed of former squirrels, bears, deer, and so forth. She expressed this vision to Dak.

"Hm," he said, after she'd explained. "That could be disastrous.... There's an anti-intruder field around it to give nerve shocks, but I'm not certain that will be effective against the zombies.... Well, we'll just have to be sure we annihilate all the zombies before that happens."

"Can't you go back and make the wall higher?"

"Veela, I keep explaining to you that our resources are limited. I agree with you that the zombies must be wiped out at all costs, but that's exactly why I don't think it makes sense to expend all our energy in containing them, if it leaves us with no way to destroy them afterward."

Veela thought she'd like to be able to go up to the ship and have a gander at their resources, herself. If only she knew how to decipher the read-outs; it wasn't her specialty. She said, "I don't see how you can be so calm and collected, considering those things hitched a ride back in time with us, through our carelessness. Not to mention...."

But her throat closed up; she could not bring herself even to speak of the other thing they'd done.

Dak said, "I don't see how feeling guilty will change things. We did what we could to survive, not to mention preserve the last two members of the human race. Maybe we did an imperfect job, but the circumstances were not exactly amenable to careful planning, if you recall. As for the other side-effect, certainly it is unfortunate...."

"Unfortunate?!"

"In any case, it isn't our immediate concern—we and our descendants will have dozens of millennia to worry over it, assuming we can survive and destroy the present infestation. So let's concentrate on the zombies at hand, shall we?"

He outlined his plan. She was dubious, but couldn't think of anything better.

"Now," said Dak, "there is a chance I won't be able to round up all the zombies and one or two more strays may cross your path...."

"Yes, I was just thinking that."

"To provide for such an eventuality, it's best you start thinking how to defend yourself."

"If the sensors show a zombie coming near me, can't you just blast it with the laser?"

"We've just been through that. Besides, this is a dangerous world, and we'll need to survive on it even if our equipment fails or malfunctions. Shouldn't we get started figuring out how to do so?"

"Dak, I don't guess there's any chance of accessing that cache anytime soon?" asked Veela, hopelessly. That store of drones, blasters, and batteries would come in pretty handy right around now.

"I've told you," said Dak, with an ostentatious air of patience. "The code-lock on that hold is very sophisticated. It will take the computer many, many trillions of iterations before it can decipher it. And we don't have unlimited processing power."

Veela didn't see why the only other ship's tasks she knew of, building the wall and tracking the zombies, should eat up so much processing power. But she supposed she wasn't being fair. Now that Dak had hijacked a spaceship and propelled it forty-five millennia back in time, it seemed like he ought to be able to unlock a damn door. But the bottom line, of course, was that she didn't know what she was talking about, and Dak did. And so he could set the rules, and she couldn't argue.

And there was no point complaining about that. It wasn't like it was Dak's fault she'd never rigorously studied physics, higher math, or cryptography.

"I know your situation is dangerous," said Dak. "But it wasn't my idea to have you down there alone, if you recall. Nor is it my fault you have no weapon."

"Yes," snapped Veela, her mouth twisting with embarrassment.

"We haven't many in the first place, you know, what with the hold being locked. So frankly the fact that you—"

"Yes, thank you! Once again, I'm sorry! Let's not talk about it again, thanks!... You were talking about learning to defend ourselves. Where should we start?"

"You must learn how to make a spear."

Veela suppressed a childish groan. Her whole life had conditioned her to say, *Isn't that somebody else's job? I'm a linguist.*

She frowned at her surroundings. "How do I even start?" she said. "Just get a piece of wood or something?"

"For the shaft, you mean? Well, first you'll need a blade with which to fashion the wood."

"Oh, crap." She remembered the weapons Chert and the Jaw had ditched. For a moment she hesitated, but she knew her mere horror at the corpse of the zombie deer in no way justified not going back for them. Dak asked her why she was turning around, and when she explained he was disgusted she'd left them behind in the first place.

"Yeah, well, I'm a little worried that you didn't already know I'd dumped them. You talk about how you can see every little detail of what's going on down here, but you sure do seem to miss a bunch, don't you?"

Dak didn't respond to that.

For the first time it really occurred to her that maybe she shouldn't piss Dak off. Because, after all, he was up there with the ship and she was down here among the zombies and the cavemen, with nothing but a couple of derelict spears and a pretty sturdy helmet, which she'd attached to the clip on her belt because she was tired of wearing it. The sudden doubt in her partner made her shiver in the warm sun.

At first she'd believed she and Dak would become friends, probably even lovers—she'd figured they wouldn't have much choice. They'd been strangers when he'd rescued her from one of the last pressurized rooms at Luna University—he'd told her he only had life support for one more, and that a linguist most suited the needs of his plan. She'd been relieved that anyone thought a linguist might be valuable enough to rescue, now that the apocalypse was here. It wasn't like she had any family she could urge him to save. What few friends she'd had had already been killed or zombified, either on Earth or the Moon.

Dak had set a course from the Moon all the way out to the Cantor-Gould Collider, nearly ten percent of the way to Mars. The little ship he'd commandeered hadn't been built for a journey like that, and it took weeks. During the trip they monitored the increasingly grim and sporadic radio traffic from Earth and the Moon, till it became clear that there were no more pressurized environments on the Moon at all, that Earth was a swarming hive of zombies, maybe a billion of them zombified humans and billions more made up of zombified members of every species of land-going vertebrate. Shit, probably something had managed to bite and zombify a fish and now the seas were full of them too, giant blue whales sending their green glow up to the surface of the water as they scoured their realm for brains, screaming a hungry whalesong. Humanity existed only as pockets of survivors in ships like theirs, watching their life support rations dwindle.

They'd reached the Collider, hanging there lonely in interplanetary space, its crew having abandoned it in their rush to get home and, Veela supposed, die with their families. Once they'd arrived it hadn't taken Dak long to set up the Collider according to his mad scheme. Veela hadn't been competent to help. She'd had zero faith that the plan would work, zero faith that the solar system's largest particle accelerator could generate an effect that would send them back in time.

Lo and behold, it *had* worked—though the energy drain nearly killed them and it took them even more weeks to limp back to this Earth. During the long quiet trip Dak had done some more math, and had one day announced, almost casually, the effect he believed their escape to have had.

Veela had still not been able to respond to it. It wasn't as if she didn't believe Dak—she wasn't competent to check his equations, but she had no reason not to believe it. She supposed she was in shock.

Anyway, in the almost three months it had taken to crawl back to Earth from the Collider—or, rather, from the point where the Collider would someday be, or might someday be— she'd had time to process the catastrophe somewhat. Everyone she'd ever known had died (or would die, rather), along with her whole civilization—there was a lot of grieving to be done, and she'd gotten started on it.

On the other hand, she'd been very lonely for many years, first on the Earth and then on the Moon, so it wasn't like she had close friends to miss. And then there was the excitement, danger, and fear of this new great adventure to distract her. When she'd left her own time, humanity had been for all practical purposes extinct, plus there was the far graver catastrophe that she and Dak had initiated. But now there were forty-five thousand years before that happened.

And then they'd landed and it turned out there had been a god damned zombie mouse in one of the holds—not the one that was locked but an exterior hold. It had come scuttling out the moment they'd popped the hold's hatch, small, black, hissing. At that moment it would have been easy enough to kill, but Veela had frozen with terror, snapping out of it only in time to see the zombie mouse go skittering under the cover of dry leaves. Then it was like it had never been there. Until the other undead had started showing up.

Now it was all happening again. Or, rather, for the first time.

Veela reached the campsite and fetched the spears, but wouldn't pause to closely examine them till she was once more far from the zombie deer, much to Dak's annoyance. She sat on a rock in the shade and hefted one of the spears, looking it over. "Doesn't seem too complicated."

"It will take more practice than you probably think."

"I guess I just find some rocks and chip at one till it's sharp, right? And shaped like a spearhead? And then I can use that to shape a long piece of wood. That should be easy to find, I'm in a forest. And then I'll tie the spearhead to the piece of wood." As she spoke, she tried to gauge how long each step was going to take. She had no clue, but she suspected a while.

"What are you going to attach the spearhead with?"

"Um. It looks like this one's attached with animal hide." Pretty firmly attached, too. Veela admired, and was intimidated by, the complicated knot. "I guess I would have to complete the spear before I could kill and skin an animal." That prospect didn't exactly make her queasy, not after everything she'd lived through, but she did wonder how she was going to learn to properly skin something, unless she found those two guys again and they taught her. Not to mention that the skins must have been treated somehow to turn them into binding material, otherwise they would have just rotted. "So I'll use some vines to tie this first one."

"Where will you find the vines?"

"I don't know, I'm in a forest, there must be vines around! Anyway, there must have been a first caveman to ever make a spear, and *he* didn't have any animal skins to work with, or know how to do it. We'll figure it out."

"Actually, I already did figure it out—that is, I called it up from the databanks. There are plenty of anthropology books featuring reconstructions of the process."

He had been asking his questions not out of curiosity, or because he was thinking aloud, but as a pompous, time-wasting Socratic game. Veela smoldered with resentment. "All right," she said. "That's good."

"There's a bed of chert only about eighty meters from you, north-northwest."

Of course, Dak said "chert" in their own language, so Veela had no idea it was the same word as Chert's name, translated. Besides, even in her own language, she didn't know the word: "What's 'chert'?"

"A type of stone. That weapon you're holding has a chert spearhead."

"Okay. And is north-northwest to my left, or my right?"

Dak guided Veela to the bed of chert. Naturally, no vegetation grew from the stone, and she peered around fearfully before leaving the cover of the trees. Veela put her helmet on and lowered the visor in preparation for chipping at the stone, thinking there might be flying rock chips.

"All right," said Dak. "Now, find a boulder, one you can pick up and rest in your lap...."

"I beg your pardon?"

"Veela, please. Obviously I don't mean a boulder in the vulgar sense, that of a rock weighing a ton or so. I'm using the proper, geological sense. Find an egg-shaped or slightly elongated boulder weighing about five pounds. Place this boulder upon your leg, and, using a stone that is smaller but harder than the boulder, strike the wider end off at a right angle to the longest axis. Don't give in to the temptation to use an anvil stone at this early stage, for that tends to create an opposing force on the opposite side, resulting in an unpredictable fracture of the boulder. Now, keep striking until you wind up with a nicely flattened end, that is to say a striking platform—it should form a right angle with the sides of the boulder. All quite obvious, when you think about it. Now, here comes the most crucial part...."

Two hours later, Veela had two bleeding, dusty, bruised hands, one serviceable spearhead, and no more clear idea than before of how to secure it to a wooden shaft. "You're going to need to do better than that," said Dak, disapprovingly.

"So I'll practice," she said. "Anyway, what about you? How good are you at this? Have you been floating around up there, knocking pieces of chert together?"

"Oh, I'm sure once I get to the planet surface I'll get the hang of it soon enough."

Veela trudged to a relatively flat stone and lay on it on her back, face basking in the sun. "Let me know if there are any zombies or humans or big animals approaching, please, Dak."

"Of course."

She tried to let some of the tension melt in the sun and ooze out of her like butter, with limited success. "We need allies," she muttered. "We need friends."

"Perhaps you should go after your two renegades," advised Dak. "I can tell you where they're headed and you can meet them at the wall. Perhaps by the time you catch them I'll have finished setting the trap at the hill; perhaps it'll even be sprung."

"I don't know," she said, hoping to hide her yearning behind a casual tone. "They didn't seem too eager to hang around with me."

"Well. They retreated in the face of that marauding zombie deer, not from you, per se. Hardly chivalrous, but I wouldn't take it personally. Besides, whether they know it or not, they do need us if they ever want to get beyond the perimeter wall. So you'll be doing them a favor, if you go hunting for them."

That was true. Veela continued to brood on that runaway pair. The younger one she missed (she was thinking of him as being roughly her age, early thirties—it had not occurred to her that that hardened, weathered hulk of a man, with his eyes that were sometimes innocent and sometimes world-weary, almost deadly, could be only fifteen). The older one gave her the creeps. Also, he'd been the one to run off and leave her for the zombie deer. Then again, he had clearly done it for the not completely unlaudable purpose of saving the Jaw (she was pretty sure his name included their version of a definite article, though she had no clue why). "Do you suppose they could be father and son?"

Veela couldn't be sure without seeing his face, but she thought she heard a smirk in his voice. "I highly doubt that's the nature of the bond between them. You're looking at the situation through anachronistic prejudices. People in this time period don't form that kind of kinship bond—they don't even understand the father's role in conception."

"How do you know?"

"I told you, I've been perusing our anthology books."

"Yeah, well, I'm the one actually down here on the surface."

"And which of us is the one who knows how to make a spearhead?"

Veela kept her mouth shut, despite being tempted to retort that while she might not yet know how to make a spear perfectly, she did know how to sit in a comfortable spaceship and read instructions on how to do it to someone else. During their long trek back from the Cantor-Gould Collider, she'd come to feel there was something so cold about Dak—it wasn't that he'd been unfriendly—in fact, part of what had unnerved Veela was that he'd been almost cheerful, as if it was a shame about the extinction of the human race but the bright side was that he got to commandeer the Collider for an experiment that he would never have been able to get approval for otherwise. He'd shown no sexual interest in her—in fact, he'd shown little more than a merely polite interest. And recently she suspected that not even that was real. Given how unperturbed he seemed to feel at the death of all humanity, as long as he'd escaped—and the death of a lot more than that—how could she expect him to care about her, personally?

She got up to leave the chert bed and head back into the forest, in the direction Dak said Chert and the Jaw had gone. "Anyway," she said, "I should be able to bring them around to helping us, once I learn the language well enough to explain the ultimate stakes."

"Er, I wouldn't count on them actually believing you about those ultimate stakes."

"I'll have to win their trust, obviously."

"Might be more involved than that. I doubt their primitive minds will be able to grasp what you're talking about at all."

"They're just as intelligent as we are!"

"But hardly the beneficiaries of rigorous post-graduate educations. I'm sorry, dear, but all I'm saying is that these are primitive people, so it might make more sense to establish a bond in some primitive way."

"For instance?"

"Well, Veela, I think surely you know that I'm referring to a sexual bond."

"Ah."

"Don't be touchy, I'm merely being pragmatic. Besides, I thought I sensed in you a certain affection for the pair."

"Do you have a recommendation as to which of them I should pick?"

"Well, on the one hand, the younger might be the more valuable of the two, since he may be physically stronger."

"I don't know about that." Veela was thinking of the way Chert had picked the Jaw up and run off with him like he weighed nothing. Also of how she'd thought her head might snap off, when he'd hit her in the visor with that rock.

"True. And I was about to say that the older one might be more valuable, anyway, because of his greater knowledge and experience. Although, given the average human life-span in this era, his best years may already be behind him."

"Gee, maybe I ought to stay on the safe side and fuck them both."

"I detect your unhelpful sarcasm, but as a matter of fact that could be ideal, if the sexual mores of their particular culture allow it. My fear is that sharing you would prove divisive, leaving the group as a whole more vulnerable than ever. One of them could kill the other for your sake, and then there would be one less ally. Worse, sharing your body might so cheapen you that they wouldn't see the point in risking their lives on behalf of such a low-value female."

"Have no fear, Dak, because I was only kidding."

"You really must stop taking offense. We're in a desperate situation, and if we're going to survive we have to take an honest tally of all our available resources."

"I prefer not to think of what I'm carrying around between my legs as a 'resource.'"

"Regardless of your enlightened, civilized preferences, we're going to have to get used to living in a brutal, unforgiving world. Both of us will. I'm sure there are going to be adjustments I'll find painful, as well."

"Okay. Convince me later, please." Veela was on the verge of pointing out that Dak had yet to make any of those adjustments, drifting around as he was in his invulnerable, climate-controlled spaceship. What stopped her was once again her sense that Dak just might up and fly around to the other side of the planet and set himself up as a god to be worshiped by their easily impressed ancestors, once he'd established to his satisfaction that all the zombies had been destroyed. Perhaps he'd establish a little empire for himself, humanity's first. In his place, Veela would never have been able to even consider such a course of action, partly because of the intense experience they'd shared as fellow survivors, partly out of simple humanity. But something warned her not to assume that Dak would feel the same compunctions.

Anyway, he might be right. Sex might be an effective binding strategy. Part of what bugged her was that she'd already been mulling over a similar idea in relation to the Jaw, and not feeling too dreadful about it either. Now, if it did happen, she was afraid she'd feel she was doing it at Dak's prompting.

Eight

The People had moved deeper and lower into the caves, away from the mouth and, as Gash-Eye told them, the bands of unkillables still roving around. By the light of some burning brands (the People had never invented proper torches) they found a big chamber, one where they could light a fire; the smoke had enough room to diffuse and not suffocate them, though it stung the eyes.

It was a sad group, these survivors of the mostly-destroyed People, bewildered, clumped together in the cold stinking smoky darkness, praying for the slave they'd spat on yesterday to tell them when they might leave.

Gash-Eye, meanwhile, hunched in a dark corner of the cave. The firelight drove most of the animals away, into darkness, so that the People's hunters could not see them, though they might occasionally hear them. But Gash-Eye, with her Big-Brow vision, could still see them when they approached, at the edge of the light's reach, a dim zone that for the People was pitch black. So far she'd caught a lizard and a salamander, both of which she'd given to them. She wasn't hungry.

Sometimes the cave's mysterious wind wafted in a patch of air that was gaggingly rotten, sometimes sweet—often the odor would be mephitic, urinous—sulfurous—sometimes it left the People, and Gash-Eye, woozy, light-headed, confused, as certain plants could do.

Earlier a swarm of bats had swooped by overhead—many of the People had screamed and cowered, ready to be terrified by anything now. A few of the quicker hunters had had the presence of mind to jump up and snatch some of the lower-flying bats, like wild living fruit. They'd torn into the animals with their teeth, ripping them apart while they were still alive. The event had given Gash-Eye pause—if bats kept flying overhead and hunters kept catching them, the People would have no more need of her for food. But it only happened that once.

There had been a skittering sound before. She was waiting for it to recur. It would be easy to hear. The People were hardly talking.

Though they needed her for now, she didn't trust them. She had been tempted to sneak away from them, to just go sit in the darkness alone and die, but she worried what would become of Quarry. So she stayed, biding her time, maintaining enough control over them with her made-up visions to keep herself alive and Quarry safe, hoping she would figure out a next step eventually. Although the longer they stayed in this cursed cave, with its darkness and its heavy black stone sky, the more she had trouble remembering there was a world outside at all, the more it seemed they would all just rot here.

Other than Quarry, Hoof was the only one whom she might have put faith in. But he was gone. There had been some commotion—Hoof had said something, Gash-Eye didn't know what, and Spear had shrieked that he was a coward and chased him from the fire. Whatever he'd said, Gash-Eye was sure it hadn't been cowardly, just sensible. Everyone had expected Hoof to wait till Spear calmed down and then head back again, without so much as holding a grudge. But he hadn't come back. The chances of him willingly remaining absent for so long, far from any fire, were low. Probably something had gotten him.

The noise came again. A shadow scurried past against a background of paler shadow. Gash-Eye grabbed the thing by the back half and whipped it against the stone. It twitched. Gash-Eye picked up the rock she had ready and brought it smashing down on the thing's head, which she could only just make out. She wanted to be sure it was dead before she picked it up. It was small, but not too small, and apart from that and the fact that it had hair, Gash-Eye had no idea what sort of animal it was.

Except that it also had a long, hairless tail, as she discovered from feeling around. It was some kind of big rodent. She picked it up by the tail and brought it back to the fire. The People had heard the noise and were looking back in her direction, glum and expectant. The small sounds of blood and brain dripping on stone could be heard as she drew near.

All eyes were on the beast as soon as it came into view, but no one molested her as she carried it to Stick. She held the meager, mangy creature a bit higher as she presented it to him, and said, "Accept this meat, Stick, on behalf of the People."

Stick looked at the dirty hairy rodent without enthusiasm. But he said, "Thank you, Petal-Drift. The People live by your service, while we remain trapped in this darkness." He accepted the animal from her, set it on the ground between himself and the fire and simply stared at it, as if wondering how he would ever be able to divide the raggedy thing among all these people, few though they were.

In reply to his unvoiced worry, Gash-Eye said, "I know this will not serve the needs of the People. I will continue to gather what creatures I can find, till there is enough for all. Meanwhile, divide this among whoever you find fit to be the first to eat."

Stick nodded, without looking up at her. "This I shall do, Petal-Drift," he said.

Each time he called her "Petal-Drift," his voice stuck a bit. This was in part because of his long habit of calling her the traditional name, "Gash-Eye." Also, she was sure, it was because the name "Petal-Drift" suggested something beautiful, and to Stick and the rest of his kind a full-blooded Big-Brow could never be anything but ugly.

Not even Gash-Eye could think of herself by that name, Petal-Drift. She tried, but she had been Gash-Eye for too long. But she was glad she could make the proud People call her by the name she'd had before ever meeting them.

Letting her eye rove over the People first, taking in how they cowered closer to that small center of illumination, helpless against the dark, she turned and started back to the darkness at the edge of the chamber.

Behind her she heard movement, footsteps advancing on her swiftly. She turned to face whoever it was, and saw Spear there; he tossed the rodent into her face and slapped her across the cheek, hard as he could.

"Take back your trash! Rat might be suitable food for Big-Brows. But we humans eat game! We're hunters, not jackals!"

He paused, glaring into her face, breathing hard in his fury, waiting to see what she would do.

She regarded him with almost a stupid expression. Finally she said, "Very well, Spear." She crouched down, picked up the rodent, stood again. Spear watched her closely, hatefully. She pitched her voice over Spear's shoulder and said, "Stick. Stick, and all you People. Spear says the food I bring is fit only for Big-Brows and not the likes of you. Very well, I will catch and eat my Big-Brow food alone. I meant no offense."

"There was no offense, Petal-Drift," said Stick. Gash-Eye relished the anxiety in his voice. "Spear does not speak for the People."

"Then the People should not let Spear speak for them."

"I speak as I wish," said Spear.

"Very well. Hunt game where you wish, as well."

Gash-Eye turned and began to walk away from him. Spear growled, grabbed her shoulder, and spun her around. Gash-Eye didn't resist; she waited to see if someone from the People would intervene.

Someone did. "Leave her alone, Spear!" screamed Horn, one of the hunters.

His scream echoed and roiled through the cave, its volume eerily amplified. The People clenched in on themselves more tightly, as if they were afraid the scream would cause the ceiling to vibrate and fall in on them.

But Gash-Eye knew that what they were really waiting for was to see if she would refuse to catch any more food. The hunters could take dim, smoldering brands far enough to find water by themselves—there were pools here and there, and a scout had already brought back word of a huge subterranean lake not far away. But the fire would frighten away whatever food there was, before the People could get close enough to see it.

The scream had startled Spear. Once he recovered, it disgusted him. He sneered at Gash-Eye, and said, "Fine. Go back to your rat-catching, Big-Brow." He turned and sauntered back to the fire.

Gash-Eye watched him go, then kept watching even after he'd sat back down. One of the hunters scampered out, grabbed the rodent, and returned to the fire without looking at her. The People were conversing among themselves in murmurs now. Already they'd forgotten the confrontation—they were content to let her go back to her rat-catching, and they'd be happy to eat the results when she was done.

She walked back to the circle around the fire. Some looked up with trepidation, afraid she was still angry—some looked up hungrily, and were disappointed to see she brought no more food.

The conversations ceased. She stood looking down at Stick, who looked up to meet her gaze. He waited with resignation for her to speak.

"Am I to be beaten for bringing meat to the People?" she said.

"No, Petal-Drift. I am sorry Spear hit you." He turned to Spear. "Spear, I say you shall not hit her again."

Unbelievably, Spear didn't protest, though he looked like he was having to chew off his own tongue to avoid doing so.

But Gash-Eye said, "I honor you, Stick. But what you say isn't good enough. Spear wanted to kill me before the unkillables attacked. Spear beat me right after we took shelter in this cave. And now Spear beats me when I bring meat to the People. Each time, Stick has said words to restrain him, but always Spear beats me again."

"I'll show you a beating, you Big-Brow animal," said Spear, no longer able to hold his peace. "Are we truly going to sit and let this Gash-Eye talk to us this way? Talk to Stick this way— Stick, whom till now we always held to be the strongest and the wisest? Are we going to let this Gash-Eye talk to us at all?! By the bone, I'd rather starve to death! Or, better, die fighting those unkillables! If they even are still out there!"

Some of the People were hissing at him to be silent. Keeping her eyes on Stick, Gash-Eye said, "They are indeed still out there. I will tell you when they're not. You know I can see the truth of it, for you captured me and have held me all these years thanks to my Sight." She turned to the rest of the band. "If the People's pride tells them they must not take aid from a Big-Brow, I will no longer give offense by offering it."

Desperate assurances came from around the circle that she gave no offense. Stick's eyes seemed no longer to see as he held his face in her direction. "Tell us what it is you wish, Petal-Drift."

"Spear's life."

Stick showed not the slightest quiver of surprise. But the rest of the circle burst into an uproar, and Spear and his good friends leaped to their feet, some with spears or knives in hand. "Never!" shouted one of the hunters—it was small, wiry young Tooth. "Never could the People surrender one of their hunters because this Gash-Eye slave requested it! Never! Such a thing is unimaginable!"

"I don't expect you to do it," she said. "I only said that was the only condition upon which I'd feed you."

Tooth sneered. "And what if your scavenging food for us is the only condition upon which I won't gut you now, Big-Brow?"

Moving faster than she had done in years, Gash-Eye grabbed Tooth by the throat and the skins he wore, hoisted him all the way up over her head, and almost before anyone realized what she was doing, she slammed him down hard onto his back, right into the middle of the fire.

The burns weren't bad enough to kill him, but he flailed and made noises that would have been shrieks if he hadn't had the air knocked from his lungs. Others screamed for him. They dragged him out of the flames, which his body had not extinguished but had much diminished. Everything was illuminated now only by a dim unstable red light.

The People were all on their feet. They made as if they would rush her, but an invisible barrier held them back. There was lots of contradictory shouting, and it was almost impossible to make out individual words.

Stick stood in the inner ring of the furious circle that had formed around Gash-Eye. He faced her and said, "What do you wish?" She could hear how it galled him to have to ask her anything.

"Kill her!" screamed Spear, hidden behind the crowd gathered around her. Gash-Eye wondered why he wasn't rushing her himself, then realized someone must be holding him back. It was hard to tell through the commotion, but she thought she heard sounds of struggle, and she wondered if not only Spear but also his friends were trying to attack her, while the more level-headed among the People stopped them. "Ask her for nothing, kill her!"

"What do you want?" repeated Stick.

"The life of the man who returned my gift of food with blows."

"She is our slave!" cried Spear. "A slave cannot give gifts!"

Now the sounds of a fight were unmistakable. Some of the People were trying to beat Spear and his friends into silence.

Stick looked at her with something almost like despair. "Thank you for the meat, Petal-Drift," he said, and the words sounded like they were being spoken to a conqueror whose foot was on his neck. "But if our only hope is to remain in this dark cave till our last days, perhaps it would be better to die soon."

"No one said you need stay down here forever. Only till the unkillables leave the hill outside."

"How long will that be?"

"Many, many nights," she bluffed. "But when it happens, I shall see it."

"Don't make her angry!" shouted someone. There were screams of outrage at this cravenness, then shouts of support for its good common sense.

"Spear's always been a bastard anyway!" shouted someone else.

"Quiet!" shouted Stick. "I say, quiet!" Some obeyed, but it was only a mild lessening of the hubbub. Stick glared at Gash-

Eye—in the red light, it almost looked like his eyes were wet. He said, "I don't know whether it is right or wrong to kill Spear for your pleasure. I do not wish for the People to all die out, forever. But I feel it would be wrong, and that the shame of it would follow us always."

He paused and watched Gash-Eye, as if hoping his words might provoke some mercy. She met his gaze steadily. The idea of the People living under the cloud of an eternal shame provoked in her nothing but a satisfaction as dark, red, and smoldering as the fire she'd thrown Tooth into.

Stick dropped his eyes. His body seemed to shrink. He said, "It cannot be my voice that says these words. If it must be, it must be the whole People."

Someone rushed from the circle at Gash-Eye. At first she tensed, readying herself to fight. Then she saw how small the on-comer was; it was Quarry. The child took her hand. Tears in her voice, she said, "Don't make us do that, Gash-Eye."

Gash-Eye stared down at Quarry, her face frozen and unreadable. She didn't even notice that Quarry called her, not the name she'd insisted on, but the one by which she'd always been known among them.

"I know he deserves it," said Quarry. "But please don't make us do it. Please."

Gash-Eye kept looking at the girl. For some reason she thought of the Jaw. She imagined that he had survived. She thought of how, if he had been trapped in here with them, she could have used the opportunity presented by her bluff to try to create a web of obligations that might keep him safe forever. Maybe she could have made the People grateful to her, maybe she could have used her new power to transform herself from a tool into a different sort of asset, a person of value. Then she would have been able to interact with her son, without either of them worrying that such interaction would contaminate him, would alienate him from the rest of the People even more violently than the mere fact of their kinship already did.

For some reason she had the urge to touch Quarry's face. She didn't do it, of course.

"Let Spear live," she said. "Let him live, I don't care what happens to him." She turned and shouldered her way through the crowd. They hesitated to let her by, as if uncertain what they ought to do with her—thank her, punish her, supplicate her—but finally they made room. She left them behind and trudged back to the dark reaches of the chamber, among the rats and moles and insects, where there wasn't any light for them to see her.

Behind her there was only a little noise for a while. Most of it came from the People trying to help the injured Tooth as best they could, without any herbs or potions. There was some hushed arguing over how much of their small store of wood should be used in rebuilding the fire—in the end they settled for a smaller blaze. Gash-Eye had talked like they would be down here a long time, so they would need to conserve their supplies. But she had also been careful to convey an impression that they would eventually be able to leave. If the People became hopeless, they might decide to go out and die fighting those unkillable things, or commit suicide, or some other desperate act. In any case, Gash-Eye would no longer be able to control them.

She huddled in the shadows by the wall. Blind animals scurried and crept over her and she ignored them. The People had split into clumps, she saw. Spear and his faction sat together, talking quietly and intently. Even if it turned out they were working out a plot to kill her, she didn't give a damn.

Quarry wandered the chamber floor. The dark scared her, but she went as far as she could without passing completely out of the light visible to her. "Gash-Eye?" she would whisper, her small sibilant voice carrying far into the echoey chamber. "Petal-Drift?" she would whisper then, remembering the strange new name.

Gash-Eye never responded or let the child know where she hid. But she never took her eyes off her, either.

***

93

She awoke to a flaming stick being shoved near her face. Though she'd thought she'd reached a state where living or dying were matters of indifference to her, her body tried to recoil in panic from the flames. But she couldn't recoil—there were four strong hunters holding her tight, one for each limb.

The flame was drawn back somewhat, but stayed blindingly close to her face. She heard Spear's voice: "Now what say I burn out this Big-Brow slave's rebellious eyes?"

Cries of protest. "We need her!" pleaded someone. "We need her to find food. We need her to look into the hidden places, so we can know when it's safe to leave...."

"Shut up!" said Spear. "I'm sick of hearing you gullible fools prattle about the hidden places! Can't you see that's a game she's playing to humiliate you?"

"But we know she sees the hidden things!" That was Tooth! "That's why we keep the Gash-Eye in the first place!"

"Shut up! And stay back, all you cowards, or I'll stick your Big-Brow master right here."

Gash-Eye felt a cold stone blade at her throat. She stopped struggling. Now that someone was actively planning to kill her, she found her will to live returning. But the only way to escape was to wait and see if an opportunity would present itself. Where was Quarry?

There were more cries and pleas from the People.

"If you cowards don't be quiet I'm not going to kill the Big-Brow, I'm going to start killing you!" That quieted some of them.

"What is your plan, Spear?" That was Stick.

"My plan? It's a simple one. I'm going to lead us all out of these caves." Moans of protest, rallying shouts of encouragement. "Those of my faction are going to stamp out the fire as we go, so if any of you cowards choose to stay and snivel here, you can do it in the dark. Meanwhile, we're going to go outside. I tell you, those unkillables will have moved on. Even if they haven't, we'll be ready for them this time. They move slow, before they've started eating anyway, we'll see them and slip back into the cave again." Gash-Eye was blinded as the brand was again shoved close to her face. "What do you think of that, Big-Brow? Still promising the unkillables won't have passed back into the forest from whence they came?"

Gash-Eye could think of nothing better than to stick with her original gambit. "Death awaits outside."

"Bah! The dark is the natural place for you. Rats and bugs are your rightful diet. But we are men, and women!... What say you, Stick?"

Stick's voice was hard and merciless: "If, once outside, we find that Gash-Eye has deceived us, in that case I say she dies."

"No!" That was Quarry. From the way her cry was cut off, Gash-Eye knew someone had clapped a hand over her mouth. She surprised herself by almost shouting at them to leave the girl alone, but held back. Best not to let them know that was a knife they could twist in her flank.

Gash-Eye felt herself being lifted. She kept her eyes closed, although the brand was so close that the flames shone almost as brightly through her lids.

She was carried through the cave. Even without seeing anything, she could tell when they were out of the big chamber and back in the tunnel; the air pressure changed, the clamorous shouting echoed differently. Those carrying her grunted with the extra effort of following the slope upward.

She had little doubt that once they got outside, the unkillables would have moved on. They had seemed such insatiable creatures, and there was bound to be more prey in the forest. For Quarry's sake, she was even glad this interlude in the cave was coming to an end. Well, it was all right that they were going to kill her. She'd been meant to die days ago. All that remained in these last minutes was to decide whether it was likely to go easier with Quarry if she went down fighting, or quietly. Quietly, probably.

The fire was moved away from her face. "Open your eyes, slave," Spear growled, close to her ears. "We're almost at the mouth of the cave. I want you to point out this death you've been scaring us with, before going to meet your own."

Gash-Eye obeyed. But it was still by sound alone that she knew they were nearing the mouth of the cave. Though her eyes were open, she could still make out little more than blotchy red and blue afterimages of the flames that had been so close. She blinked rapidly, trying to clear her vision. It suddenly seemed to her that, since she was about to see for the very last time, it would be nice to see clearly.

There was a crackling boom.

The People all came to a halt. Gash-Eye was jolted by the way the four men carrying her stopped at slightly different moments. A few moans went up from the women and children and some of the men.

"Shut up!" said Spear. "It's just thunder!"

"Spear...." That was Stick. Even he was scared.

"It's just thunder, damn it! Are you afraid of thunder now?! Do you think the warring thunder spirits are more likely to take notice of earth creatures today than they were yesterday? Have you ever heard of earthly creatures whose fighting made a sound like thunder, unkillable or not? So how can that sound be made by earthly creatures? Now move!"

They started forward again. From protests and shouts behind her Gash-Eye came to realize that the People were being marched forward mostly against their will, by Spear's friends.

Her vision was coming back, but she still couldn't see what they were screaming about the next moment. Partly because her head was still facing the ceiling.

"It's just lightning!" shouted Spear. "It's just lightning! The mouth is just around the bend!"

"But it makes a sound different from any thunder I ever heard!"

"It's lightning, I tell you!"

"If it's lightning then why is it red?!"

"That's from our damned eyes drying out in the Big-Brow's poisoned cave! I tell you, that's lightning! Lightning! Lightning! Lightning!"

Now they were turning her so that her body was upright—two men apiece held her by the arms now, and her feet dragged along the floor. She picked them up and began walking along to keep the tops from being scraped. She didn't struggle. Sure enough, up ahead she could see the bend, the last corner before the mouth of the cave. It must be night. The People wouldn't have been able to see the bend if not for the brands, and if not for the flashes of light from outside the mouth, which reflected off the rock wall. Spear was right, their eyes were no doubt still confused by the long sojourn in darkness, but she did think the so-called lightning looked red.

They rounded the corner. The dark cave mouth opened into the nighttime before them. Stars glittered in the sky—no clouds. Spear leaned in close to Gash-Eye and growled, "You're about to die."

Pitching her voice for his ears only, she said, "I don't care."

As they drew right up to the mouth of the cave there seemed nothing outside but a peaceful, tranquil night. Gasps of cautious joy could be heard. They approached the crystalline stars and the small but peaceful patch of grass visible in the moonlight, and Gash-Eye knew they were about to kill her.

Then a lightning bolt sizzled down with a crash the instant before they exited the cave. At least, Gash-Eye supposed it was lightning; it was impossibly straight, and definitely red. The boom it made was not quite like thunder.

Those in the very front halted again. But Spear's allies in the back must have been determined to push forward no matter what, and to keep from being trampled those in the front had to start moving again. As those who'd first left the cave started screaming, the ones in the back continued spilling out, shoving them.

The small patch of outside they'd been able to see from within the cave had looked calm. But chaos raged everywhere around that patch. Unkillables streamed or shuffled up the hill, according to their strength; the black ones were illuminated by the glowing green ones. Gash-Eye's captors released her, in their shock. She turned around to look back up the hill to see what the unkillables were heading toward. There was a huge mound of something organic-looking that shouldn't be there, glistening in the starlight. The mound was momentarily lit by another red bolt, and Gash-Eye felt like she might vomit—though she couldn't be certain, though it was impossible, she felt suddenly sure that what she was looking at was a massive heap of animal brains.

What sort of monster would kill more animals than anyone could ever eat and then leave only the brains, heaped on a hillside?

Someone screamed and she whipped her head around to see that a black unkillable had grabbed Stick by the arm with his teeth, and was using his hands to pull the old hunter and his brain closer. Before any of the People could raise a spear to help, one of the stronger, green unkillables leaped forward and ripped Stick's head off, stealing the prize from its hungry brethren. The green unkillable raised Stick's head to its mouth and chomped down hard, biting through Stick's skull like it was the skin of a fruit. As it munched out chunks of the hunter's brain and gulped them whole, Gash-Eye and the People could see it glow brighter and stronger. Then with a deafening crackle another red bolt destroyed the green unkillable, exploding its head, then a second bolt hit the head of the black unkillable still tearing in futile, frustrated rage at Stick's headless body.

Gash-Eye looked up, to see where the red bolts were coming from. There was something like a huge, impossibly regular stone floating overhead.

The smell of smoke and burning rotten flesh. Underneath the screams the deafening crackles of the big red bolts. Gash-Eye looked back uphill at the mound of what might be brains. Some of the unkillables had reached it and were leaning their whole bodies into it, arms outstretched as if hugging it. They glowed an impossibly bright green; Gash-Eye could not see their mouths, but she imagined them munching, munching, munching their ways into the mound.

She realized that some of the People had been bitten by the unkillables and were flopping on the ground, the black webs spreading across their bodies. Most of the unkillables who had bitten them had not bothered to break their skulls. They must have been drawn too irresistibly by that mountain of brains above.

Something crashed into Gash-Eye and threw its arms around her waist. She was about to club it in terror when it screamed, in Quarry's voice, "Gash-Eye!"

Gash-Eye awoke from her trance. How could she possibly have cared about looking at the chaos and trying to figure out what was going on? Escaping from it was all that mattered. She picked the child up and clutched her to her chest. "People!" she cried. "If you can hear, back to the cave!"

Some had already gone, not needing the invitation. But others were disoriented by the terror, noise, smoke, and flashing lights; nearly blinded by their long days in the dark, and then by these searing red bolts of fire, they had lost their sense of where shelter was. Now, hearing Gash-Eye, they rallied to her.

She backed into the cave. The People came after her. "Follow my voice if you cannot see!" A bit of inspiration struck her, and she added, "I shall be your eyes, as before!"

"Follow Gash-Eye! Follow Gash-Eye!" some of them screamed. And one said, "Follow Petal-Drift!"

She wondered if Spear were still with them. Maybe he and his friends had been taken by those things outside.

She ran deeper back into the cave, careful to keep her balance on the downward incline. The floor shook, Gash-Eye suspected from the impact of another red bolt. There was a rumbling crash and some screams—the ceiling had collapsed behind them.

From behind them came more screams. Something had followed them in. Her first instinct was to keep running, but the unkillable thing, and all its spawn, would be trapped in here with Quarry, as well.

Gash-Eye set Quarry down; "Run," she hissed, then turned without waiting to see if the child obeyed.

She cast around for two fist-sized stones, then waded against the stream of fleeing People. The only light came from a few burning sticks that had been dropped. An unkillable was beginning to glow as it ate its victim's brain. By its own glow she could see its eyes fix on her, but it either didn't consider her a threat or else couldn't tear itself away from its meal. Gash-Eye clapped the stones together into the creature's temples, as hard as she could; the thing's head popped. Never had Gash-Eye heard of such soft-headed beings. Again she sealed her lips, but some of the spraying gunk hit her high on the cheek, almost getting in her eye. With horror she wiped her face with her forearm. Opening her eyes again she saw that two of the People were flopping on the floor, the black veins spreading like webs across their bodies. She clapped the stones together against their temples, too. Their skulls didn't yet pop open the way the full unkillables' did, and she had to strike them repeatedly; though she did think she could already detect a bit more give than one would expect.

She ran after Quarry, afraid the girl would need protection if Spear and his friends took their frustrations out on her.

Back in the big chamber the embers of the fire still glowed a faint red—Spear's men had failed to completely extinguish it. Some of the People screamed as her dark bulk came running in, but someone else cried, "It's her! It's Petal-Drift!" People surrounded her, hands clutched her. "Help us!" "Save us!"

"Where's Quarry?!"

"Here she is!"

"We kept her safe for you!"

"I'm here!" That was Quarry's voice, weeping. The crowd parted for her. She flew into Gash-Eye's arms, clutching her.

Gash-Eye rested, holding the child close. For the moment she was almost unconscious of the People surrounding her, the monsters outside.

"What should we do, Petal-Drift?" someone ventured timorously.

Only now did Gash-Eye begin to appreciate the advantages of her predictions having proven true. She almost wondered if she did have some gift of prescience, after all.

If she did, it gave her no more idea than before of what to do about the monsters outside, except continue to cower in the caves.

In fact, that seemed like a better idea than ever. But there was one threat she could use her newfound power to do away with.

"Where's Spear?" she demanded.

"He ran!" That was Tooth. "We tried to hold him and his friends, but they ran!"

So. They were lurking in the dark, lost, as blind as they had threatened to make Gash-Eye. A horrible fate, but she would waste no energy feeling sorry for them. Besides, they weren't dead yet, not necessarily. "Didn't I warn you Spear's way was dangerous?" she said balefully.

"You did, you did." "You did, Petal-Drift."

She studied the survivors. Most of the older, braver men were gone—so were all of the children. What was left was mainly women and the weaker hunters. And Tooth, whose spirit she had wounded far worse than she had his body.

"Who was it who fed more of you to the unkillables? Who turned more of you into unkillables, which in turn may claim still more victims? Wasn't that Spear?"

"Yes, yes." "Yes, Petal-Drift." "Yes, you were right, we're sorry."

She raised one hand for silence. The other hand remained on Quarry. She said, "Never mind all that. Only say: is not my enemy your enemy?"

"Yes, Petal-Drift," many voices said.

"I will stand watch against the unkillables," she said. "I will look where you cannot see. I will hunt on your behalf what little food there is in these caves. We shall go together to the underground lake. The dark shall be dreary and the water stale, but we shall survive. I shall keep one eye in the shadows of this world, watching for enemies, and one eye in the world of shadows, watching for when we may safely leave these caves. But only on one condition. My enemies are your enemies, as your enemies are mine."

"Our enemies are each other's!" someone cried, and others took up the cry.

She was the leader of this People now. The world had turned upside-down and they had all become her slaves. But she reflected with bitterness that if ever they escaped back up to the world of the sun, she should expect no gratitude. The People would remember their groveling with humiliation, and take revenge for it.

"Very well," she said, "let us go to the lake. Some of you take a brand from the fire. Some others take the firewood. Let he who takes the brand lead the way. I'll walk in the rear, to be sure nothing follows." She added, "And if any of you comes across Spear, or any of his followers, cut me off their heads."

Multiple voices swore that they would.

Nine

Veela found Chert and the Jaw two days after the attack of the zombie deer, some hours before the People made their disastrous escape attempt. Who knew how long it would have taken her without the help of Dak and his scanners—the zombie zone they'd walled off was a circle with a diameter of more than twenty miles, and it wasn't like she could possibly track whatever faint trail those guys might leave. (The zone had to be sufficiently vast to contain the outbreak—it was calculated on the distance that animals and humans could roam after having been bitten by that zombie mouse at the original landing site, taking into account the motor debilitation that accompanied zombification, especially in the blackened hungry state, and that would prevent, say, a zombie bird from being able to fly long distances, or a deer from being able to bound along at its normal speed.)

Still, Dak griped over having even that much of his resources diverted. He was preparing the mound of animal brains for the trap he was going to spring that night, the one that Gash-Eye and the remnants of the People were going to wander into. He was in a bad mood because he had to use up most of their stock of Rejuvenatrix in soaking the brain-pile, to keep the brains alive enough for the zombies to hear their brainsong.

When she came upon them, Chert and the Jaw were slumped dejectedly in front of the white perimeter wall. When Chert had first seen it, he had run at it to punch it, and had been beyond furious when he'd realized he couldn't get within arm's reach without the air itself biting him. All the trees within five man-lengths of the wall were gone, there was only a gray fine ash where they should have been, so they couldn't climb anything from which to leap to the other side; there were no branches poking over from beyond the barrier, so presumably the trees there had met the same fate. The wall curved around into the distance in both directions. It seemed to enclose them. As soon as they regained enough spirit, they were going to pick a direction and start walking that way, looking for a gap. Chert couldn't think of what else to do.

"Hey, guys," called Veela in her own language when she saw them. She waved, having no idea how close Chert was to earnestly trying to kill her. Part of what enraged him was the unnatural white of the hides she wore, white like that damned wall (or whatever it was—Chert and the Jaw didn't even have a word for "wall").

The Jaw, though, was glad to see her.

Exhausted from her hike, Veela plopped down to sit with them, all smiles. She'd decided to act like, the last time they'd seen her, they hadn't run off and left her to die at the snout of that deer. To accent her friendliness, she wasn't even wearing her visor down, reckless as that might be. She wanted allies who could show her the ropes, could show her how to make a spear and could potentially decide to stay and fight alongside her the *next* time a zombie deer popped up. She wanted it badly enough to gamble that they all knew each other well enough now that Chert wouldn't hit her in the face with a rock again.

"I'm going to kill her," snarled Chert.

"Then I'll try to kill you," said the Jaw. He hadn't forgiven his father for abandoning Veela.

Chert backed down. He glowered at Veela, resenting her for creating still more friction between himself and his son.

Veela hadn't understood the exchange, but she tried not to squirm under that formidable glare. She'd been about to take off her helmet, which she'd kept on ever since the deer had caught her undefended; Chert's murderous look gave her pause. But it was important to send any signals she could that she was a friend, someone who felt comfortable with them and with whom they should feel comfortable, so she took it off and set it on her lap. Immediately the Jaw took it from her. She thought, with near-panic, that he was confiscating it, but soon saw he only wanted to examine it curiously.

While the Jaw was rapping on the helmet with his knuckles and trying to squeeze his too-big head into it, Chert demanded, "What is this?," pointing at the wall.

She tried to meet his glare meekly, remembering how he'd hit her in the face with a rock. For the next little while she tried to explain to Chert what the wall was, but of course she couldn't know the word for "wall" when the language didn't even have one; she thought "cliff" might have worked, sort of, but she didn't know that word either; so she tried telling Chert it was a kind of a long hill, which only confused him more and made him even angrier. Finally she opted for defining it according to its function: "Purpose: no-die, can't move."

"We can't move either, damn you! It's keeping us here with your damn no-dies!"

"Fear, is having no need," she soothed. "My friend, kill all no-dies, very soon." She held up the communicator. "My friend. All no-dies, kill soon."

Chert and the Jaw eyed the strange nut dubiously. They still were not quite willing to believe the little man inside could destroy all the undead, but after the last couple days they were also unwilling to completely discredit anything. The Jaw hoped that the extraordinary little man would one day leave his enclosure, so they could meet him.

Chert said, "I thought you said you needed *our* help, to kill the no-dies?"

Veela paused, trying to think of a diplomatic way to explain that she wanted a backup plan, because she didn't completely trust Dak—she certainly didn't trust him to keep their equipment running, since he still wasn't able to get at the hold with the extra drones, weapons, and power packs, and now she couldn't even land the ship. That magic technology was the only thing that gave her and Dak an edge, and if it went south they really would need these guys.

But telling them that wouldn't exactly inspire confidence; and it would be particularly tricky, since even though Dak was silent, the communicator always maintained an open channel.

To change the subject, she pointed at Chert's spear. "Teach," she said. "Teach. Teach."

Chert looked at her blankly.

Veela got up and began looking around on the ground, moving into the trees beyond the zone where everything had been vaporized. The two men watched her. She poked around till she found two stones, a smaller one and one about five pounds, then came back to sit in the ash. "Teach to make," she insisted, and began banging the rocks together more or less the way Dak had tried to explain.

Both men burst out laughing, even Chert. They rolled around, holding their bellies. Veela grinned. It was worth being laughed at, if it lightened the mood and helped make them all friends. "Teach make," she repeated, and banged the rocks together again to make them laugh some more.

Once their glee had subsided, the Jaw held up her helmet and said, "Teach *us* to make *this*. Anyone can make a spear."

Veela hesitated, wondering how much to reveal. She decided to be as honest as possible: "Other ones make. I no make. I, other skills."

Chert pointed at her communicator. "Did the little man make it?"

"No. Other ones."

Chert and the Jaw exchanged a look. There were more of these strange new people. Chert had an inkling that the arrival of Veela and her ilk might prove even more dangerous to his way of life than the undead.

"So there are more of you?" said the Jaw. "More than just you and the little man?"

After another silent inner debate, Veela decided to continue being honest. "No," she said. "Only he. Only I."

Chert brought his fist wrathfully down into the ash. Veela started with fear. "You just said there were others! Who made the white stone for your head, if it's only you and the little man?!"

"Only he, only I, now," said Veela. "For the others—no-dies."

So her people, too, had been wiped out by the undead. The Jaw's face softened and grew distant, though his eyes remained on Veela—as if he were simultaneously seeing her, and the destruction of his People, as if he were hearing the death cry of his mother.

Chert reflected that if Veela's people, with all their magic, had been no match for the undead, then it really did behoove them to find some way to the other side of that white air-biting thing, and flee the monsters.

He said, "I suppose your people built this white air-biting thing before the no-dies killed them?"

Veela couldn't make out the words "air-biting," but it was plain what Chert meant. She held up the communicator, pointing at it, and said, "No. He build. He build."

Chert and the Jaw gaped in stupefaction at the small strange nut that enclosed the tiny man.

The Jaw said, "You said you had other skills. What are your skills?"

"Me skill is, tongues-speaking."

Once they'd deciphered that, Chert and the Jaw laughed even harder than they had at her attempt to make a spearhead. They clapped each other on the backs and for a moment nearly forgot the undead and all their dead friends. Veela laughed, too.

They moved from the corridor of ash into the shade of the trees, and the men taught Veela some rudiments of stonework. Actually, Chert let the Jaw do it, since he didn't have the patience to mollycoddle the ignorant, possibly retarded woman. But watching the rapport develop between the two, he began to regret leaving her to the Jaw. Maybe it would be a good thing, having her as a link to whatever powerful force it was that had built the white air-biting thing. For some reason, though, the sight of them laughing together made him uneasy.

As they worked, the Jaw told Veela he was sorry he'd roared in her face when they'd first met.

Veela, her hands bruised and dirty and bleeding a little, finally made a passable spearhead. The pleasure of success washed away the pain in her hands, and she gave a cheer.

The Jaw laughed, and cheered too. Still grinning at her, he put his big palm on her knee.

Veela's laughter trickled out, but she didn't stop smiling. She looked at his big, grinning head. *Is he making a pass at me?* she wondered. *Is this big Neanderthal going to kiss me?*

It wouldn't be so bad, she figured; not so bad at all. He was kind of cute in a rough, exotic way—his breath was terrible, but she'd had worse dates. And she vastly preferred him to his more conventionally handsome but occasionally creepy older companion, who might or might not be his father.

But it would definitely complicate things here below, in her dealings with these two. And she sensed that it would also complicate things with Dak. Not that he would be sexually jealous. But, as he'd made clear in their earlier conversation, he would consider her sexual relationship with one of the natives as a new resource, that he should be able to exploit.

While she was trying to decide whether a physical relationship with the Jaw would be wise, or desirable, or neither, or both, his grip on her knee tightened, and his grin got dreamier. With sudden trepidation, it occurred to her that he might not necessarily consider that it was up to her. The guy was a fucking Neanderthal, after all.

But he took his hand off her knee and sat back. Though he let the moment pass, he regarded her with a friendly, satisfied smirk, as if he'd seen something responsive in her face that pleased him.

Veela let her eyes slip from the Jaw to Chert and shuddered. He did not look nearly so pleased.

The Jaw seemed not to notice his father's displeasure. Pointing at the spearhead she'd made, getting back to business, he said, "We taught you something. Now you teach us something."

Veela made the stupid mistake of saying, "You want learn, what?"

"The strong tight fire," said the Jaw immediately.

"Yes," said Chert. "The strong tight fire."

Dammit. Veela tried to think of a way to squirm out of having to produce a laser just yet. "Long time will need," she said.

"Of course it may take a long time," said Chert scornfully. "Who knows, it may take us even longer to learn the strong tight fire than it did you to fashion a spearhead about as skilfully as could a child of the People, still at its mother's teat."

Veela didn't catch all that, but she got the gist. Realizing there was no way she could make a convincing excuse, she decided to come clean about this as well. Holding up the communicator, she pointed at it. "*He*, strong tight fire holds," she said. "Him give it, not yet. I, other things can teach, maybe."

Chert ignored that last sentence. Baring his teeth at the strange nut, leaning forward so that the tiny man could see him through the air holes, he shouted, "You'll give me that strong tight fire, damn you, or I'll swallow you whole!"

"What's that?" asked Dak in his and Veela's tongue. Veela hadn't thought he was even listening. "What's he yelling about all of a sudden?"

"He's yelling at you, because I just told them you wouldn't teach them the secret of lasers yet."

"Yelling at *me*?! Oh!" And Dak started to laugh.

The sound drove Chert crazy. "Is he laughing at me?!" Without waiting for an answer he snatched the strange nut from Veela, put it on the flat surface of a nearby stone, and began hammering it with one of Veela's practice rocks.

Dak must have been watching on the sensors, because he laughed even harder. That drove Chert to new heights of fury—he screamed and beat the communicator as hard as he could.

"Stop!" shouted the Jaw. "Don't kill him, we need him!"

He was about to try to physically restrain Chert, but Veela grabbed his elbow to stop him. Although the Jaw couldn't know, as she did, that Chert's chances of damaging the communicator were close to nil, he nevertheless trusted her enough to let her touch hold him back.

Dak was still laughing. He sounded almost crazy, the hilarity had taken such hold of him. "Stop it, Dak!" shouted Veela.

Dak gasped and spluttered, trying to get hold of himself as Chert continued to bash the communicator. "I'm sorry," he managed, "it's just so funny—I mean, he thinks I'm *in the communicator.*"

"Yes. He does," said Veela. "Which means he's in the middle of a homicidal rampage, as far as he's concerned." Every time Chert brought the rock down again, Veela imagined what it would look like if, instead of the communicator, it were a face he was hitting. "We need these people, Dak! These are our only allies in the whole world, remember?" *And I'm the one down here with them*, she silently added, yet again.

"Oh, all right, all right. Tell him I apologize, will you?" Veela translated for Chert. But the two paleolithic men could hear the smug mockery in Dak's voice.

Chert stood, breathing hard, the rock still in his hand. He glared down at the strange nut that protected Veela's friend. He said to the Jaw, "I have a score that needs settling with that little man."

The Jaw nodded, and turned to Veela. "I like you," he said. "But if your tiny friend doesn't look out, I may help my father kill him someday."

Chert advanced on Veela. "You must teach us something," he warned, "or otherwise prove your worth. So far you're dead weight. You don't ever explain any of these mysteries, you just appear alongside them."

"True, Chert's saying," admitted Veela. She tried to think of some point that might qualify this admission, but nothing came to mind.

"Veela," said the Jaw. He sounded both gentle and anxious, as if her safety depended on her producing something, and he was afraid she wouldn't pull it off. "You must give my father something. If you can bring your own meat to the circle, my father and I will hunt alongside you. But you must bring something. Something besides questions, strange garb, and an evil little man in a nut."

110

Veela nodded. She didn't think of anything to say, though.

The Jaw took a step towards her. Almost pleadingly, he said, "Veela. Just the first step. What is the first thing one must do, when making the magic of the strong tight fire?"

Veela hoped she was managing to keep her fear hidden. She had no clue how to go about making a laser gun, much less making one out of mud, wood, and stone....

Then a crazy inspiration hit her: *All he's asking for is the first step....*

What was the first step of engineering, of physics, of everything?

With great solemnity, she said, "Teach you this magic, I can. From path's first step. But path is long. Long, long, long. Want you it do?"

"Yes," said the Jaw.

"Of course we want to do it," said Chert.

"Long time. More long than hundred times the time for me to learn spear. More long than thousand times."

When she said this, she had to use the words for "hundred" and "thousand" from her own native language. Not only did she not know those words in the People's tongue, but, as she had anticipated, the People's tongue did not even have such words. Chert and the Jaw both twisted up their faces in confusion. "What's 'hundred'?" asked the Jaw. "What's 'thousand'?"

"Ah!" said Veela. "That question, first step is. First step, of magic path."

She sat down again. Chert and the Jaw followed suit, watching her uncertainly. She gestured out at the forest. "Trees," she said. "How much?"

"Very much," replied Chert, in a tone that said he was still listening, but his patience would soon run out.

Fortunately, Veela had chanced upon a word meaning something like "exact" during an earlier session, so she was able to say, "No—how much, with exactness?" Even if she had known the language perfectly, she would not have been able to ask "how many," because they had no word for "many." While they did have the rough concept of numbers, it wasn't developed enough for them to need much vocabulary related to counting or exact quantifications.

The Jaw frowned at the trees. "How can anyone say how much, exactly?"

"And what does it have to do with the strong tight fire?" pressed Chert.

"Do this," said Veela, and held up two lightly closed fists. "Do this."

The Jaw obeyed. So did Chert, reluctantly.

Veela poked up the index finger of her right hand. "What this, you call? Word for this, there is?"

The People did have words for counting up to ten, though the word list ran out along with their fingers. Even so, Veela's question was confusing, because when they did count they started with their thumbs.

"Finger," ventured Chert.

But the Jaw got it. "One?" he said.

Veela ran through all ten fingers. When she tried moving on to toes, they looked at her like she was crazy. So: they only counted up to ten.

She decided to go ahead and teach them her own words for the first ten numbers, figuring that things would ultimately be less confusing if she imported her own mathematical vocabulary wholesale.

Then she taught them the numbers eleven through twenty. That was harder. The way she did it was to have the Jaw hold up his two fists while she did the same. Once again she cycled through her ten fingers, then touched the Jaw's fingers. For the first finger she touched on his hand, she said, "Eleven."

"No," he said. "One. You said that was one."

Veela shook her head and repeated the new word: "Eleven." Quickly she counted to ten again on her fingers, then touched the Jaw's finger and said, "Eleven."

"The bitch can't even count!" shouted Chert.

The Jaw ignored his father, face straining toward Veela, trying to understand. "That's my one," he insisted. "Why should my one be different from your one?"

Veela counted to twenty on their hands again, but this time she started with his hands, and designated her own fingers as eleven through twenty.

The Jaw tried to understand what she was doing but couldn't. Unlike his impatient father, though, he sensed there was *something* she was trying to explain to him, something real and new.

"Sometimes your finger is 'one,'" he said. "Sometimes my finger is 'one.' Why? What decides whose finger gets to be 'one'? What changes? I can't see any change. And I still don't understand why sometimes it's 'one,' and sometimes 'eleven'. Why is 'two' sometimes 'twelve'?"

"'One,' different from finger," Veela said. "Even if no finger is, 'one' is existing."

She got up and ran to a tree. She ran from one to another of them, touching each one and when she touched it counting from one to twenty. She scooped up a handful of pebbles and sat back down with the two men and counted out a little pile of twenty pebbles.

"This is stupid," said Chert. "Let's kill her."

"Number *is*." Veela slapped the pile of twenty pebbles. They clattered into the underbrush. "Before rock, number is. Before finger, number is. Before world, number is. In darkness, is number. Number is power. Number is *only* power."

"What is she talking about?" demanded Chert.

"Shut up," said the Jaw, without tearing his eyes from Veela. "Shut up." He was concentrating so hard, beads of sweat popped from his forehead.

"Number is bones of the world. Number is the magic language."

"But," began the Jaw, then had so many questions he couldn't find the sentence. Desperately, he said, "But how can you keep track of the numbers? If you don't use your fingers? If there are more numbers than there are fingers?"

113

Veela grabbed a twig and jumped up, gesturing for them to follow her out to the ash. They did.

They sat together. Veela held out her hands and again cycled from one through ten. Then, in a column in the ash, she wrote the Arabic numerals for one through ten, saying each number as she went.

Then she held up both hands, leaving the fists closed, and said, "Zero. Zero." She kept doing it until the Jaw, still confused, mimicked her. Chert refused to.

Then she took her stick again and wrote a zero in the ash atop her column of numerals. "Zero," she said again. She faced the two men and held up her closed fists again and again said, "Zero."

The Jaw noticed that the circle she'd drawn to represent a zero was also half of the two-part mark she'd made to represent "ten." Then he noticed that the other half of the mark was that which represented "one."

"Zero, hidden number is," she said. "But most powerful number is."

"Powerful things have no need to hide," said Chert.

"Is strange," she said. "But is true."

She wrote down the numbers for eleven through twenty, saying them aloud as she went. Having noticed that the "ten" was made of a "one" fronting a "zero," it was not lost on the Jaw that this new set was just the old set fronted by a "one" each time. He was expecting the same thing to happen when she wrote "twenty," so that the mark would be "one, one, zero," and was surprised when instead it was a "two, zero." His eyes ran up the column again. He noted, with only a groping idea of its significance, that this appearance of a "two, zero" for twenty after the "one, zero" for ten seemed to mirror the sequence of the one and the two in the original column.

Veela looked at the Jaw's face to see if he understood. She couldn't tell whether he was close to it or not, but he was clearly trying.

She continued writing the sequence, saying the numbers aloud as she went. "Twenty-two. Twenty-three. Twenty-four."

She had to move along the ash field to find room to write. Chert and the Jaw followed her.

Chert was so annoyed that he wanted to stop her by force. But it seemed that the Jaw was seeing something in all this nonsense, and Chert felt uncharacteristically unsure of himself.

Shortly after Veela got to the the thirties the Jaw realized with a gasp that this new string of marks, fronted by the mark for "three," also mirrored the sequence of the original string. "Next is four!" he shouted, voice breaking. Veela looked at him. He'd spoken too excitedly for her to make out the words. The Jaw started to hurry back to the original string, then realized he didn't have to go that far and stopped at the place where she'd written "twenty-four." He pointed down at the second half of the mark, the "four," and shouted, "Next is four!" He looked at Veela in appeal, waiting to hear if he'd gotten it right.

"Yes!" she shouted. "Yes!" She wrote more quickly, hurrying to get through the thirties' subset of the sequence so that she could get to the forties, to reward the Jaw.

He walked beside her as she wrote. When she got to the forties, and he saw he'd been right, that he'd predicted the pattern, his body shook with emotion. He put his hand over his eyes. Voice hoarse, he said, "Next is five. Next is five."

Veela kept writing on into the fifties. Her voice was getting hoarse too, as she continued to name each number. She was exultantly shouting them now.

Chert stared in astonishment at his son, who for some reason was actually crying over these scratchings in the dirt. "How long will you go on?" he demanded of Veela. "Where do these scratchings end?"

She straightened and turned to face him. She said, "They end at the strong tight fire."

As she was about to finish the sixties, the Jaw took the stick from her and took over the sequence. Having never written before—having never conceived of the notion of writing until today—his scratchings were barely legible. But it was plain that he had grasped the principle of the sequence—he made his way into the seventies with no problem, then the eighties. Veela walked alongside him, saying the name of each number as he wrote it.

Once he'd written "ninety-nine," he looked up at her uncertainly. She took the stick from him and wrote a one and two zeros. "One hundred," she said.

"Is that the end?" he asked.

"No end. Never end."

The Jaw breathed out softly. He gazed up at the dimming sky and seemed to no longer even notice the nearby wall.

While there was still light Veela sat the Jaw down with her in a fresh patch of ash. Chert hung back—Veela wasn't going to waste time begging him to pay attention when the Jaw was so enthusiastic.

In the ash she wrote a ten, and below it she wrote an "x" beside a two. Under them both she drew a line, and below it she wrote a twenty. The Jaw stared, face scrunched in concentration.

She held her two closed fists up, and flashed her ten fingers open twice in quick succession, saying, "Ten. Twenty." She repeated the action, this time saying, "One. Two." She repeated the whole thing several times, using both pairs.

Then she pointed down at the newly written symbols. One the Jaw's attention was there, she held her two closed fists beside the symbols. She opened her fingers. "Ten," she said. Then she flashed her fingers closed and open twice. "One, two," she said. "Two." Then she pointed at the symbols written in ash, pointing at each relevant marking in turn. "Ten. Two times. Is twenty."

She repeated this many times. The Jaw, scowling in concentration, followed along with the symbols, watching her flashing fingers, muttered along after her. He would look up at her face, looking for help. She continued repeating the lesson, patiently.

At last he gave that gasp of comprehension. He leaned far forward, supporting himself with his hands and bringing his face close to the markings.

With his finger he crudely wrote, next to Veela's markings, the symbols for "ten times three equals thirty." Before he could even look up at her for approval, she screamed for joy and threw her arms around him.

In a dim way, he grasped that this had something to do with why she had said zero was the most powerful number. It designated magnitude ... but of course the Jaw had no words for this.

He was right, but Veela had also meant that the concept of zero served as a gateway from the idea of natural numbers to the idea of integers. But she would have been delighted enough with the Jaw's insight.

They called it a night after that. Just as well—Veela wanted to spend time planning the next lessons better. For instance, why had she gone straight to multiplication, without even pausing for addition and subtraction?... The Jaw seemed to have a knack for this stuff, considering that a couple hours ago he'd had no notion of a number as an entity existing independent of any contingent physical phenomena, as pure pattern. But knack or no knack, she should be able to keep him on his toes. Her mathematical background might be laughable compared to Dak's, but she'd been good at it in college and was confident she could teach someone all the way up to calculus.

Chert eyed her, where she lay resting in the ash. He suspected she'd played a trick on his son, and felt angry at her on the Jaw's behalf; he speculated, a little sadly, that perhaps the Jaw's Big-Brow blood made him gullible.

The Jaw wandered, almost staggered, through the corridor of ash, head tilted back as he counted the stars. He felt he himself had been cracked open to reveal a beautiful terror within. All of a sudden there was an abstract pattern underpinning the world. The Jaw felt instinctively that it transcended himself, that it transcended all the spirits and people and animals and plants he had ever known. If the universe disappeared tomorrow, that eternal pattern would remain.

He went to where Veela was resting and knelt beside her. "Thank you for showing me."

She smiled, and put her hand upon his arm. Earlier she'd feared that the attraction he obviously felt for her might manifest itself as rape. Now, looking at his grateful, humble, awed face, she knew she wouldn't have to worry about that. As far as the Jaw was concerned, she called the shots from now on.

Ten

The monster-woman Veela really had driven Chert's son crazy. Now that his frustration had faded and he'd calmed down, he was willing to concede that there was a strong enough possibility of her having some value after all, for them not to necessarily kill her outright. But something had to be done to break this hold that she had over the Jaw.

Chert could understand being fascinated by a female, and if the Jaw would just take her, like a normal person, the fact that he had chosen this particular female would have been merely annoying. But he followed her around like he was still a mewling whelp and she a master hunter. He barely seemed to notice Chert anymore, he was so busy mooning over her and repeating her endless incantations over her scratchings in the dirt. She had definitely bewitched him. Since that first night, Chert had avoided even looking at her scratchings, for fear that this time he might not prove strong enough to withstand their magic.

But he knew she wasn't entirely bluffing—she really did understand things that he would have liked to understand. The night that she made the Jaw swoon over her scratchings in the dirt, there was a terrible commotion and red flashes that must have been the strong tight fire, back the way they'd come. Chert and the Jaw had tried not to show how frightened they were by it all—but Veela stood with her hands on her hips, grinning in the direction of the red flashes.

When they asked her what was going on, she held her hands up with the palms facing each other. "No-dies," she said, nodding to indicate the space between her palms. Then she pressed her hands together.

So it was a trap. Chert wondered what spirits were undertaking it, and who had cajoled them into it. The strange unbreakable nut was still here with them, so it couldn't have been the little man.

Screams began to come from the hill, mixed in with the strange humming crash of the strong tight fire. Veela looked shocked, then somber. The Jaw looked at Chert. "Those are the People," he said. "There were survivors."

"I suppose there were," said Chert. He left his gaze forward. When the Jaw wouldn't look away, Chert met his eyes and said, "What do you care? There was only one of them you gave a damn about. She wasn't even of the People, and anyway I tell you she's dead."

The Jaw left his hard glare upon him, breathing heavily. For a second Chert thought his son might try to kill him. Finally the Jaw stalked off instead.

Chert watched the boy's back as he went. It wasn't fair. What had Chert done? His only sin had been to rescue the boy and nobody else. But when those undead had attacked, Chert had realized that there was no one else among the People he cared about very much. Was that such a terrible thing, to have saved only his son, when he'd barely been able to manage even that?

He didn't think it was so terrible. In fact, he was beginning to think that maybe he ought to be thanked.

Veela, meanwhile, ignored the men's exchange, lost in thoughts of her own. Eventually she went looking for the Jaw—despite his angry grief and her linguistic limitations, he gradually realized she wanted to know where he thought the screaming humans had appeared from. After much more back-and-forth, he managed to explain about the cave up on the hill, that the People had been trying to escape into during the first no-die attack.

Dak hadn't mentioned any cave.

She couldn't understand how there could have been human survivors in the caves, if there had been zombies there too. Humans needed light to navigate; zombies needed light, as well, except when it came to brains. The refugees in the caves wouldn't have been able to see the zombies coming, whereas the zombies would have been drawn inexorably by their brainsong.... Veela supposed the humans must have had torches, and then been constantly on the move to keep one step ahead of the undead.

She contacted Dak about it. Both of the guys were moping and sullen, so it was easy to get some privacy from them.

"They're all dead now," Dak assured her. "It's true that there did turn out to be a cave, with some humans hiding inside. But all who came out were killed or zombified, and the ship's lasers destroyed the zombified ones."

"How can you be sure of that?"

"Because, Veela, I had the ship's computer keep track of the humans as they exited the cave, and they were all accounted for. There could be some still hiding inside, I suppose, but I doubt it."

Veela didn't see why he was so certain. Besides, if humans had been able to slip into the cave complex in the first place, zombies might have done the same, and that could be a disaster of untold magnitude. If the zombies were in a vast enough cave system, with egresses potentially many miles away, then the perimeter wall wouldn't mean shit.

She had a hard time hiding her annoyance at the spot he'd picked for his trap. Even if the hilltop was the nearest forest clearing to the zombie epicenter, and thus the easiest place for the lasers to operate, luring them so close to the cave mouth had been reckless. She wondered if Dak had even known the cave was there. If not, it didn't speak well of his ability to use the equipment with as much expertise as he claimed, especially considering his inability to open that hold filled with drones and weapons, and the fact that now he couldn't even land the ship.

And if for some reason he had known the cave was there, and had picked that site anyway ... well, that would be even stranger.

The next morning Chert killed a rabbit, skinned it, built a small fire, and cooked it. The Jaw and Veela tore into it ravenously. Chert watched them.

Veela paused in her eating. "You, no eat?" she asked Chert.

He only shrugged in reply. He didn't much feel like eating with the woman.

As they were licking the bones clean, the Jaw said, "What now? Do you think the trap worked? Do you think all the zombies are destroyed?" Veela had taught them that new word, "zombies."

"My hope, is. Our hope, is."

Chert had given up trying to understand her explanations of the trap. Something about a gigantic pile of brains, and a big flying something that used the strong tight fire (presumably the stone he and the Jaw had seen the other day). Like everything she said, it made no sense. Even if it was all true, Chert wished that she would explain herself in such a way that a sane person could believe her.

"How do the no-dies know the pile of brains is there?" the Jaw had asked. "They can smell it?"

"No," Veela had said, and then had launched into a long confused babble. The gist appeared to be that living brains "sang," and the no-dies were drawn to the song. Human brains sang the loudest, but any brain was audible to them, and a huge pile of brains harvested from deer, bears, foxes, squirrels, lizards, and so on, she assured them, would blare at the no-dies throughout the forest, wherever they were within the wall.

Chert pointed out that a pile of disembodied brains was hardly likely to be "living." Veela gave a reply that made no sense—she seemed to be saying that she and the little man had some kind of juice that could keep an organ alive a few hours, in a halfway fashion, even outside of a body.

To explain all this even as well as she had, Veela had had to sing, since "sing" was a word they'd not yet taught each other. As she sang, the Jaw had gazed at her with such stupid adoring awe that Chert had felt he might throw up.

"Why are the no-dies such a dark black when they're hungry?" asked the Jaw. "And why do they glow bright green when they eat a brain?"

Once Veela had deciphered the question, she knew its answer was going to be a doozy. How to explain that the zombie venom kickstarted the production of the cthuloid fluid, which transformed the blood into a black ichor that stained its way through every vein and capillary, till finally it had soaked through the entirety of the victim's flesh? And then further explain that the ingestion of cerebral fluid set off a whole symphony of metabolic reactions in the zombie, the most visible of which was the brief and spectacular activation of the cthuloid fluid's phosphorescent quality? "Magic," she finally settled for, with a shrug.

Chert and, mainly, the Jaw taught Veela how to make a knife, and a spear. They taught her the most basic rudiments of tracking, the kind of things they were used to teaching toddlers only beginning to walk, not full-grown adults. She caught on pretty quickly. That only bewildered Chert even more. He'd assumed she was simply an idiot, albeit a very unusual sort of idiot. Now it turned out that her problem was that she had never learned the most basic lessons of being human. It was as if a full-grown woman had never gotten around to learning how to walk, out of laziness.

Two days after she'd made her first spear, she killed her first animal. At first she danced around, inordinately pleased with herself for having killed a mere rabbit. Then she picked the thing up, holding it at a distance and making a displeased face at it, a sure way to offend its spirit. The Jaw, who had been beaming at her throughout the kill, actually had to tell her to thank the rabbit's spirit before they skinned it.

Chert was disgusted. It would be one thing if her particular rites of thanksgiving had been different from the People's. But not thinking to thank the animal at all betrayed a lack of decency.

In the middle of the Jaw showing her how to skin the rabbit, Veela excused herself. She insisted on hiding in the bushes to urinate. The Jaw was content to accept this as simply another of her eccentricities; Chert was convinced she was concealing something sinister under that white garb.

123

While she was gone Chert approached the Jaw. He was happily dressing the monster woman's kill for her: a bitter reminder to Chert that slave blood ran in his son's veins. He said, "We're supposed to be teaching her in exchange for something. When is she going to start giving us something in return?"

The Jaw stared at Chert in unfeigned shock. "She's giving us the math," he said.

"Math" was what she called her prattlings and scratchings. Chert regarded his son sullenly and without speaking, then walked away from him.

Meanwhile, as Veela was urinating she noticed that she'd happened to pick a spot near a patch of those purple shrooms that Chert had been so gung-ho to keep her away from. She picked one, and with four taps on the communicator—two shorts, a long, then two more shorts—she caused a tiny needle to pop out, then stuck that needle into the shroom. The needle would sample and decode the mushroom's DNA, and send the genome up to Dak. He should be able to model how the fungus was likely to interact with human biochemistry. And then they would have at least a clue as to what the exact flavor of the experience was, when her new buddies were tripping balls. That might be interesting, maybe.

Veela and the Jaw talked all the time, he trying to learn the math and she trying to learn the language. But he wanted to learn about her, as well. "Why are you here, alone?" he asked. "Alone with no band, except the little man in the nut? With no weapon you can control, yourself?"

Veela hung on his words, translating them. Once she'd processed his question, bitter humiliation spread through her face like a stain, prompted by the memories his questions evoked.

Not humiliation at her decision to stay on the planet surface—she felt no shame over that, although it would not be quite true to say she hadn't regretted it a few times, and she still couldn't believe she'd done it.

She replayed the moment in her head—Dak had brought the ship down for a landing, by night so they wouldn't be seen, in a deserted forest spot at the center of what was now the walled perimeter. At dawn, they'd stepped out, with no protection but their white therma-fix jumpsuits and their sturdy helmets, and Veela's rudimentary grasp of the basics of Group B's language. And two laser-blasters, the only two that weren't locked away in that hold. They'd walked around the side of the ship, to open a side-hold and get a pack's worth of perma-meals … and that fucking zombie mouse had streaked out, hissing and slithering as it zipped under the carpet of dead leaves and disappeared.

Veela had given a yelping shriek and leaped into the arms of Dak, her unlikely hero. He had extricated himself from her embrace, and blithely said, "Ah, well, that's unfortunate. We shall have to go back up, now. If the undead are going to be loose here in prehistory, there's no time to lose in building a perimeter wall to contain them. Eradicating the infected will be the second priority."

Eradicating the infected, Veela had repeated to herself, as Dak combed through the hold with his instruments, making sure there were no more stowaways from the future. Everything he had just said was absolutely correct; now that they had committed this fuck-up (how had a mouse ever snuck into the hold in the first place, much less a zombie mouse?!), their number-one priority had to be nipping an apocalypse in the bud. Both morally and in terms of their own survival, that was the only thing that made sense.

But there were people down here. Unsuspecting humans. As Dak was finishing up his sensor sweep of the hold and heading back to the main hatch, she'd heard herself say, "I'm staying down here."

The slightly immature pleasure of seeing Dak at a loss almost made up for the crippling terror of what she was about to do. "What?"

"The people," she said. "I speak some of one of the three linguistic group's lingo, and someone has to warn them what's

125

coming. Has to tell them how dangerous these things are, has to explain that their only vulnerable point is the brain. Stuff like that."

He was still staring at her. "They're primitives," he said. "They'll rape and eat you."

"Only if they're primitives and also dickheads."

He spent a little more time trying to dissuade her, but she was raring to go try to catch up with the Overhill group before any of its members became infected. Also before her nerve failed. She was almost touched by how upset Dak seemed at the prospect of her heading into danger alone, although maybe he was just pissed that she was taking one of their only two hand-held laser blasters. For a second she thought he might refuse to hand it over.

When they'd parted, Veela had said, "All right, I'm going to go find Group B. They're north, right?" She pointed.

"Yes, they are to the north, but you're pointing west, for goodness' sake. Once again, I must protest this reckless and tactically useless notion of yours."

Once she had it clear which direction north was, she'd marched off that way, trying to quell the fearful tremblings in her belly, unable even to look up over her shoulder at the ship as it hummed smoothly and safely into the sky.... And then how had she lost that blaster? What use had she, the brave and intrepid rescuer, made of fully half their available hand-held weaponry? With her belly bubbling in fear the way it was, she hadn't gone many yards before she'd realized she was going to have to take a shit. And then she'd realized, appalled, that she had no idea how to go about it. Never before in her whole life had she even once relieved herself in an environment not engineered and built for that explicit purpose. She'd looked around at the forest: what, was she just supposed to go out here? In daylight, on the ground? In some irrational but powerful way it was simply unthinkable, even aside from the possibility of a lurking zombie mouse. She tried to recall a scene from some adventure vid or some historical novel where a character in the wild had taken a dump, so she could remember how they'd managed. She couldn't think of any such scene, though.

Nearby was the sound of running water. She'd walked to it and found a pretty brisk stream with what she supposed was a fairly strong current, not that she'd ever before seen a stream that wasn't man-made. The running water had made the set-up feel sort of like plumbing. After a nervous look around, Veela had opened the back flap of her jumpsuit and copped a squat, poking her bottom out over the water—just in time, too. There were a few towelettes stored in the lining of her jumpsuit that she'd used to clean herself, wondering all the while what she was going to do when *those* ran out.... Did people here in prehistory just use leaves? How many centuries did that go on?

She'd managed to walk a pretty long way before she even noticed that her blaster holster was empty, and remembered that, before sticking her butt out over that stream, she hadn't thought to fasten the holster. Horrified, she'd run back to the spot. But the quick little stream's current had been strong enough to whisk the light plastic-and-synthcrystal weapon away already.

Now, with the Jaw, she replied to his question: "To explain, is difficult." And when it looked like he was going to press the issue, she distracted him with multiplication drills.

Eleven

Veela was learning the People's tongue fast—she spent all her time practicing, which was another way of saying she was forever babbling. Chert was going to go insane listening to her. Whenever he tried to steer her to some interesting topic, she started talking about her math again. And then the Jaw would hang on her every word.

The Jaw grew more pathetic with each passing moment. She'd let him take that protective head-protecting stone of hers, called a "helmet," since it fascinated him so much. The Jaw had torn loose a strip of the hide he wore and tied it to the helmet, so that now it hung from his garment, getting in the way. It was as if he was so fascinated that he wanted some fetish of hers always at hand, in addition to her actual presence. Chert hated the sight of that bizarre stone, hanging off his son and bobbing clumsily as they walked.

Two days after the red flashings, his second full day of getting an earful of the math, Chert raised his hand to the Jaw's chest, to halt their progress.

The Jaw stopped. It was plain from his face that he expected nothing good from whatever his father was going to say. Veela kept walking, till she noticed that they'd stopped.

"Who are you to hold this female for yourself?" said Chert.

The Jaw didn't respond, except to tighten his mouth and the muscles around his eyes.

"Am I not the older?" said Chert. "Am I not the father? I have the right to use the captured woman, too."

"She's not our captive, Father."

The Jaw had gotten into the habit of calling Chert "Father" when he wanted to soften him. But Chert could see there was no affection behind the title, certainly not this time, and the trick only made him more resentful.

"Are we her captives, then?"

"No, Father. Maybe we're...." The Jaw trailed off. He had been going to say "equals," but knew the mockery he'd face if he suggested to Chert that they be equals with a female, even one as extraordinary as Veela. In truth, the notion struck the Jaw himself as bizarre, when he tried to articulate it.

Chert waited for him to finish. When the Jaw didn't say anything, Chert said, "She's not a member of our band. She's not of the People. Thus, either she is our captive or we are hers. And I will be no woman's captive. So: she is ours. If she is our captive, we have three choices: kill her; free her; or use her. You don't want to kill her. As for releasing her, I doubt we could persuade her to go, and even if we did she's so ignorant that she would soon die in the forest. So we only have one choice left."

Veela's listening comprehension had advanced far enough that she could make out the vague drift of Chert's words. For now, she merely moved her eyes uneasily from one man to the other, waiting to see how they would decide it between them before taking any action herself.

The Jaw's face looked like it was about to explode. Barely able to move his tight-gripped teeth enough to get the words out, he said, "Say you're right, Father. Say she is our captive. There's plenty of use to be gotten out of her, going on as we are. She is our link to the strong tight fire and the flying stone. And you don't understand the math, but I do, and I tell you it's good."

"Don't remind me of how she's fogged your mind with that math magic, you'll only convince me that the best thing is to kill her after all."

The Jaw took a step closer to him. "I say again that you'll not kill her, Chert. Or touch her at all."

Chert wondered if he would have hated his own father, as the Jaw was coming to hate him, as Spear had once hated his. Probably not—not enough to kill him, at least. Anyway, he would never know. Chert's father had been mauled to death by a bear, back when he and the other hunters still towered twice Chert's height.

He tried to keep the note of pleading from his voice. "Son. If you want to keep her for your own use, if you ask me for that, I will renounce my right to her. I have no desire for this female, anyway. Only, make use of her yourself, at least. I can't stand to see you debase yourself like this. This is not the use to be made of the life I gave you."

"The life you gave me?" the Jaw repeated. "And what was the purpose of that life, I ask you? Was I not destined to be a slave? To be used? Was it not my sole purpose to be killed by the People whenever they saw fit to punish my mother for some trifle?"

Chert raised his hand to the Jaw's elbow. Incredibly, his eyes had grown wet. "But I wouldn't let them, my son," he said. "Do remember that."

"How will we ever know if your resolve would have held?"

"Don't be a fool. You know."

"I know I'm half Big-Brow. How long would it have taken Spear and the rest to refocus your eyes on that hated half? If the unkillables hadn't come, perhaps I'd be dead now. Either you all would have executed me, or I would have died trying to stop you from killing my Big-Brow mother, whom you once used as you'd like to use Veela now."

Chert was losing patience. "This is foolishness. All I'm trying to do is get you to do what men have done since the world began. And if you don't know how, I'll show you."

Dry leaves crackled as Veela backed away from them. She raised the nut to her mouth and said something softly to the little man, who didn't reply.

Chert stepped toward her. "I swear I'll kill that little man of yours!"

The Jaw clapped a hand on Chert's shoulder to halt him. "I'll kill *you*," he said. "If you lay a hand on her, I swear I will."

"You can't kill me, I'm stronger than you!" Chert wheeled

around to face his son. "And you can't kill me for a reason like that, anyway! Women don't come between men! They don't come between us!"

Veela, hissing something angrily at the little man in the nut, turned and ran.

"Veela!" shouted the Jaw, and pushed past his father to go after her.

Chert grabbed his son by the arm, yanking him back. "Let her go! We're better without—"

The Jaw smashed his father in the face, hard enough to knock him loose—yet Chert retained enough control to grab hold of the Jaw and pull him down along with him. The Jaw landed atop him and tried to pound him again. If the blows had connected they might have done real damage, but the Jaw was in a tearful rage and his fists flew wildly, connecting with nothing as Chert dodged them. Chert bucked his hips and rolled on top of the Jaw, then slithered around behind him as the Jaw tried to turn over, and got him in a chokehold. The helmet got torn loose.

From beyond the near trees, Veela screamed. Panicked, she shouted something in her own language.

The Jaw struggled even more fiercely, but all he could do was land weak punches on the back of his father's head. He had to reach around behind himself to punch. The blows hurt, and they would soon add up, but for now Chert was able to wait them out.

Veela screamed again, this time in the People's tongue: "No-die!"

The Jaw let out a desperate wheeze, and fought even more vigorously to break free. But Chert held tight.

"No-die!" she screamed again.

"Sh," Chert said. "Shhh. It's for the best. Let her go. If she can't defeat one undead, or no-die, or zombie, or whatever they are, then she's no good to us anyway." The Jaw unleashed another burst of thrashing. "Shhh," said his father again, squeezing his neck tighter. "When you wake up, it'll all be over."

The Jaw struggled as long as he could. Then he slumped, unconscious.

As Chert got up Veela screamed again. Hopefully whatever she'd come across would kill her before the Jaw awoke.

He cautiously made his way to her. What with the path she'd torn through the forest and the sounds of her struggle, she wasn't hard to find.

He saw her and one of the undead. Chert realized with a shock that he recognized it—this thing had once been Horn. He was black now, his head had that indefinably misshapen quality of the no-dies. The thing that had been Horn glared at Veela as if indignant that she would dare withhold her brain. She had her spear pointed inexpertly at it. As Chert leaned against a tree to watch, she jabbed at it, coming nowhere near its body. "Help me!" she shouted at Chert. "Help me!"

He watched her impassively. Even avoiding the risk that she, too, would be changed into a zombie he'd have to fight, was not worth the trouble of helping her. Right now, Chert felt he would gladly allow the personal danger to himself to increase, in exchange for seeing Veela dispatched.

She was only still alive because the zombie was even clumsier than her, and because they were in a stand of saplings that blocked what limited mobility it had. They blocked Veela's too, though. "Help!" she said once more, hopelessly, then returned her full attention to fending the creature off.

This might prove to be a rare chance to calmly observe one of these zombies fighting, Chert thought. Again he noted how it led with its teeth—more precisely with its out-jutting jaws. It swiped at Veela with its arms, too, but almost as an afterthought.

"Dak!" shouted Veela. That, Chert and the Jaw had figured out from listening to her foreign chatter, was the name of the little man in the nut. He still didn't respond to her.

Fear must have aided her concentration. She landed two good thrusts, driving the spear into the zombie's ribs. She couldn't kill the creature with the spear, but she could keep shoving it back till she got unlucky or exhausted. But the second blow nearly got her killed; the spearhead stuck between the zombie's ribs, and if the zombie had thought to grab the shaft while Veela was trying to yank it out, it could have disarmed her. But the zombie proved almost as stupid as its prey, and too preoccupied with lunging uselessly at her head to press its advantage.

Veela pulled the spear out and circled around the thing, spear up. The thing spun after her. Chert saw what she was trying to do, and admitted that it wasn't a bad idea, though she didn't seem very aware of where her spear was in relation to the trees.

She waited till the right moment, till the zombie's neck was lined up with a sapling behind it, though Chert could see how hard it was for her to hold back, how terror made her want to strike prematurely.

When everything was aligned, she thrust forward with the spear, putting all her strength into it, all her hope. Her aim was true—the spear pierced the zombie's neck and passed through into the tree behind—the zombie's swiping twisted hands nearly caught Veela, but she managed to stay just out of their range. The zombie was pinned to the tree. Considering how pathetic Veela had been two days ago, Chert was willing to admit that this was relatively impressive.

Even with its neck pierced the zombie continued trying to breathe. Most of the air whistled in and out through the hole incompletely plugged by the spear. Obviously the thing no longer needed to breathe but continued to do it, out of habit perhaps. Instead of using its arms to tear the spear from its neck, the idiotic creature continued to claw at Veela.

Gasping from exertion and terror, she hunted for stones big enough to do damage but small enough to easily handle. She looked at Chert as if she again had the urge to plead for help, but knew better than to waste her breath. She found two suitable stones. She circled around behind the zombie. It expected her to come back around on the other side, its right, and sent its arms flailing and swiping in that direction. Veela, feinting to the right just close enough for the thing to spot her and strain its energies in that direction, doubled back and sprang upon the creature from the left. She spun around, pounding the rock in her left hand as hard as she could into the zombie's head, then following up with the stone in her right.

The zombie grabbed her around the waist with its left arm, when she lunged in to bash it in the skull. To be fair, Chert wasn't sure how she could have gotten close enough to hit it in the head with the rock, without getting within arm's reach as well. Luckily for her the zombie, after having at first shown little interest in the spear, had become preoccupied with clawing at the spot on its neck where the thing held it fixed; with only the zombie's one arm around her waist, she was able to push on its chest hard enough with her left hand to keep out of range from its snapping jaws and strong teeth, while she pounded it in the forehead and temple with the rock. As she hit it she made desperate little sobbing noises, but no longer bothered to look up at Chert or call to Dak.

Chert doubted that under normal circumstances her arm would have had the strength to shatter a skull with a rock. But he saw his impression of the no-dies' rottenness confirmed now. At first he thought it might be his imagination—but, no, there were small dents in the forehead and temple, dents that grew bigger and deeper as she hit it again and again. But the damage to its head didn't seem to slow it down—on the contrary, it seemed even more determined to draw her into killing range, though still too stupid to divert its right arm for the purpose. The outcome looked certain now, and Chert decided he had little left to learn by watching. He scanned the ground for rocks of his own, planning to walk to the sapling, smash in the zombie's head, and kill Veela as well, preferably before that thing gained strength from eating her brain.

Something came crashing through the vegetation— without turning around, Chert knew it was the Jaw. He considered trying to stop the boy, but fighting each other would dangerously distract them from the no-die. It was simply bad luck that he'd woken so soon.

The Jaw barreled past his father to the tree. He grabbed the zombie's arm and pulled it off Veela; he bent it back around the tree, screaming in rage and exertion. There were popping and cracking noises as the zombie's arm and shoulder snapped in multiple places. The creature howled, but Chert was sure it was in frustration at having its meal torn from its grasp, not out of pain. Veela pounded its head with renewed ferocity, and its skull and face got more and more deformed and misshapen. Finally the Jaw pulled her away from the zombie and snatched both stones from her. As the zombie clawed at him, he slammed both rocks together so that they met in the center of the zombie's brain. The soft, rotted insides of its head sprayed everywhere.

Veela shouted something, reverting in her panic to her own language; then she said, in the People's tongue, "No swallow! No swallow!"

The warning was unnecessary. The Jaw was already wiping and scrubbing with his forearms at the places on his face where the zombie's head-matter had splattered onto him. Veela gathered handfuls of dry leaves and handed them to him, and he scraped them across his face over and over, eyes still squeezed shut.

As the Jaw finished cleaning himself as best he could, Veela glared at Chert. He met her gaze. It looked like she was about to say something to him, but decided not to bother.

Once he was relatively clean, the Jaw marched over to his father, fists bunched. "You were going to stand and watch her die."

Although Chert maintained the appearance of lounging against the tree, his muscles tensed in readiness. "Yes. I was. If she can't defend herself, she can't travel with us."

"Since when does a mighty hunter stand back and let a woman do her own fighting?"

"Ah, but she's no ordinary woman. Right? I thought she was a powerful sorceress."

Chert kept his tone relaxed and disdainful. But it was to mask the weary sadness he felt at the prospect of yet more physical combat with his son.

Veela shouted, "Stop your fight! Find zombies. No-dies, we fight!" She was tearing around in the bushes, for no reason Chert could discern. "Where it came from? Must fight them!"

"We *can't* keep fighting these things!" shouted Chert. "One, maybe two, perhaps we'll get lucky and survive. But if we run into more than that we're dead. We have to get across the white air-biting thing!"

"No! Never! Never until all no-dies die!"

"*We'll* die, if there are many more of those things in here with us!"

"Yes! We die! If need is, we die, to fight the no-dies! To kill the zombies!"

"You see?" snarled Chert to the Jaw. "I was only trying to grant her wish."

The Jaw had been distracted by Veela's rant—now he turned on his father again. Veela ran over and grabbed his arm. "Damn your fight!" she said. "Damn your fight! Is nothing! Help with *other* fight!"

"What do you know of our fight?" said Chert.

"Your fight, for always. Always, this fight will happen, of father of son, again and again, for all of human time. But only if we kill the no-dies."

"Perhaps we ought to let your zombies wipe us out, then, since we're only good for squabbling."

Veela paused, looked at him. His bitter joke did not amuse her. She held up the strange nut and said, "Like Dak, you sound sometimes."

She managed to gall him anew every time she opened her mouth. He had not forgotten his vow to stomp that little man to paste.

By tugging on his arm, Veela managed to pull the Jaw away from his father and their incipient brawl. "Must find where zombie came from," she kept repeating.

The Jaw's nerves were so frayed that even he was short with Veela. "What do you mean, where it came from? It could have been wandering through the woods for days! Years, for all I know!"

But Veela remembered what Dak had said about the caves. The zombies had gone in, but come straight back out—he'd been oh so sure of that. And since the ship's sensors wouldn't penetrate the planet surface, he wouldn't be much help even if he did eventually deign to answer her hail. "Search holes," she said, pointing at the ground. "Search holes."

The Jaw stared at the ground. "What holes am I supposed to be searching?" he asked.

Veela stopped and squeezed her eyes shut, trying to remember the prepositions she'd picked up. She'd like to see Dak learn a whole fucking language in just a few days! Chert, too. "Search in holes," she tried. The Jaw continued to just look at her. "Search *on* holes." The Jaw looked more bewildered than ever. "Search *for* holes!" she finally shouted. "Search *for* holes!"

The Jaw was still confused, but at least he understood well enough that he started scanning the ground for holes.

Veela waved at Chert. "You, also!" she said. "No each other fight, now. Now is to fight zombies."

Chert merely looked at her and remained aloof.

Veela returned to scanning the ground. As she did so she kept talking in her own language into the communicator: "Dak—Dak, come in, Dak. Dak, you've got to come in."

There was no answer, which sent her beyond worry. Something had to be wrong—surely not even Dak could be so irresponsible as to leave the communicator off? Even if he was asleep, surely not even he would neglect to program an alarm to go off if she were hailing him. Although who knew.... That son of a bitch had driven the zombies underground. That would leave them in much more long-term danger than when the undead had roamed the planet surface—that unmapped cave complex might easily head to other cave mouths well beyond the perimeter wall. Dak's amazing plan might turn out to have totally fucked all of human history. She'd be willing to bet he'd been so convinced of the flawlessness of his own operation, that he'd hypnotized himself into actually *seeing* the zombies come right back out again, regardless of reality.

She realized that the Jaw was trying almost timidly to get her attention, so she quit hailing Dak for a moment. "What?" she said, trying not to be curt.

"Are we looking for a hole because you think the zombie came out of one?" he asked uncertainly.

"Yes."

"So the purpose is to track the zombie back to where it came from?"

"Yes!" Jesus, what was it with these guys?! Did they have no clue what was going on at all?!

"Well," the Jaw suggested humbly, "maybe we should follow the trail that the zombie made? If it came out of a hole, the trail must lead back there."

Veela blushed. "You can follow its trail?"

The Jaw gaped at her. "Of course." A blind person could follow the trails left by those clumsy, shuffling, undead things.

It was Veela's turn to feel humbled. She touched the Jaw's arm gratefully and tilted her head down. "Yes," she said, "thank you. Please, follow it."

The Jaw led the way, backtracking along the trail—no matter how long he'd wondered why she didn't follow it back to the zombie's lair, it might never have occurred to him that the reason was she couldn't see it. Chert fell in behind them. "You see?" he called to his son. "She's stupid."

Seeing the way the Jaw's shoulders tensed at his father's voice, Veela was afraid they were going to get into it again. But he let it go. Veela felt stupid enough not to take offense. Following the Jaw now, she realized that the trail was, in fact, dramatic enough that she should have been able to see it herself, after all the lessons of the last couple days.

Trailing behind them both, Chert kept his grim eyes on Veela's back. The woman was going to get his son and himself killed. As soon as the Jaw was distracted, Chert was going to get rid of her.

As predicted, the trail led back to a fissure in the earth. It was a great stone lurching up out of the soil like a whale frozen in time as it broke the surface of a dirt sea, with a dark light-gobbling crevice wide enough for a human or zombie to wriggle through. "Goddammit," she muttered, and raised the communicator to her mouth again. "Dak? Dak, goddammit, you have to answer me!"

The Jaw watched her worriedly. He had no idea what was going on or what it had to do with the little man, but he could tell something was terribly wrong.

"Dak!" she cried, so angry she was near tears. "The zombies are underground, Dak! They're in the fucking caves! It's going to take work and technology to even try to clean them out, so I need you to respond to me!"

She had walked a few paces away, out of a sense that it didn't look good for her and Dak to fight openly in front of the natives; meanwhile the Jaw was running his hands over the stone fissure from which the zombie must have come. She was watching him, and was just about to tell him to be careful, in case another zombie sprang out of the hole. The Jaw turned to look over his shoulder at her, did a double-take, and shouted a warning. Veela had barely registered it or had time to feel any fear, when there was a massive blow to the back of her head. She was unconscious before her face hit the dirt.

Twelve

The remnants of the People lived under the guidance of Gash-Eye on the stony shore of the subterranean lake, even deeper down than when Spear and Stick had still been with them. One fire spluttered and smoked beside the stale water. They weren't permitted more than one, because no one knew when they would be able to go outside again to gather more wood.

Gash-Eye sat trying to get a grasp of this new world they'd entered. There was that chamber where she'd thrown Tooth into the fire, and this one by the lake. In both the floor was relatively dry, not too slick, only a few stalactites dotting the rooms. Connecting these chambers was a sort of passageway—not a straightforward tunnel, but a winding corridor with branchings off. Some of those branches were tight fissures, but others were sizable doorways one could easily wander into, without realizing one was leaving the main artery. The People and Gash-Eye found the terrain there treacherous, but that was only because they'd had so little experience inside caves—they'd actually gotten very lucky.

When hunting, Gash-Eye had nearly been tricked by one of these branchings. That had rattled her. It would be easy to get lost forever here.

Soon no one could say how long they'd been underground. These were people who'd spent their entire lives outside, entering caves only to escape rain or snow, or to hide from animals or other people, and never straying far from the mouth. Their new environment would have been trying, even excruciating for almost any human from any society throughout history, but for them it proved physically and mentally debilitating.

Gash-Eye watched them deteriorate. Though she didn't harbor an excessive amount of love for the People, their sufferings were too great for her to gloat. Especially since she shared in their sufferings. More importantly, so did Quarry.

On the one hand, Gash-Eye felt guilty because part of the reason Quarry was stuck down here was Gash-Eye's fraudulent prophesying. On the other, last time they'd gone outside the world really had been full of unkillable monsters and red fire streaming down from the heavens, so, fraudulent or not, she'd apparently been right.

Regardless, she could feel a dangerous shift taking place in the People. Just after their most recent escape they had been grateful and anxious to please her. But their fear and dependence had mixed to form something new. From feeling that they were dependent on Gash-Eye, it was not such a long emotional leap to feel she was responsible for them, and from that to feel she was responsible for everything. Shortly after Spear's disastrous attempt to lead the People from the cave, when they had asked when they might go outside again, they had asked appealingly, beseechingly. Now there was the hint of a demand to the question, as if they were asking not for information but for permission. Then, when she'd brought them food, they'd been fawning. Now, they accepted it almost sullenly, as if it were her fault they weren't still living off steamingly fresh game.

Sometimes she resented the fact that so much of their gratitude had worn off after only a few days underground. Other moments she thought it was understandable, considering how many weeks they'd been down here. Her time sense was as garbled as anyone's.

Now she was hunting, far from the fire, just around the curve leading from the chamber into the tunnel, at the very edge of her vision's range. Quarry was with her—Gash-Eye had done her best to leave the girl near the fire, but more and more Quarry insisted on accompanying her everywhere. Since the disastrous attempt to leave the cave, the girl seemed to feel that her only hope of safety lay with the Big-Brow.

Out here the girl was blind—they had rounded the corner of a tunnel leading away from the grand chamber at the shore of the lake, and they were standing completely still, listening for prey. Quarry, wrapped in the bearskin she'd inherited from her mother, held onto the thinner skin Gash-Eye wore, to avoid being separated. Quarry's bearskin should have kept her warm, but both of them nevertheless shivered in the cold underground air. By the faint glimmerings of the fire that managed to round the corner, Gash-Eye could only just make out the child's form beside her.

"Gash-Eye?" whispered Quarry. Unlike all the People, who tried to flatter her despite their fear and hatred, Quarry had not adopted the strange new name "Petal-Drift." It seemed to never occur to her to use it.

"Sh," said Gash-Eye, and caressed the child to take the edge off her reproach. Moments ago she'd heard something scrape along the rock floor, further up the tunnel. Hopefully it was an animal, more food, and she didn't want to warn it off by making any noise.

And if it turned out to be a wandering unkillable, she didn't want to make any noise that might attract it.

Quarry obediently fell silent. But a moment later she coughed; a huge volley of chest-rattling bursts whose echoes rolled through the caves.

Gash-Eye sighed. That had practically been loud enough for the unkillables up on the surface to hear. Then she looked down at Quarry's dark form with concern, feeling guilty for her annoyance. There was no point asking if the girl was all right. The cold and the damp had invaded her lungs, like they had everyone else's. Gash-Eye reached down and pulled the bearskin tighter around the girl's shoulders.

"Gash-Eye?"

"What is it?" whispered Gash-Eye gently.

"Have you seen yet when we will be able to leave?" From Quarry, the question had none of the accusatory quality the rest of the People gave it. There was only a toneless despair.

Gash-Eye would have loved to be able to confide her fraud to Quarry, and Quarry alone. That she didn't was not because she didn't trust the girl, nor because she thought Quarry would find fault with the ploy. She just didn't want to burden her with the secret.

"No," Gash-Eye said, "not yet," and caressed the girl again. Quarry was trembling and feverish—only slightly, but it would get worse.

Quarry nodded in quiet acceptance. Then she whispered, "I know you can't help it, Gash-Eye. I know you can't make the spirits show you anything, and I know you didn't bring the unkillables. But you should be careful. Because some of the People, if they don't get to leave the caves soon, they're going to blame you."

"I know."

"I think they're awful. I think they're ugly. If it weren't for you we'd all be dead. You ought to have left us all and let us die, after the way we always treated you. But all that, I think it only makes them hate you more now. I don't know why, but I think it does."

For a moment Gash-Eye only looked at her, the girl-shaped shadow in the darkness. Then she pulled her in close: "I'll never leave you," she whispered.

Quarry hugged her back, but Gash-Eye could feel how slack her muscles were, and her voice was distant as she said, "Soon, I think my eyes won't work anymore, even if we do ever go back outside."

That scraping noise reappeared, closer this time, and Gash-Eye put her hand over Quarry's mouth, then removed it once she was sure the girl had the idea. Whatever was making the noise, now that it was close Gash-Eye realized it was bigger than a rodent. Maybe it was Spear. Or an unkillable. If it were an unkillable, at least she wouldn't have to worry about any of the People siding with it against her.

Gash-Eye became aware of dark splotches moving towards them along the wall she was facing. Heart hammering, she gently put her hand over Quarry's mouth again and slowly, slowly stepped backwards, willing the girl to follow, and to remain absolutely silent as she did so. They crept till Gash-Eye felt the rock wall at her back, and then they stood still. Gash-Eye held her breath.

The splotches took form. There were five of them, definitely human-shaped. At first she was afraid they were more unkillables, because of their strange twitchings and hunched postures. But they didn't have the absent shuffle of the unkillables, that could explode into action when prey was near. These were merely humans who had been broken by days spent in terror and total darkness. As they groped their way along the opposite wall, Gash-Eye felt almost sure she could make out Spear's features. They all wheezed slightly as they breathed—the damp cold air must have been even harder on them than on the rest of the People, since they'd been without wood to make a fire.

Once Spear and his friends passed Gash-Eye and Quarry, they were able to see the glimmers of the fire. Gash-Eye heard their gasps and whimpers of desperate excitement, then Spear shushed them and began hissing his plan. The People were unlikely to hear the approachers, huddled around the fire as they were—for one thing they were too far away, for another the fire's crackling and the echo of its crackling would mask the intruders' noise. After some quick whispered instructions, Spear led his men around the corner.

Now that they were out of sight, Gash-Eye dared lean her mouth down towards Quarry's ear. She whispered, "I'm going to go see what they're doing. You wait here...."

"No! Take me with you...."

"Sh! You wait here, it isn't safe...."

"No, no, take me, take me with you...." Quarry started to cry.

Gash-Eye didn't think anyone else would be able to hear the girl's panicked snufflings, yet, but she was still desperate to get her to stop. "All right," she whispered, "all right, but quiet, please. They'll kill us if they hear."

Quarry got herself under control. They crept to the corner where Spear and his men had just been standing, and peered around it. Gash-Eye could see the men, silhouettes against the dim light of the weak fire, moving in on the People. It seemed incredible to her that the People didn't see them; she wasn't about to risk Quarry's life by calling out a warning. To be safe she had her hand over the girl's mouth again.

Finally someone noticed the on-comers and let out a shout. Now that they'd been discovered, Spear and the rest of them ran in at speed—they'd held onto their stone knives, apparently, for they fell upon the People and hacked crazily at them. Quarry's teeth sank involuntarily into Gash-Eye's palm—Gash-Eye felt her drawing blood, but kept her hand clapped over the child's mouth anyway. It was Spear, Oak, Boar, Club, and Granite. Though they were outnumbered, it didn't take long for Spear and his friends to kill all the men; they kept the girls alive. Spear singled Tooth out for special attention and spent a while with him. If there were any unkillables left in the cave complex, Gash-Eye felt sure the howls of Spear's old friend would draw them.

By the time Spear finally finished killing Tooth, his friend Oak had Maple on her back. He was trying to rape her, but thanks to hunger, days spent in darkness, fear-born madness, and who knew what else, he couldn't get an erection. Spear kicked him hard in the ribs to get him off the girl, then stared at his bloody cohorts. They all blinked at each other; it was amazing that they'd managed to fall upon the People so disastrously, blind as they must have been. The strength of their furious insanity had carried them through.

"Where's Thorn?" barked Spear. His voice was hoarse and raspy, as if this was the first time in days that he'd spoken above a whisper. Besides, his lungs were irritated like everyone else's.

The men blinked stupidly at him.

"Where's Thorn?! Where's Thorn, damn you all?!"

"I haven't seen him," said Granite.

"Of course you haven't *seen* him! No one's seen anything in days! Now tell me where he is or I'll do you all like I did these traitors!"

Oak started to cry. "It's not our fault if he got lost!" shouted Boar.

Spear cuffed Boar, and when Boar tried to stand to hit him back Spear knocked him down. "We're going back to find Thorn!" he commanded.

"What if one of the unkillables got him?" said Oak, the weeping rapist.

Spear kicked him again. "Don't worry, you can stay here with the women since you like them so much. But let one of them escape and we'll do you the way you tried to do Maple! The rest of you, we're going back for Thorn. Hold hands and spread out! We're going back the way we came and we're not going to pass anything unnoticed."

"But what if we run into unkillables, out there in the dark?"

"Then we'll die! Better that than cowering here the way these scum were doing, kowtowing to their own slave!" Spear raised his voice: "Do you hear that, Big-Brow? I haven't forgotten you! We know you're out there, and soon we'll be seeing to you and your adopted whelp!"

Granite spoke, his voice trembling: "Spear, maybe let's wait. Maybe let's stay in the light a little bit longer. Don't you think it's too soon to go right back out into the dark?"

"Thorn's out there in the dark! Tell me, when it's your turn to be lost, will *you* be so patient to be rescued? Now come on! Join hands!"

"Spear, we should bring the fire...."

"Then the unkillables will see us before we can see them! Or that Big-Brow bitch will. Trust me! Be brave, and we have a better chance to live."

They joined hands and began to move out of the grand chamber, toward Gash-Eye and Quarry. Gash-Eye picked the child up and swung her around onto her back, and Quarry held her around the shoulders and pressed her knees into her flanks. "Don't make a sound," Gash-Eye hissed. She loped down the tunnel till they were too far from the fire for even her to see well enough to run safely, then she slowed to a walk, running her fingers along the stone wall.

She could hear Spear and the rest of them behind her. But they were falling behind—they couldn't see at all, and it slowed them down even more to all hold hands. She was able to make better time. Maybe now was the moment she should risk taking the girl back up outside. Surely it would be better than being hunted down and tortured to death without ever again having seen the sun.

This passage was a fairly straightforward tunnel. That was why Gash-Eye usually liked to do her hunting here—now, though, she thought it would be a good idea if she could find some cranny or niche for herself and Quarry to hide in, till Spear and the others had passed by. As long as they didn't wind up backed into a corner they couldn't escape from.

Before long they were far away enough from the fire that Gash-Eye couldn't see by its ambient light at all. She felt that graspy terror in her chest and the base of her throat, that Quarry and the rest of the people had grown even more familiar with. Yes, Gash-Eye told herself—she had to get the child outside, regardless of the risk.

Then again, perhaps some kinds of light were even worse than darkness.

Feeling along the wall, moving as fast as she dared, Gash-Eye became aware of something like a hint of light ahead, a dream of light. She thought it was a hallucination, her sight-hungry spirit conjuring things to see. But, as she felt along, she became aware that she was approaching a turn, and that what she had seen had been the faint reflection of a pale greenish light, reflecting off the wall from around the corner. As she crept around the corner she saw that this light shone through a narrow fissure she'd never noticed before. The fissure led into a chamber in which there was an unkillable, glowing green as it held the head of Thorn's corpse up to its mouth and chomped at the brain through the shattered skull. Thorn's feet still stuck out the over the threshold of the fissure. Elsewhere in the chamber were two other unkillables, glowing more dimly as they fed on the sorts of lizards and rodents Gash-Eye had been catching for the People. A fourth unkillable, still black, shuffled desperately along the chamber wall, searching for food.

Gash-Eye felt Quarry's breathing change at the sight of the monsters. If only the girl could keep silent, they might survive.

But up ahead, further along the tunnel they'd been traveling along, the one that led back to the cave mouth, she heard a shuffling sound. There was another unkillable somewhere up there, she was sure, one she couldn't see at all. Better to slip past ones she could make out, perhaps.

Or they could turn and run back the way they'd come—but, again, they were bound to receive a more unpleasant death at the hands of Spear than at the hands of the unkillables. It might even be possible to let the unkillables take care of Spear for them. Maybe all she had to do was get the creatures between herself and Spear.

She edged into the room with the unkillables, hoping Quarry wouldn't panic. The girl did breathe harder and grip Gash-Eye's skins even more tightly, but that was all.

A scenario presented itself in Gash-Eye's mind: these unkillables had been wandering hungrily through the cave for days; they only glowed when they ate, it seemed, and Gash-Eye had spotted no sign of any greenish light during her hunting expeditions. Perhaps this clump of them had wandered hours or days ago into this chamber, by chance; Thorn had gotten separated from his friends and for some reason entered the chamber, maybe because he heard the unkillables moving and mistook them for Spear and the others; one of the unkillables had attacked Thorn's brain; the other two had caught their cave-dwelling rodents and lizards thanks to the illumination created by the first unkillable's feeding; and any other food had been scared off by the light and noise before the unlucky fourth unkillable could catch it.

Any other food, that is, except herself and Quarry. The green unkillable still glowed enough for Gash-Eye to see, but just barely. Her hope was that the unkillables' eyesight would be even worse than the People's, allowing her to slip by unnoticed.

She had only intuitive reasons to think so: something about the quality of their clumsiness, as if they had no clear notion of their surroundings; a vague sense that dead things ought not to see as well as live ones.

But basically, Gash-Eye saw no choice but to act as if the unkillables in that chamber couldn't see her. She wouldn't wait here for Spear, and she believed there was another unkillable ahead in the narrow passageway, one she couldn't see at all. Even if the unkillables did spot them, they would either grant a quick death, or else turn them into things that would wreak some much-deserved mayhem on Spear and the others.

The green one's glow was very dim. Her plan was to get on the other side of them, then hope that after the unkillables all went dark Spear would run into them before he got to her. This way there was at least a chance of getting rid of him. Hopefully, once they were past these unkillables, Gash-Eye would luck upon some other path to the surface.

She stepped over Thorn and fought the urge to hurry through the chamber, concentrating on moving noiselessly instead. On the other hand, she wanted to be out of the room before Spear got there. Hopefully, with their weaker vision, Spear and the rest wouldn't be able to see the reflection of the green against the rock wall (the rodent-fed unkillables had already faded back to black), and would just come crashing in. If that happened, and the unkillables noticed and attacked them, there would be lots of thrashing and confusion. One of the unkillables might bump into Gash-Eye and Quarry—or, for that matter, one of Spear and his men might—or else one of the glowing unkillables might move close enough to her that she might be spotted.

As she came all the way around to the other side of the chamber, though, so that she'd done nearly half a circuit, ropes of sick dread began knotting themselves together in her belly. There was no other egress, as far as she could tell. The unkillables had fumbled their way in here, in the dark, but then had been too stupid to find their way back out of the dead-end room. Gash-Eye wondered how long they would have wasted away there, if Thorn had not gotten separated and, disoriented, wandered straight into one—maybe they would have stumbled back upon the entrance eventually, but Gash-Eye had a sudden feeling that even if they'd gotten too hungry to keep shuffling around, they could have sat down and waited forever, more or less inert, but ready to be hungry again even if they had to wait till the cave cracked open at the end of the world.

There was nothing to be done now—it was too late to attempt to creep back the way they'd come, she could already hear the approach of Spear and the others. They were noisier than Gash-Eye had been, and the heads of the unkillables all began to twitch—especially that of the now very faintly glowing one, as if with sustenance came not only greater physical strength, but greater strength of the senses.

Quarry was still hanging off Gash-Eye's back. Gash-Eye tried to position herself so that her body completely shielded the girl from the unkillables. She reached up and held the child's hands.

The men were trying to move quietly, but their self-control had decayed over the last days spent underground, and they were making enough noise that they would have scared off a boar, if they'd been hunting one. The unkillables heard their progress.

Gash-Eye knew Spear would be unable to see the now almost invisible glow, and so would not wander through the fissure. She risked saying the word, "Spear," when she heard him just beyond the fissure.

The unkillables' heads all twitched in her direction and they rose. If Spear had kept walking and not entered, Gash-Eye and Quarry would have been dead.

Following her voice, the men burst into the chamber, pitch-dark to them. Granite was first in the room, and he had enough time to scream before the unkillable who'd eaten Thorn's brain pounced and took his skull in his jaws, and shook it like a dog. By the time Granite's skull was open, his neck had already snapped.

151

Spear, Boar, Club, and Granite leaped to their right as the other unkillables leaped at them—one bit Boar on the shoulder, who tore himself away—he screamed, and collapsed to the floor in the throes of the seizure. Another chomped Boar's head before his brain could die, and immediately lit up green. Seeing the fight had moved briefly away from the entrance of the chamber, Gash-Eye made a break for it.

She collided with Spear, who had just jumped out of range of an unkillable's snapping jaws. In the glow he looked at her, shocked, as if he'd forgotten she'd been what he was hunting: "You!"

She backhanded him in the neck and kicked him in the knee, then shoved past him. She swung Quarry off her back, getting ready to push her through the fissure they'd entered from, before following herself. As Gash-Eye shoved her through the crack in the wall, Quarry broke her silence for the first time since Spear's appearance, with a scream. Gash-Eye looked back to see a green unkillable lunging for her with its snapping teeth. She stepped out of range and into the fissure just in time. Not smart enough to turn its body sideways as Gash-Eye had, and thus make itself thin enough to get through the passage, the unkillable thrust its head through but was blocked by its shoulders.

Inspiration struck Gash-Eye. She grabbed the thing with both hands under its jaws. Its frenzy grew even greater as it snapped its teeth, but it couldn't reach her hands and it couldn't move its head forward any closer. She put her feet on the rock wall and, still holding the thing by the hand, she pulled its head right off, flying backwards. Quarry screamed again. The severed head continued to bite crazily in Gash-Eye's hands—she was careful to hold it at a safe distance. It didn't bleed much, only a slow-oozing gunk. It continued to glow green as it stared at her and snapped its jaws. Gash-Eye wondered if the thing could still see. She recognized it—the head had once belonged to a hunter named Fox.

Its body blocked the escape route. Neither Spear nor the unkillables could get through the fissure and at Gash-Eye or

Quarry, for the moment; nor could Spear get away from the unkillables.

Gash-Eye adjusted her grip on the unkillable's head so that she was holding it by the hair and out in front, its snapping visage facing away from her. Now that she only needed one hand to hold the head, she drew Quarry to her again. By the light of her undead lamp, she saw that the girl was silently weeping.

"Shh," she said, "shh," and stroked her hair and kissed her gently on the temple. There was time for nothing else. From the corpse-blocked fissure still came screams and the sounds of Spear, Granite, and Club fighting. "Come on," she hissed, tugging on the girl's hand, "Spear may manage to move that unkillable's body out of the way before the others kill him, and then they will all be able to come after us." To try to cheer the girl, Gash-Eye nodded at the wildly animated, savage head. "We've got a light now, at least," she said. "We can carry it with us. All we have to do is every once in a while feed it a bit of brain to keep it glowing, the way those Big-Brows were doing in the forest."

They raced back the way they'd come. Gash-Eye wanted to kill Oak before he realized his friends weren't coming back. It would take time for Gash-Eye to dig through the cave-in back to the mouth, assuming she could manage it at all, and she couldn't risk having Oak attack her from behind. They could move much faster now that they had the light of the unkillable head to see by.

When they were nearing the camp, Gash-Eye stopped. "We have to hide the light before we get too close," she whispered to Quarry. She started to take off the skins she wore, then paused. They weren't especially thick, and she had no reason to expect the unkillable to stop snapping its teeth anytime soon. Even if an unkillable bite muffled by the skins didn't transform her, it could do injury if there wasn't enough cushioning.

Gash-Eye looked reluctantly at Quarry's thick bearskin. "I'm sorry," she said. "But I think we have to use your skins to wrap this head in."

Quarry shrugged her bearskin off immediately. Gash-Eye wrapped the unkillable head up and tied the skin into a bag. The head was still moving around in there, but not very energetically, and the skin seemed thick enough that it posed little danger.

Quarry was shivering in the cold. Gash-Eye took off her own skin and wrapped it around the girl's shoulders: "Here. It isn't as good as yours, but it'll do for a while. And soon we'll leave these caves, I promise."

Quary gave no sign of whether or not she believed that claim; she said, "But what about you? Now you'll be cold...."

"No I won't," said Gash-Eye, already trembling. "We'll take turns wearing it," she lied. "You can go first.... Now come on. We have to go kill Oak, or he may come after us later."

"I'm so tired of people being killed, though."

"I know you are, sweet one. There are only a few more to go."

Gash-Eye crept around the corner, the unkillable head stirring and biting in the impromptu bearskin bag. Before them was the opening into the big chamber where Oak still guarded the three surviving women beside the dying fire. Even if he'd been able to see in the dark, Oak wouldn't have noticed their approach; he was slumped over, staring with dumb despair into the low flames. Good—staring into the fire would render him almost completely blind if he finally did hear her coming at him. He was gripping his spear—the rest of his body seemed as loose as a propped-up corpse's, but the muscles of his arms were engaged and his hands squeezed tight. The girls huddled together, clutching each other, unwilling to look directly at Oak but unable to keep their gazes from being dragged towards him.

Gash-Eye eased into the big chamber, bringing Quarry along. Her plan was to leave Quarry here by the entrance, with her face to the wall. She didn't want the girl seeing what she was about to do to Oak—she was going to try to be quiet, partly for the sake of stealth, but also because she didn't want Quarry hearing too much. Of course, the terrorized, maddened women were bound to start screaming.

Gash-Eye wasn't sure what she ought to do about the women. One might decide her loyalties lay more with Spear than with the Big-Brow slave, even despite all that had happened, and she could decide to stick a vengeful knife in Gash-Eye's back. At the very least, guiding them would complicate the task of getting out of here (for Gash-Eye had decided that, whatever the risks, Quarry's health depended on getting free of these caves). And now that they knew there were unkillables wandering through the caverns, it was hard not to see the girls as potential unkillables themselves, if they should happen to be bitten. Unkillables that Gash-Eye would only have to deal with later.

There was a commotion behind them, running feet slapping stone. Damn! Gash-Eye ushered Quarry down the wall, away from the entrance. Oak looked up in their direction as he heard the approaching noise, but she didn't think he'd seen them. His captives looked up a moment after he did.

Spear came running in. Gash-Eye couldn't believe it. If she hadn't had Quarry to worry about, she would have screamed in rage and flown at him, just to have it all over with one way or the other.

Oak was on his feet with his weapon up by the time Spear got there; the girls huddled closer together, trying to make their clump smaller and lower to the ground. "It's me!" shouted Spear.

Oak blinked, still paranoid but looking less ready to attack. Spear was followed by Club. After a brief hesitation, Gash-Eye squeezed Quarry's hand and began leading her back towards the passageway. As bad for the child as the dark might be, Gash-Eye didn't think things would go well if she attacked all three of these men, instead of only Oak by himself. Not to mention that she still didn't trust the girls.

Spear was saying, "That Big-Brow led us right into a nest of unkillables!"

"Where are the others?" asked Oak, with a shaky voice.

"Dead," said Spear.

The girls set up a wail. "Where are they?!" said Oak, almost shrieking.

"Left them in the room where they died," said Club.

"The unkillables are too stupid to get out," said Spear. "We left the brainless corpses of our friends to block the entry."

"Too stupid to get out!" screamed Oak. "What do you mean, too stupid to get out! They got in there, didn't they! Now they're in here with us! We may as well have stayed outside if they're going to—"

Spear slapped him twice, hard. Club took this as permission to vent his own fury and terror—he punched Oak and, once he had fallen, kicked him in the ribs.

Spear pulled Club off. "Stop it!" he shouted over the screams of the girls. He feinted a kick in their direction to silence them. "Now where's that Big-Brow and her pet?"

By this time Gash-Eye had led Quarry back down the passageway, to where it curved around the bend. She waited, dividing her attention between Spear and the rest around one corner, and the darkness around the other, from out of which an unkillable might come shambling.

Club was staring at Spear in shock. Even Oak was shaking his head up at him from where he lay curled on the floor. Club said, "Spear, who cares about the Big-Brow? Much less about the little girl? It's the unkillables we've got to worry about."

"It's both."

"Spear, that's—"

"*It's both.* The unkillables are demonic spirits. Fine. Let them run havoc as they're meant to do, and let us try to survive. That's the natural way. But that Gash-Eye is our slave. She's thwarted me, and thwarted me, and thwarted me, and I say she dies before we leave here."

That was enough for Gash-Eye. While Oak and Club were still staring at Spear, she drew Quarry back deeper into the gloom. Once again she hoisted the girl up onto her back, and hurried back through the caves, groping along the walls, still moving at almost a run even after she'd lost the ambient light. She'd been in these caves so long, she felt like soon she'd have them memorized.

Quarry's hands started to slip from her naked shoulders. Gash-Eye came to a halt, grabbed the girl's wrists. "What's wrong?" she hissed.

Sounding as if she were waking up, Quarry said, "What?"

"Why were you letting go of me?"

"I was? I'm sorry, Gash-Eye."

She had to get the girl out of these caves. Who knew what strange maladies and under-earth spirits they were inviting in by staying so long? Gash-Eye knew the girl was feverish, but she couldn't tell by touch how hot she was because Gash-Eye was feverish, herself. Her throat was hot and thirsty all the time now, no matter how much cold sour water she scooped from the occasional puddle or pool into her mouth. "Hold tight to me," she whispered. "Press your knees into my sides and hold tight." She herself kept holding tightly to Quarry's wrist with her free hand while feeling her way along the wall with the other as she hurried back the way she'd come.

In the dark they ran by the corpse-sealed chamber with the trapped unkillables; they ran through the big chamber where she'd thrown Tooth into the fire; soon they were back in the narrow passageway that led to the mouth.

As Gash-Eye had hoped, the cave-in had not completely sealed them off. The rocks didn't go all the way to the ceiling—the gaps were too tight for her or even Quarry to squeeze through, but the stones were small enough that she should be able to dig free.

Gash-Eye climbed to the top of the pile and put her face to one of the gaps. Outside it was nighttime, but moonlight seeped into the cave. Perhaps there were unkillables lurking out there in the deep shadows cast by the rocks, but now that was equally true of this side of the rubble barrier. The world outside sounded peaceful—Gash-Eye could even hear birds. She thought that if there had been a lot of unkillables crawling around out there, the birds would have stayed away.

She started digging with her hands, pushing and pulling the rubble and pebbles through so that they cascaded noisily down both sides of the pile. She hoped she wouldn't destabilize the pile so that it rolled out from under her, and turned to make sure Quarry wasn't so close that she'd be crushed if that should happen. "Don't worry," she hissed. "I'll have you out of here soon."

"Gash-Eye?" said Quarry.

Quarry's voice was too weak to be heard well over the noise of Gash-Eye's digging, so she reluctantly stopped. Now that she'd begun making noise, she wanted to hurry and get through the task before the sounds attracted either Spear or an unkillable. "Yes?" she said, trying to keep the impatience from her voice. "Yes, Quarry, what is it?"

It took the girl a long time to reply. Finally, she said, "Are we going to leave the caves?"

"Yes. Don't worry, we're going to leave. I have to dig us out first, is all."

"But what about the unkillables, Gash-Eye?"

"I think they're all dead, Quarry. The red fire we saw coming from the sky was hunting them—I don't see how even the unkillables could have survived that. I know I said it wasn't safe to go outside, but that was because...." She trailed off, ashamed.

Quarry said, "But what about the unkillables here in the cave?"

"Well. We're running away from them." Gash-Eye wondered with a sinking feeling if Quarry's fever was worse than she'd thought. "Pull that skin around you tighter, child."

"But what if the unkillables get out of the cave?"

"Then they won't find us, because we're going to run. You don't have to worry. I'm going to take you as far away as my legs will go."

"But what if they get out after we've gone, and attack different people? People from another band?"

"Well ... but ... you mean, strangers? But if it's strangers, then who cares? In that case, it's not our problem, is it?... Besides, the unkillables really are stupid and clumsy. I think Spear may have been right—I think they really might remain trapped in that small room forever. Even if they do happen to get out, even if they do somehow manage to wander in the dark until they stumble upon the mouth of the cave here, I think that will be a long time from now. Many snows will fall and melt before ever that happens, and you and I may be long gone anyway."

Gash-Eye decided that if the girl still wanted to talk she was going to shush or at least ignore her. Nothing rivaled the importance of digging through this pile of rock.

But for some reason, when Quarry began speaking again, Gash-Eye listened anyway.

"I had a dream," Quarry said. "Actually, I keep having it. Sometimes I have it when I'm asleep. Sometimes I have it when I'm awake. I think I was having it again, when you stopped me from slipping off your back.

"In my dream it's many winters from now, and you and I are both asleep and at peace somewhere far away in the ground. But the world is still alive. The winds blow and blow and blow. They blow so long that at last this hill, this hill our cave is in, it gets tired of standing and sinks down and melts away. And in my dream there are still unkillables here, sleeping in the dark. And when the hill melts away, after more winters than anyone has ever seen, the sunlight hits those sleeping unkillables, and they wake up, and remember they're hungry.

"And in my dream the unkillables leave this melted hill and they go forth, hungrier than ever. The forest is different, the people in it are different. But not *so* different. The unkillables come upon them, and bite them. For some, they eat their brains. But there are others whom they merely bite, whom they change into other unkillables. As we've seen them do.

"And then—and this is the part of my dream that's truly hard to explain, because I know that it could simply never be, though I see it clearly—and then, the new unkillables go forth and bite others, and though some have their brains eaten, others are changed into more unkillables, and so on, and so on. And they bite, and bite, and bite, until none are left unbitten.

"I know that that could never be—I know it couldn't, yet I believe it could, for I see it so clearly. All the world is transformed or dead. And though you and I are asleep in the earth, the earth we sleep in is no longer peaceful and alive. It is an earth I would not spend the ages in.

"We have to destroy the unkillables, Gash-Eye. I'm sorry.

I'm sorry, because I'm too weak to help much. And I'm sorry, because it's not fair to ask you to help a world that's been cruel to you. But I won't leave this cave if it means leaving the unkillables for later people, unwarned people."

The girl finished talking. Gash-Eye, who was still naked and freezing herself, watched Quarry shivering feverishly in the scraps of moonlight that reached the cave interior. A complex mixture of emotions roiled within her, and she didn't bother trying to sort them out. "The world hasn't been only cruel to me," she said. Then, "In your dream. How can you see all these things?"

"You mean the things that are yet to come?"

"No. I mean the other people. How can you see the connections to people you don't even know, who won't even be born till after we're dead?"

Quarry didn't reply. But she turned her face up toward Gash-Eye. Gash-Eye didn't think Quarry could make her out in this scant light, but it seemed her unseeing eyes were pointed straight at her. Gash-Eye remembered the strange way she herself had suddenly cared about those Big-Brows, that night before the catastrophe—how she'd felt a responsibility for them, despite their being strangers.

"Let me dig us out and leave you outside, at least," said Gash-Eye, with a heavy heart. "Then I'll return and fight the unkillables."

"No," said Quarry, shaking her head. "Maybe I can help somehow. Maybe not. Either way, I won't leave you alone in the caves with the monsters, while I get to go outside. It wouldn't be fair."

"Forget about fair. You're a child. And you're sick. You need the sun, don't you?"

Quarry started to cry. Gash-Eye climbed down from the rock pile to hold her, first using her foot to nudge the bundle with the animated head out of the way. "Yes," Quarry said. "Yes, I do need it. But don't you, too? I won't leave, Gash-Eye. I won't leave, till it's done."

Gash-Eye held the girl close till her weeping had stopped. Surreptitiously, she wiped her own eyes. "All right," she said. "We'll have to kill them as quickly as we can, then."

Thirteen

Chert stared at the Jaw. His head was still immobilized, and the strain of keeping his eyeballs turned toward his son was starting to hurt. He was watching to make sure the boy managed to retain his sanity. Truth be told, he was probably also concentrating on him as a way of maintaining his own.

They were bound in a cave of cool stone that gleamed like ice or crystal. Embedded in the stone walls were winking, multicolored stars, mainly green, red, yellow, and blue. Chert couldn't begin to make a tally of everything he saw, even without being able to budge his head. Never in his life had he seen so many made things.

For he didn't doubt the things here were made, by someone. Even the cave itself—why someone would want to *make a cave*, he could not imagine, but he was certain someone had fashioned the walls, floor, and ceiling; they were so outrageously regular and smooth. It must have taken a whole band of people years, merely to chisel and polish the walls. The People had gotten a lot of use out of Gash-Eye and her predecessors, but Chert was developing a dim glimmer of just how much use a stronger group might be able to squeeze out of slavery, on an impossibly grander scale.

The things he and the Jaw were sitting on were made things, too. Naturally, he could not see his own, but he could see the Jaw's—it was made up of four long, thin, white, cylindrical stones, attached to a flat stone that the rump rested on, and then another flat long cool stone that pressed against the sitter's back. Chert would have guessed that the purpose of this last stone was to have something to attach the bindings to. But Dak and

Veela sat on similar things, that also had the stone that pressed against the back, and they were not bound. Instead of having the four long thin stones for the structure to rest upon, their sitting-things were supported by one thick cylindrical stone, and the flat stones under their rumps were able to spin upon the cylindrical stone, so that Veela and Dak could turn as they sat. Chert didn't know what the purpose was of being able to do that, but as an engineering feat it was fearsomely awe-inspiring.

As for what his and the Jaw's bindings and gags were made of, Chert had no idea. Some kind of hide, he supposed. They were blue.

Seeing how at-home Veela was in this fabulous, unimaginable environment, Chert felt more afraid than he ever had before in his life. She seemed to have shrugged off his blow to the back of her head—Chert thought that had something to do with the strange object Dak had stuck her neck with when he'd kidnapped Chert and the Jaw—it had been a thing like a rigid ice-colored pine needle, and Veela had awoken at its touch.

They were inside that floating stone, he understood. It had come down from the sky just as he was hitting Veela. It had come down so fast, like some great spirit had dropped it—but then it had somehow landed light as a feather. Then Dak had stepped out of it and pointed something at Chert and the Jaw and they'd fallen down, unable to move.

Chert was glad he was gagged, because if he hadn't been he might have pleaded with Veela, might have assured her that he would never, ever have threatened or challenged her if he had realized just how stupendous were the resources she had access to. He was glad he wasn't able to say those things.

Not that she was in charge. Dak clearly was the one deciding things, and though she seemed to be trying to get him to change his mind about something, she was having no success. They were speaking their own language, of which Chert and the Jaw knew nothing, except a few words like "math" and "zombie." Chert wondered what they were arguing over. He imagined she wanted to kill him, and Dak was resistant.

162

Right at that moment, Dak was repeating, "I just think we should get rid of them."

"No, Dak!" Veela said yet again.

But Chert had no idea those were the words coming from their mouths. He rolled his eyes towards the Jaw again. His son seemed to have calmed, though he still didn't look at Chert. They wouldn't kill the Jaw, too, would they? Ungrateful bitch! To leave the Jaw tied up that way after he'd been so loyal to her, after he'd defied his own father for her sake!

He looked at Dak again. Although he, like Veela, was taller than an average human, Chert had no doubt that this was the little man Veela had been carrying inside the strange, indestructible nut: his voice was the same, and every once in a while in the midst of the babble he made out that Veela was calling him "Dak."

He was in some ways an ordinary person, albeit obviously no kin to the People with his curly hair and unbelievably pale skin. There was something almost extraordinarily bland about him. Chert found it difficult to guess his age—of course, never could he have guessed that the well-preserved, well-fed, well-rested Dak, with his lifetime of climate-controlled environments and preventative medical care, was older than him; but there was more to it than that, and people from Dak's own time and place had been known to think there was something blurry about him.

In addition to his blandness, Chert found the man almost offensively soft. His skin looked like it had never been touched by wind or sun; Chert kept staring at his hands, which looked more delicate than feathers; there was a certain looseness to his mouth and, though Chert had never seen the expression before, he instinctively recognized it as that of a man who had never suffered.

Chert reminded himself that he'd sworn to kill this man. Focusing on that, on his anger and on the insult he'd suffered, helped stave off and redirect his fear.

Veela, too, had finally recognized the look of Dak's face for what it was. Maybe it was something about having spent time with the two guys that allowed her to finally see it. Maybe it had been harder to see during her long weeks alone with Dak, when he was both her savior and the only other living human she knew of. Or maybe he was changing, so that that unconcerned, unreachable aspect was becoming more prominent, less hidden.

Besides, in addition to Veela's growing worry that he might be sociopathic, she was feeling less and less assured that his intellectual prowess was going to be enough to keep them alive. Dak was clearly a hell of a physicist, but Veela wasn't so sure about his practical abilities. A month ago she'd still been in awe of him, what with his last-minute rescue of herself and his inspired, mad time-travel gambit. But, though he'd apparently gotten the hang of the ship and its weapons, she'd gradually come to realize with dread that he was nearly as klutzy as she was, and in some ways perhaps even worse with machines. As long as he paid attention, everything went fine; but sometimes he seemed not to deign to pay attention. It was as if he simply couldn't be bothered to deal with problems that were excessively simple. The upshot was that he was the kind of guy who could figure out how to travel forty-five thousand years back in time, but might have no idea that his flashlight's battery was running low.

"At least take their gags off," Veela was saying, again.

"No," said Dak. His voice had the mildness of someone who does not need to argue or persuade, who knows as a matter of course that his plans will be followed, his opinion deferred to (eventually, at least). "And have them start barking at me again?"

"I'm sure the Jaw won't, at least."

"Veela, dear, how would you know? You were unconscious when I intervened—thereby, by the way, saving your life. Both of them barked up a storm. Had to be stunned. Then had to be restrained."

"You waited long enough to save my life. Or even answer my fucking hail."

"I told you, I needed absolute concentration while trying to decipher the code locking up those drones and weapons. That took priority. I thought you'd be happier to hear that I gained access to them."

Instead of looking happy, Veela narrowed her eyes. "It seems convenient that you managed to also fix the landing apparatus just at that moment." Maybe he wasn't *really* so klutzy after all, she speculated.

"It was lucky, certainly. That primitive was going to kill you. I trust the meds took care of the swelling? And the painkiller's working?"

"No offense, but I can't help wonder if there was ever a problem with the apparatus at all. Maybe you just knew that if you picked me up I'd insist on bringing the guys with me, and you didn't want the distraction. Or maybe you didn't want *me* to be distracted, from expanding my grasp of their language."

"In fact that suggestion *is* quite offensive, since it's tantamount to calling me a liar, but no matter. As always, I am an open book. You're welcome to check the data records, if you'd like to confirm the malfunction and my repairs."

Veela tried not to bare her teeth. "Unfortunately, I don't currently have the expertise necessary to check those records. But once everything settles down I intend to start teaching myself."

"A fine idea. Let me remind you, it was not I who stopped you from commencing such study during our long voyage to and from the Cantor-Gould Collider. You were the one who chose to spend that time moping."

Veela couldn't protest. He was right, the cold-blooded prick.

The other subject of their conversation was the purple-capped mushroom. There was a chemical in that shroom of theirs that, after repeated doses, permanently muffled brainsong. Without impairing cognitive function, it seemed to render brains mute.

That was how humans had been able to survive in the caves with zombies. Once the humans' brainsong went quiet, the zombies were as blind as they were; blinder, since the humans had the benefit of their intelligence.

"That's why that zombie deer went for me, and not the guys," said Veela. "In the dark it couldn't see any of us well. But me, it could still hear."

"I suppose it is possible that, primitive though they are, this attribute might potentially render our guests useful as scouts, once we go into the caves," mused Dak. "Of course, we no longer have much need of scouts, now that I've got the extra drones working."

Veela returned to her earlier point. "Anyway. I'm not sure you had to restrain them."

"Oh, no? What do you think they would do to me if they were loose? Look at that one, look at his eyes."

Veela looked at Chert. It was hard not to admit Dak had a point.

But all she said was, "They were scared, Dak. Can't you put yourself in their shoes?"

"I'm afraid I'd have to revert quite a way to put myself in their shoes. Which, by the way, they have yet to invent."

Veela just looked at him. *Motherfucker.* "Just let me talk to them."

"Oh, you're welcome to talk to them! Only, leave the gags on, please. I'm not in the mood to put up with any more of that racket."

All right. Part of Veela wanted to rebel, to point out that Dak had no actual rank, and that while neither of them could be called experts on the natives, she was still a hell of a lot closer than he was. But she didn't say anything. Dak was the one who really knew how to pilot the ship, though she could fake her way through it. He was the only one adept enough with the laser cannon to know how to blast zombies without starting a forest fire (not that she would much regret a forest fire if it managed to wipe out the zombies, but still). And Veela wondered more and more if he would feel the slightest hesitation, if it suddenly struck his fancy to abandon her and start a new life in Canada or wherever.

She tried to give Chert a reassuring smile, to let him know there were no hard feelings. That wasn't necessarily true, but she thought things might go more smoothly if they put behind them the fact that he'd tried to kill her by bashing her in the back of the head with a rock. She wanted to keep the Jaw on her side, and killing his father didn't strike her as the best way to accomplish that. Chert looked back at her like he didn't give a shit whether she had hard feelings. He'd regained control of himself and gave no more signs of fear; captive that he was, he watched her and Dak with an almost royal disdain.

She rolled her chair over closer to them. At first she wondered what new thing was suddenly freaking them out; then she realized it was the rolling chair. They'd never seen anything like it. She thought about trying to explain its function, and how it worked. But if she let herself get hung up on swivel chairs, how would she ever get around to time travel, the zombification of the human race and all other vertebrate life, and the destruction of the universe?

She gazed into the Jaw's eyes, staring out at her from inside his gagged and immobilized head. In spite of his fear, she saw trust there. He knew it wasn't she who'd stunned him, who'd tied him up, it wasn't she who chose to leave him that way. That trust awoke in her a sense of obligation.

She opened her mouth to speak, then said nothing. It wasn't a mere problem of translation. The Jaw and Chert had some notion of time; as, say, the medium actions moved through. But how to explain time travel to someone who had no conception, not only of science, but of history?

She gave it a first shot: "Dak, and I. We come from after."

The Jaw frowned in confusion. *After what?*, she could practically hear him asking. The difference between his expression and Chert's was that Chert looked like he hadn't expected her to make sense, and so wasn't disappointed.

"After everything," she said.

They kept looking at her, with no sign of comprehension. They didn't look like they even comprehended that that was the end of her sentence.

Veela was about to try again when Dak preempted her: "I think *I* have a solution to the communication problem."

His smug tone made her skin crawl. She turned to face him. "I would be very interested to hear what that is."

Chert was impressed by her expression. He had no idea what was going on, but she hadn't looked half as fierce when she'd fought any of those zombies.

Dak was showing them something that looked to Chert and the Jaw like another strange nut, like the one he'd lived in when he was small. Veela recognized it as a modified communicator. "It's a translator," said Dak, pleased with himself. "I've been having the computer record and collate your conversations with the primitives, and now we have the ability to talk directly to them, without bothering with the clumsy, human-powered translation process."

Veela looked at the communicator dubiously. "You just whipped that up?" she said. "Cyber-centric linguistic analysis has always been one of the more challenging programming fields. I didn't know you had a strong background in artificial intelligence."

"Well, anyone can read a few books on the subject, Veela."

"Kind of my point."

Dak was annoyed. "Excuse me, but I think I can handle making a communicator that understands the most primitive known human language. Did I not save us from a zombie apocalypse and bring us back through time forty-five thousand years? Do you think making a communicator is likely to be more complicated than that?"

Actually, Veela was certain it was. Physics, as far as she could tell, was vastly simpler than linguistics, regardless of which field she personally understood better. Physics' relative simplicity was what allowed one to make predictions about the behavior of physical objects—try making such precise and detailed predictions of linguistic events, and see how far you got. A star was a much simpler phenomenon than a haiku, and translating a haiku from Japanese into French was a more complex operation than traveling back in time. It was just that traveling back in time required vast shitloads more money and energy.

She didn't mention any of this to Dak, though. For one thing, he wouldn't have wanted to hear it. For another, maybe he really was the genius he thought he was, and the communicator would work fine. To Dak and Chert, she said, "This nut, translate Dak's words, it will."

Dak flicked a toggle on the communicator, took a white fold-out tray from a compartment hidden in the wall, set the tray up beside the Jaw, and put the communicator on top of it. Chert and the Jaw were much more astounded and intrigued by the fold-out tray than they were by the communicator. "There!" said Dak, clapping his hands together in pleasure and smiling at the captives. "Now you'll understand me."

In the People's tongue, the communicator said, "Now under me you shall stand."

Chert and the Jaw glared fiercely at Dak. They already knew they were his prisoners and subject to his will, but did he have to gloat? Veela frowned at the communicator. There had been something wrong with its translation, but she didn't speak the People's tongue well enough yet to be sure what it was.

"My name is Dak," Dak explained.

The communicator said, "Dak is mine to be naming."

Now the captive men's faces went from anger back to confusion. Veela knelt between them and began murmuring translations of Dak's speech as best she could; Dak seemed oblivious to her aid.

He continued talking, and she tried to keep up: "In the future, about forty-five thousand years from now—or 'winters,' I think you people call them—anyway, in the future, there was a zombie plague that swept across the Earth and all its possessions, and which wiped out all human life except for myself. And Veela, of course, whom I rescued.

"How did the plague come about, you ask? It sprang originally from a noble intention—that eternal human desire to extend one's span and influence. In fact, when you think of it objectively, the so-called zombie plague represents a huge advance for the biological sciences, and for all mankind. For does it not seem to have accomplished the primary goal of the project directors: personal, individual immortality? There are some deeply unfortunate side-effects, obviously. But I'm confident that my colleagues would have overcome those hurdles, if only they'd had the chance to proceed with their research in a professional, orthodox fashion."

Veela had quickly given up trying to translate exactly what Dak said and was simply murmuring her own account to the men. That was confusing enough. She intended her words for both paleolithics, but unconsciously favored the Jaw, so Chert heard less of the explanation. The nonsense issuing from the communicator was distracting; its rendering of "a professional, orthodox fashion" was particularly Dada-esque. Things would have been easier if the communicator had been switched off, but Veela knew Dak would take offense at the suggestion.

He kept talking: "My colleagues in the biological sciences had managed to produce a serum that did indeed cause immortality in mice, rats, and then primates. Of course, it was a zombie immortality, such as you've seen. The subjects, while potentially never susceptible to death, wander through a dim world, seeing everything through a black haze of hunger, devoid of thought, devoid of emotion, devoid of personality. Though the body lives on, the mind is in such shambles it scarcely deserves the designation 'mind' at all, and in fact the mind possessed by the subject prior to his or her ingestion of the serum genuinely has ceased to exist. All that having been said, you have to admit that it was a very impressive start!

"Now, these unfortunate side-effects were, of course, kept on a need-to-know basis. For one thing, if the state of the newly-immortalized subjects had gotten out, it might have created a certain nervousness among less daring segments of the population. Also, there were funding issues to be considered. And then, of course, the project as a whole had to be kept secret, because, even once the immortality serum had been perfected, obviously they would not have been able to administer it to everyone. Even with off-world immigration, the Earth was already over-crowded—only a carefully selected elite would have been eligible for immortality.

"At the same time, rumors made their rounds. In the end, the secrecy served only to garble what information *was* leaking out. People knew there was an immortality serum that seemed to work—they didn't realize it changed you into a zombie. One enterprising lab employee, a rather low-level one, managed to nab a vial of the serum. By the time lab security realized what had happened, the young man was already at the New York Mega-Terminal, a major transportation hub. He drank the serum and flew into something of a rage, biting people left and right. But, with the early strain of the plague, it took more than a day after being bitten for the victims to change into zombies themselves. Meaning at least a dozen of them were able to get on airplanes and go to their far-flung destinations. And that, as the expression puts it, was all she wrote."

As Veela murmured her own account in the People's tongue, she remembered all the times she'd been annoyed that Dak was safely back on the ship, and reflected that now she was glad he'd been separated from the guys. He showed an almost psychotic lack of awareness that the two paleolithic-era men might need more context than this. He would have made a shitty ambassador, just as he made a shitty linguist. She had managed to catch his big miraculous revolutionary translation program's version of "vial of serum": it came out as "cupped-hands of spirit." Jesus Christ. Though that was better than its rendering of "all she wrote" into a pre-literate language.

The other thing that bugged her was that Dak spoke as if he'd been on the inside of all these developments. But he'd had nothing to do with it—he was a physicist, a scholar of an unrelated discipline—he'd been at a totally different university than the one at which the zombie plague had been concocted. What he was telling the guys was a mixture of public knowledge, public rumor, and stuff they'd pieced together during their long weeks in space. Yet listening to him now, Veela grew more and more certain that he was remembering himself as having been, if not actually on the team that had been researching immortality, then one of its close advisers.

Dak had paused, and seemed to be thinking of what to say. While he was quiet, Veela murmured to the Jaw, in the People's tongue, "Not all he says, exact truth. Later, explain I will."

Veela had no fear that Dak would understand anything she said in the People's tongue. However, it had not occurred to her that, once he himself had stopped talking, his translator would focus on her, the quieter, secondary speaker, and try to render speech back the other way. But as soon as she'd finished speaking, it said, "He lies. I'll explain later."

Dak froze. So did Veela. His eyes drifted over to catch hold of hers. After a long moment, he smiled strangely.

"I lie, do I?" he said.

"I told you," said Veela, angry because she was frightened. "Your translator doesn't work."

She was about to go into a list of its errors and their philosophical and sociolinguistic roots, but Dak waved his hand in dismissal. "Never mind, never mind," he said, "it means less than nothing."

She could feel the anger trying to scratch its way out from behind her face. Somehow she hadn't been angry like this even when Chert had left her to fend off that zombie on her own, in the hopes she would die—at least she could understand that from Chert's point of view, she was an alien invader. Dak was supposed to have been her partner, though. "Since the communicator's garbling everything," she said, "maybe we should turn it off and concentrate on me translating for them...."

"Yes, but I don't know what you're saying, do I?" he snapped.

He paused a moment, pacing, collecting himself. Then he stopped before the two captives, hands behind his back.

He said, "Of course, our escape into the past incurred its own unintended side-effects."

He began pacing again.

He paused, and his eyes darted back and forth between Chert and the Jaw. "Tell me," he said. "Have either of you ever wondered why you've never met a time traveler from the future, until us?"

For one thing they had their gags on, so obviously they couldn't answer. For another, the idea that these two paleolithics had spent a lot of time idly wondering why they'd never been visited by time travelers from some distant post-industrial future was clearly absurd. Dak seemed to take none of this into account. He kept looking at them like his question hadn't been rhetorical, apparently waiting for a reply, and then, when they said nothing, he shrugged and continued his pacing.

"I, too, often wondered about that," he said. "I had done a lot of research into time travel. It had always fascinated me—I never could understand why I should be bound by the contingent strictures of any particular time or place. It seemed only fair that my body should be just as free to roam as was my spirit.

"Standing upon the shoulders of the giants who had come before me, I began to see a way through the thickets of equations that might lead to total temporal freedom. Excited though I was, I kept my work secret. Partly because I feared it might be stolen. But also because, certain as I was that I was right, I couldn't discount the possibility I might be wrong. The equations indeed indicated that, given enough energy, I should be able to travel backwards in time. But if that were true, why had the past never been visited by intrepid voyagers from the more technologically developed future? Moreover, why did I keep hitting a theoretical wall when I tried to figure out how to move forward, into the future, instead of only the past?

"I was still grappling with these great questions when the zombie plague hit. Only then did I realize how fortuitous it was that I had followed this particular obsession; never could I have imagined that my quest would prove the key to human survival itself. Suddenly I had, not only the freedom, but the necessity to try out my hypotheses. I took the time to rescue Veela from the Linguistics Department at Luna University, not realizing how easy it would be for me simply to dream up a translation program on my own. We headed out to the Cantor-Gould Collider, which proved itself capable of creating the energy burst necessary to fuel our temporal journey. Through all the long trip to the Collider, and then after our journey back through the eons, I continued to labor over the equations. Until at last, a few days after our arrival in this time, I had it. I hit upon the answer—I knew why no one had ever traveled back from the future to meet us—and I saw why there was an invisible wall preventing us from jumping forward in time, despite all my ingenuity."

Dak stopped pacing. He faced his audience again, trembling with the enormity of his revelation.

"It turns out that when you force the space-time continuum in this way, when you do it the violence of shoving yourself back in time, you set up a reaction in the other direction. Something like a splash, a destructive wave, spreading into the future, the *entire* future. A destructive wave, crashing through all of the eternity that lies on the other side of your jump point and leaving it ash. I'm speaking metaphorically, of course—there are no ashes lying to the future side of our jump point— there's nothing at all. Traveling back through time destroys the universe. There is no instant that follows the one in which I used the Collider to travel back to this time. I am the bookend of Creation."

The two paleolithics stared at him blankly. Even Veela, who understood him, couldn't muster a reaction. Her soul couldn't configure itself into an appropriate attitude. But beyond her blank surface, she felt a sad horror. She did believe him about his findings. Now that they had proven time travel into the past was possible, she couldn't see any other reason why no one had ever met voyagers from a more advanced future. She and Dak had killed that future. According to Dak, they had killed it not merely in the vicinity of Earth—every galaxy was doomed to wink out at exactly the same moment she and Dak traveled back here (whatever "exactly the same moment" might mean, when the phrase was applied to a single event taking place across the possibly infinite reaches of intergalactic space in a relativistic universe).

Dak got impatient, waiting for an appropriately awed reaction. He lifted his hands, and said, "Don't you understand what this means? The fact that no one else ever destroyed the future by traveling back into the past, means that no one had ever managed it before! Despite all the thousands of billions of intelligent species that, statistically speaking, simply must have existed, I was the first who managed to work out the equations! *I was the first in all of Creation, in all the histories of all the galaxies, only I!"*

He rocked back on his heels as if being released by something, gasping as if in the aftermath of a sexual climax. He wiped the sweat off his brow. Veela and the two captives waited for him to recover from his excitement. He sat down in a chair before the console and sighed.

"Dak, we should explain to them why we need their help," said Veela.

"Yes, of course," said Dak, and returned his attention to Chert and the Jaw. "You see, in light of the fact that some of your fellow tribesmen took refuge in the cave system—"

But Veela interrupted him: "Dak, just let me explain it, please. Your translator doesn't make any sense, it'll only confuse them."

Dak looked at her. She met his gaze. After a moment he said, "Very well. If you think that's necessary."

Veela explained to the guys that they thought some of the People who'd escaped into the caves might still be there. Or they might have been zombified. If they were simply still in the caves, though, Veela would like to have Chert and the Jaw there to help communicate with them. (She also nearly told them that, unlike hers and Dak's, their brains were mute to the zombies, but that was too complicated to explain right now.) Maybe the survivors would know where in the cave complex the zombies were, if there were any, and could guide Veela and Dak to them. Dak was certain that his two drones would be able to handle that, but Veela preferred some sort of Plan B.

Once she'd finished explaining, she said angrily to Dak, "Now that we've asked them to risk their lives for us, surely you agree that we have to take the gags off so they can answer."

"Naturally," said Dak, "now that it's necessary to let them speak."

Veela removed Chert's and the Jaw's gags. "Sorry, I am for these," she said grimly, not caring that her apology was translated back for Dak, more or less recognizably.

Once the gags were off, Chert and the Jaw moved their mouth muscles and worked their tongues, trying to expel the alien sensations of the strange new material.

Veela gave them a moment before pressing them: "Help, will you give?"

Chert remained silent. The Jaw glared first at Dak, then at Veela. He said, "You need my help? I have one condition."

Veela didn't know the word "condition," and the translator was no aid. It took some back-and-forth before she figured out what it meant. Once she had, she said, "Condition, is what?"

"Give me and my father spears," said the Jaw, "and let me kill him."

Veela blinked, not sure she'd heard right. She looked at Chert.

His eyes were red and wet. He glared at the Jaw, then turned his gaze away. "Give him a spear and let him do what he likes," he muttered. "I'll not defend myself."

For some reason Veela didn't understand, that made the Jaw all the more furious. She didn't get it that the Jaw interpreted Chert's refusal as meaning that Chert didn't think the Jaw was worthy of the People's right to fight for his father's place in the circle, and that he'd rather die than dignify his halfbreed spawn's upstart pretensions.

"Well," said Dak. "One member of this little clan may serve just as effectively as two. And the older one has tried to kill you. He could well prove a pure liability. Perhaps letting him die wouldn't be such a bad idea, particularly if it insures the younger one's gratitude and loyalty. It's their culture, after all—it's not our job to understand it."

Though there was no love lost between herself and Chert, Veela was glad the translator rendered Dak's musings as gobbledygook that the man couldn't possibly understand. Still, she forced herself to seriously consider the Jaw's demand. It

176

would do no good to try to import her exact ethical code back into this alien world where no human had yet figured out how to so much as sow a field. This was a bloody place, maybe she should get busy adapting to it.

She looked again at Chert. His fierce red eyes still stared straight ahead.

"No," Veela said to Dak, and then in the People's tongue to the Jaw, "No." He glared at her, then dropped his eyes. To Dak, she said, "He doesn't want to do that as badly as he thinks he does."

Dak shrugged. "If you say so. You're the expert on these fellows, I suppose."

Veela placed a hand on the Jaw's bound forearm, hoping it was a consoling touch. She leaned in close to him, and murmured, "You help. No condition. It is right, and you must, so you help."

Fourteen

Quarry refused to leave the cave and wait outdoors. Gash-Eye considered resting before going back to the chamber of unkillables, for the girl's sake. But the sooner they destroyed the unkillables (assuming they could), the sooner she could get the child out in the fresh air. So they crept their way back.

First she prepared a handle for their lamp. When the unkillable's head had almost dimmed to black, when there was only just barely enough green glow to locate its mouth by, Gash-Eye fed it the brain of a lizard she'd caught. She and Quarry ate the rest of the lizard's raw body. Once the head was dimly glowing again, Gash-Eye attached it to one of the sticks of firewood by sharpening it to a stake and then driving the stick through the neck. She took another sharpened stick as a weapon.

They kept the unkillable head covered most of the way back to the chamber of trapped unkillables. Gash-Eye didn't want to risk Spear, his minions, and their captives spotting her before she could spot them. She felt her way along the wall, naked and shivering, desperate necessity adding force to her memory and helping her retrace her steps. Along the way she caught another lizard and wrung its neck.

As they neared the crevice by which one entered the chamber of trapped unkillables, they moved more cautiously. There were definitely still unkillables in the chamber—she heard them shuffling. Empty-headed corpses of Spear's friends plugged the crevice leading into the room—without using the lamp she made sure the corpses were there by probing for them with her fingers. The unkillables must be too stupid to simply pull the corpses out of the entryway. Gash-Eye imagined them wandering around, bumping their faces into the wall and slowly turning to shuffle the other way. Who knew how long they might keep doing that? Even a rat would figure out that it should drag aside something that prevented its escape. Not being able to understand that was the kind of stupidity one expected from an insect. But Gash-Eye had a hunch that the unkillables were indeed closer to insects than they were to rats.

She remembered the fugitive noises she'd heard and her near-certainty that there was at least one other unkillable wandering the caves, besides those stuck in this chamber. Killing all of them, the way she'd promised Quarry, would mean finding that one as well. Nothing to do about that right now, though.

It hadn't been long since the corpses blocking the entrance to the side chamber had been killed, or beheaded in the case of the unkillable who'd provided her lamp, so they wouldn't be stiff yet, and it should be relatively easy to shove them out of the way, once she was ready.

She squeezed Quarry's hand in the dark, and ran her palm over the girl's hair. "I'm sorry," she said. "But I'm going to need to use your skins for this."

"Oh. Yes, all right," said Quarry. Everything she said now came from across a feverish distance. "It's your turn, anyway." Apparently she thought that Gash-Eye was simply asking for her turn to protect herself from the chill with the only skin they had left to wear, now that they were using one to transport the head. Quarry shrugged the garment off.

"I'll give it back to you soon."

"No, you should wear it for a while." But Gash-Eye could feel that Quarry's trembling had already grown more violent, and she could hear the girl's teeth chatter. When she took the unkillable head out of the bearskin and bundled it in Quarry's thinner one, she caught an instant's glimpse of Quarry by its dim light. She looked very sick.

Once Gash-Eye had re-wrapped the head in the thinner skin, she wrapped Quarry's original bearskin around herself.

The delicious feeling of being a little less cold distracted her a moment from the danger and horror, though the pleasure made her feel guilty, since it came from depriving Quarry of the skin.

Gash-Eye held the lizard's head in her palm. She took a breath and tossed the head over the bodies and into the chamber, aiming for where it sounded like one of the unkillables was shuffling. The lizard had been dead only a little while, hopefully its brain was still fresh enough.

There was a plopping sound as the lizard's head hit something other than stone, and then the sound of it falling to the rock floor. Gash-Eye was certain that she'd gotten lucky, and that the head had actually hit one of the unkillables directly. The quality of the shuffling of one of them changed—it moved rapidly, as if it were frantically looking for something. A few seconds later, a very dim glow emanated through the crevice.

Gash-Eye slammed herself through the opening, shoving the bodies through as she went, hoping their movement might distract and confuse the unkillables. It did—the nearest one, a black and starving creature, threw itself upon one of the empty-skulled corpses. What with the bearskin making her thicker, Gash-Eye thought for a sickening moment she was going to get stuck in the passageway, an easy meal. But she pushed herself through, as she did so bringing her whole weight down upon the sharpened firewood in her hand, penetrating the skull of the unkillable at her feet that was clawing at the corpses.

She was no hunter, and had never had the chance to hone her accuracy or prowess. But Quarry would soon die if she failed, and that knowledge sharpened her reflexes and intensified her concentration until nothing existed but the task of destroying the unkillables.

She nearly lost her balance as she jammed the stick into the crouching unkillable's brain, but turned her tumble into a low dodge, as one of the other creatures rushed at her, attracted to her motion. She retreated to the far side of the chamber, away from the crevice, so that the unkillables would be less likely to stumble upon the passageway during the struggle.

There were now two black unkillables and the dimly glowing one, which for the moment remained squatting, obsessively hunting on the floor for more brains, still so fixated on its last morsel of food and where it had been found, that it seemed not yet to have noticed the huge piece of food that had come crashing into its lair.

The two still-starving ones saw her, though, and lunged, jaws snapping. She dodged them, holding the bearskin out in front of her to make her silhouette bigger and twirling it. She didn't expect the bearskin to protect her from the bites of these living hungry unkillables the way it did from those of the sluggish severed head—their jaws could snap through skulls, after all. She mainly hoped it would serve as a visual distraction.

It worked—the two unkillables went snapping at opposite ends of the skin. Gash-Eye whipped the bearskin off herself and threw it over the head of one of them. It flailed around, blinded, unable to get the heavy fur off itself. She aimed the sharpened ichor-stained firewood at the other unkillable and jabbed at its head as if with a spear.

But she missed. It came barreling at her face, jaws snapping and arms snatching. Gash-Eye had no time to step out of the way or feint to one side; all she could do was jump back and feel herself tumble as her balance gave.

The fall nearly knocked all the air out of her, but she kept her head raised and managed to avoid banging it on the rock floor. The ravenous unkillable was coming down on top of her. By incredible luck there was a stone under her right hand. Under normal circumstances it would have been a bit too big for her to handle easily; now, she slammed it with all her strength into the unkillable's temple.

The blow would have killed any other creature. It did at least knock the unkillable off her and over to the side. She doubted it could feel stunned, exactly, but it was looking around into the darkness on the far side of her as if it hadn't been able to keep track of its own motion, and wasn't sure where it was now relative to her. If she'd had two stones she could have clapped them together upon its head; instead she pushed the left cheek of its head down onto the stone floor and wrenched its right shoulder up, pinning the other shoulder against the floor with her knee, hearing bones and ligaments snap and crackle. She'd hoped to wrench the torso away from the head so that the head would come off, but it stayed attached and the thing still bucked and struggled beneath her.

These few seconds of fighting had finally roused the glowing green unkillable from its single-minded survey of the last place it had found food. It sprang to its feet, head twitching back and forth between Gash-Eye and the other unkillable, still struggling blindly to get out from under the bearskin. There wasn't time while the unkillable decided which source of motion to attack for Gash-Eye to go retrieve her sharpened stick. She got up and, trying not to think of the risk of its teeth and venom coming into contact with her feet, jumped up and brought her naked calloused heels down as hard as she could on the head of the mangled unkillable she'd been fighting on the floor. It popped underneath her, and rotted spongy skull and lukewarm curdled brain sprayed through the room.

The green unkillable chose her as its target and sprang at her. She would have been defenseless, except her feet slipped in the slick mess that had been the black unkillable's head and she went flying onto her back again even as the green monster went gnashing overhead. It bounced off the rock wall.

Gash-Eye forced herself back up. She grabbed the bearskin-covered unkillable and swung it in between her and the lunging green one—they collided and ran into her, nearly knocking her down again. The unkillables snapped at each other. Gash-Eye knew she had only a brief moment before they each realized the thing they were snapping at lacked a living brain, and turned their attention back to hunting her. She got behind the green unkillable and, as it snapped at the one in the bearskin, used its momentum to drive its crown into the rock wall beyond. Its skull cracked open, but the brain beneath was undamaged enough that it still writhed. Keeping herself behind it as it spun around madly,

Gash-Eye grabbed her sharpened stick from the floor and drove it down in between two cracked plates of skull, into a patch of exposed brain. She worried that might not be enough damage to stop it. It was, though; the creature crumpled at her feet.

As the unkillable's brain died its glow faded fast. By the last of its light she cast around on the floor and found two fist-sized stones. Just as the black unkillable finally worked itself free of the bearskin, Gash-Eye had the two stones ready; she clapped them together upon its head, bursting it, averting her face to avoid the spray of brain, ichor, and gunk.

All the unkillables were dead. All she knew how to find, anyhow. Surely, no one could ask her for more than that.

Except she knew there was more she had to do.

"Quarry," she called. "Quarry, uncover the unkillable head. Carefully, though!"

Immediately she felt guilty for having given the child such a dangerous task. But she felt so hungry for light.

Even the ghastly faint glow that seeped in through the crevice, when Quarry had uncovered the head, felt like it might be enough to sustain her, for a while at least. Nothing was more horrible than these unkillables, yet she was grateful for the glow they brought to this cave. She imagined a world in which it really would be possible to bring light into the dark places, the way she was reputed to do, the way she had pretended to do.

Even as her body tried to rest, her mind was rushing to form the next plan. After they'd first come to the lake she'd gone on a scouting party with one of the hunters, while the rest of the People had stayed by the fire. They'd come to a large chamber, where they'd found a natural pit. She thought she could find her way back to that pit; if she could, she might be able to lure Spear there simply by calling out for him.

She found herself hoping they wouldn't meet. But if Spear ever escaped from the cave and saw Quarry, he would kill her for having befriend Gash-Eye. Besides, if she left him here in the caves, he was one more potential unkillable. And Gash-Eye had promised the child she'd get rid of all those.

She realized she hadn't heard Quarry speak yet, and grew worried. "Quarry?" she called. Her adrenaline-wracked body was bruised bone-deep, blood trickled from dirt-clogged cuts and scrapes, she was half-starved and freezing, and though she tried to force herself to go check on Quarry, she couldn't quite move. Her body was in a state of quivering, feverish rebellion, now that the immediate threat to her survival was gone. "Child? Are you all right? Answer me!"

"I'm fine," called Quarry's thin voice. Gash-Eye let out a sigh of relief.

She had managed to kill the unkillables. She wondered if it would be as hard to do the same for Spear.

Maple tried to move fast enough that Club would not have to shove her along, but it was hard to make herself go quickly in the darkness, and often she felt his palm between her shoulder blades. Each time she had to suppress a sob. It was madness to keep plummeting aimlessly into the darkness like this, without even their wicked Big-Brow to guide them.

When they'd left Club had taken the firewood and Spear had taken one of the burning brands. But Club had slipped and fallen into a deep pool in the dim light, and had unthinkingly grabbed Spear for support and dragged him into the water with him. The wood and the brand were all soaked, and now they traveled in darkness. Spear had beaten Club for that.

"Move!" Spear would rasp. "Move, or do you want the unkillables to get you?!"

Maple did not want the unkillables to get her, and each time Spear said that she knew that the only good solution was for them to all come to a halt and kill themselves. But every time she thought she would suggest that, she realized that if she opened her mouth only sobs would come out. Once she tried anyhow, and, sure enough, could only weep. Spear and Club had slapped her until she was silent and bloody, with one less tooth than before.

Where were they going? She wanted to ask the other two women, but it was somehow unthinkable. The three were not allowed to speak—they all knew it, without having needed the example of the beating given to Maple. Once they had been kin to Spear and Club, members of the same People—now there was no more People and they'd become less than Gash-Eyes.

They weren't going anywhere. That was the horror. They couldn't go outside, because of the red lightning bolts of fire and the unkillables. They couldn't stay in one place because they would go crazy. Who knew how far underground they had gone already—who knew if they weren't already so deep in the earth that they would never get free.

Truly, only death made sense now. They should stop this running and help each other die. After all, they were already in the earth. But she couldn't make herself say so.

Oak had known. In the middle of their crazed march, he had simply stopped and died, and hadn't come back to life no matter how Spear beat him.

As they were crawling blind across the uneven stones, all of them came to a sudden halt. Even Spear. A voice had called his name: "Spear!" It was Gash-Eye.

Their unseeing eyes rolled fearfully in the dark. The name echoed weirdly through the caves, it was hard to locate but seemed to come from ahead of them.

"Spear," she called again. "Why are you running, Spear? I thought you were going to kill me."

"I am going to kill you!" shrieked Spear, so savagely that Maple covered her ears, shut her eyes, and ducked her head. *"I will kill you!* You're the one who ran!"

"I'm not running now."

"Where are you?!"

"Follow my voice."

Club groped his way past the women to clutch at Spear's shoulder—Spear flung his arms out, trying to strike him. "Spear! Can't you tell it's a trap?!"

"Let that Big-Brow bitch try to trap me, if she dares! We're going after her!"

Maple could feel Club's fear and reluctance vibrating in the air. He knew it was a trap, that Gash-Eye wouldn't call Spear that way unless she had a plan to kill him, and probably his followers as well. Yet she also knew that Club wouldn't be able to stand the thought of letting Spear leave him alone.

Sure enough, as Spear rushed crazily towards the source of Gash-Eye's voice, Club lashed the women to follow, and they obeyed. Facing whatever trap Gash-Eye had prepared for them was less frightening than facing this darkness without a strong man. Even a strong man as crazy as Spear.

They were moving too fast through these lightless zones. Women and even Club kept falling, skinning and bruising their hands and knees; Spear somehow never did, and he always heard their tumbles and turned and beat them till they regained their feet. No doubt Spear scorned any contribution they might make to his fight against the Big-Brow—but they were all his possessions now, and he was unwilling to part with any of them.

From the changing acoustics Maple could tell they were progressing into a bigger, wider chamber; away from the claustrophobic terror of the tight, winding corridors where an unkillable might block their path at any moment, and into the bottomless, agoraphobic terror of a formless open space in which unkillables might converge from any and all directions.

"Keep close to me!" screamed Spear, and yanked Maple to try to make her follow closer on his heels. She was trying—if she had to stay with him, if she couldn't just let him go to destruction on his own, then she wanted to stick close so that maybe he would protect her from that destruction when they caught up with it. "Club!" he cried. "Keep up their pace!" Club frantically obliged, slapping and shoving them so much that it was a miracle they were able to maintain their footing at all.

"Good," Gash-Eye's voice called through the dark, closer now. "You're making progress, Spear. I see you approach."

"Lying bitch! Trying to scare us with your so-called powers! Not even you can see in this blackness!"

187

"The dark is my element. Haven't you said that many times, Spear? My very purpose is to see into the darkness."

That was true, Maple thought; they could not see Gash-Eye, but surely Gash-Eye could see them. Maple was certain the same wave of nauseous fear was rippling through all their little band at the thought.

But Spear shouted, "Lies! There's no light for even you to see by, Big-Brow! The one advantage you ever had is gone, and now I—"

Spear's words turned to a howl of surprise perhaps at the same moment that Maple felt herself plummeting, perhaps an instant before; she honestly didn't know. So disoriented was she by having been starved so long of light, she couldn't even be sure if she was falling for a long time or a brief one, if she was falling up or down. But she knew when she hit bottom—it was hard, and knocked the breath out of her.

Club screamed. They had all fallen, not just her. Maple could tell from his scream that Club was hurt badly.

Spear, on the other hand, recovered from the fall right away. "Big-Brow! Where are you?! Face me!"

"You want a face, do you?" she said.

Above Maple, above the lip of the depression they'd fallen into, a glowing green ball appeared. What was it? Maple fearfully recognized the quality of the light as that given off by the unkillables. She blinked furiously, trying to force her atrophied eyes to see something more than a blurry green ball, but even without being able to make out any details, she realized the moment before Gash-Eye threw it what it must be.

The snapping maw of the unkillable's head locked onto Spear's forehead upon impact; Spear had time for one short scream before he landed on his back, silenced. The unkillable head glowed a brighter green as it munched into Spear's brain. Having no lungs, it could not suck. But some of its throat had come off with its head, and it still had enough muscles there to do a lot of swallowing. All of the brain matter it ingested appeared to spill out the hole of its neck, having been milled by

188

the teeth, but the head must have absorbed something through the lining of its mouth or gums or throat—some cerebral juice, perhaps—for it glowed a brighter and stronger green as it burrowed forth into Spear's head.

Neither Maple nor any of the others in the pit with her could make out any details; with their smeary vision all they could see by the green glow was Spear, dead at its epicenter, and Club on his back, gaping at Spear in horror, as if he had managed to forget the bloody broken bone sticking at a crazy angle out of his torn shin. Gash-Eye leaped down among them, carrying a pointed stick. Club was still staring at her stupidly when she stabbed him through the throat and wrenched it back and forth as he wriggled, to be sure he was dead.

The two other women screamed and cowered from Gash-Eye, staring at her, their backs against the cold damp wall. One was begging Gash-Eye not to kill them.

Only Maple did not move. She remained where she'd landed, staring impassively up at the former slave. Not even the nearby munching head distracted her. Gash-Eye met her gaze, and Maple knew what was coming. She didn't flinch. It wasn't that she was brave—she simply couldn't see the point of struggling and even if she had, she wouldn't have been able to find the energy.

"Help us, Petal-Drift!" said one of the women. "You'll lead us out, won't you?"

Gash-Eye surveyed them all wordlessly, then said, "If I keep you with me, you'll turn on me sooner or later."

"No, no!"

"No, we'd never do that!"

Maple, meanwhile, kept silent.

Gash-Eye, as if she hadn't heard their protests, said, "And if I let you go and wander the caves by yourself, maybe you'll meet one of those things. One that escaped. And then maybe I'll have more unkillables to worry about."

She jerked the pointed stick up out of Club's body. Maple was between her and the rest of the women, and Gash-Eye began advancing her huge naked body on her. Behind Maple the others set up a wail. But Maple felt a strange calm spread through her.

"Gash-Eye!" That sounded like Quarry, crying out from the edge of the pit. "Gash-Eye, please, just let them go! Just these ones!"

Gash-Eye was looming over Maple now. "Close your eyes, Quarry!" she shouted, and raised the pointed stick. "Close your eyes," she said again.

But Maple felt no need to close them.

Fifteen

It didn't hit Gash-Eye how weak she'd become until she had to pursue Quarry through the darkness. The girl stayed at the edge of the pit, ignoring Gash-Eye's commands to close her eyes, pleading with Gash-Eye to spare the women right up until all three were dead. Then she ran away, racing wildly into the black darkness, screaming. It was by the screams that Gash-Eye tracked her through the blackness. Throughout the brief nightmarish race, Gash-Eye doubted her ability to follow the misbehaving sound, as it echoed and re-echoed; she was sure that if she tripped and fell once, she would lose what small grip she had on the trail. But it was Quarry who fell, and then lay there, still crying out for Gash-Eye to spare the already-dead women, as Gash-Eye finally caught up to her and clutched her in her arms.

After she caught her, Gash-Eye had to hold Quarry's hot feverish body a long time before she quit struggling; and after that she continued to weep for what seemed like forever.

Gash-Eye wrapped the girl more tightly in her skin, and pressed her body against her as closely as possible, to transmit some warmth. Even so, Quarry continued to shake violently. Gash-Eye had to get her out of here. Grief and delirium were combining to form a dangerous mixture.

"We'll go outside," Gash-Eye said.

"Are there more unkillables out there?"

"I don't think so. I think the red fire from the sky got them all." Gash-Eye had no idea whether or not that was true, but it seemed like the proper thing to tell the child. Then she laughed, and said, "Besides, you said that, if there are any more unkillables, we should find and destroy them, right? So if we've finished off the ones down here, we ought to be looking for more up top."

"Oh. Yes. I forgot."

She sounded so earnest. "I don't think there are any more unkillables, though," Gash-Eye said. Except there had been that fugitive shuffling she'd thought she'd heard. But she wasn't going to mention that. She was just as feverish as Quarry, she suspected, and in no condition to go thrashing around the darkness in the hopes of hitting one of those monsters. She wasn't completely certain she would live through the next few days, even if they did get out of this clammy air where she was still naked. (She had continued to use the bearskin to bundle the unkillable head in; they might need a light again before they got out of these caves. Right now the skin was still where she'd flung it beside the pit, and the head was still in the pit itself.) Waves of sickly heat kept sparking hazy multicolored hallucinations before her eyes. The surface of her body was hyper-sensitive—it was like she could feel even the irritating friction of her hair pushing through the skin as it grew—yet it also seemed very distant. As if her body were a thing she had to reach across a great distance to control, with strain and effort.

Now that the girl was calm, Gash-Eye said, "We must go. You'll stay with me? You won't run like that again?"

"Yes. I'll stay with you, Gash-Eye. I was only angry about the...." She didn't finish the sentence. "But I'll stay. I love you. And besides, you're the only other member of the People left."

Never before had Gash-Eye been considered a member of the People, not even by Quarry. But now that all the rest were dead, she supposed she would have to do.

Gash-Eye kissed her on the top of her head, and said, "Come on, sweetling. We're going to live. But first we have to get out of these caves. And you have to walk—I'm not strong enough to carry you."

Gash-Eye heaved herself up, and Quarry obediently followed suit. As soon as she was standing, Gash-Eye's head swam and for a panicked moment she thought she was actually falling. "On second thought," she gasped, "let's crawl."

"Yes," said Quarry. From her tone Gash-Eye guessed that she, too, was disoriented. There was no more excitement or immediate howling terror to distract them from the fever. If they didn't get out of these caves soon, neither one of them would be much good to the other.

But once they were on all fours, Gash-Eye had to fend off a new bubble of horror expanding through her chest. There was absolutely no light here, and she had reached this spot at the end of a headlong flight in which she'd taken stock of nothing but Quarry's screams in front of her; on top of that, the fever had addled her sense of direction. She didn't know where the pit was, with the unkillable head at the bottom of it. She strained her eyes into the darkness, forcing herself to filter out the false colors popping in front of her eyes. She turned and looked the other way, over her shoulder. Nothing. Even if they'd run a fair ways she thought she should have been able to see the green unkillable glow seeping out of the pit, so they must have been gone long enough for the brain juice to wear off and the hungry head to fade once more to black.

Trying to speak casually, as if their lives didn't depend on the girl's answer, she said, "Quarry—do you remember which direction we ran from?"

Quarry thought. Finally, she said, "No." She sounded more apologetic than frightened.

They would need some sort of light to navigate their way out, which meant they would need that head. Even then, they would have to be lucky. They could crawl until they reached the wall, then follow along it—but in which direction? Which way was the pit? Gash-Eye knew that on one side of the pit the wall curved around the bend into a narrow tunnel. If they kept feeling along the wall of that tunnel they would eventually get to the big chamber where the People had camped and built the fire she'd thrown Tooth into. But once they reached the wall, which direction should they crawl in order to reach the pit?

Dizzy and disoriented as she was, they were just as likely to wind up crawling even deeper into the endless maze.

She wanted to lay down and cry. They'd been on the verge of escape, and had come back to kill the unkillables. They'd done that, and also defeated their other enemies. And now it turned out that struggle for survival had taken too much from them. They were going to die down here in the darkness, the dry fiery thirst of fever biting inside their throats.

But she couldn't give up yet—she still had the child with her. And who knew, maybe they would get lucky and choose the right direction. "Come on," she said, gently taking hold of Quarry's arm, "let's find the wall—"

There was a noise. They both shut up.

A scuffling. A cracking. A crunching. Gash-Eye's grip on Quarry tightened. By now she didn't have to tell the girl to be quiet anymore. The sounds became very faint, they had a liquescent quality. Gash-Eye wondered if they were real or merely the games of those feverish trickster phantoms who are the heralds of delirium....

A pale green glow began to dawn.

Gash-Eye's grip became so tight that Quarry couldn't help but whimper. Gash-Eye made herself relax her hand.

The green figure ahead of them was little more than a smear. She blinked and forced her bleary disused vision back into focus. The new unkillable was Hoof, who'd run away.

By the ghastly light Gash-Eye thought she could see where the pit was, at least. The unkillable that had been Hoof was between them and it. Even with her Big-Brow vision, the outline of the depression was so faint and vague she couldn't be certain it was there, especially with her feverish swimminess.

Gash-Eye tugged silently on Quarry's arm. The girl resisted only for a moment the repugnant thought of moving toward the unkillable, not away from it. They began to creep as noiselessly as possible across the stone floor.

The unkillable had lucked upon a rat, it looked like. It hadn't taken long to clean out its skull, and the thing was still sucking and licking at that broken bowl of bone, desperately hunting for another scrap of brain or drop of its juice. At last it flung the corpse away in frustration and bent over the floor, using its own body as a lamp to hunt for more food.

This was a smart one, Gash-Eye thought. It looked like it was trying to search somewhat systematically, moving its body in ever widening circles. Of course, she didn't see how that would be effective, since it seemed any prey could just scurry back into one of the unlit patches the unkillable had already searched, but she still thought it was a pretty good idea for an unkillable. She wondered if that cleverness was thanks to some residue of Hoof's mind, but immediately choked the thought. It wouldn't do to give the unkillables names or pretend they had anything in common with whoever they'd once been.

Smart or not, the unkillable's method made it more likely that it was going to find them. The two had been moving as cautiously as possible, sacrificing speed for silence. But the unkillable's circles were bringing it closer and closer to the path they were going to have to follow to reach the pit. With a tug on Quarry's arm Gash-Eye signaled her to move faster. They managed to time it so they crawled past the unkillable when it was on the far side of its circle. The thing had its eyes fixed on the floor, looking for prey closer to the ground. Even so, Gash-Eye was so sure the thing was going to see them, that even after they were past it she had trouble believing it had not killed them after all, and that this darkness they crawled through was not a dream of dead shades.

The pit grew closer. She could even make out the sharpened stick, covered in its layer of dried gore. Behind them they heard the steady shuffle of the unkillable. Gash-Eye dared not look back—what with her fever she was afraid to take her concentration off the goal—but she listened for any change in its pace, for any sudden hurry, for any fast approach.

They made it to the pit. They made it to the sharpened stick. Gash-Eye thought about lowering Quarry into the pit, where she might be better hidden. But she was afraid that if she died, and the unkillable realized Quarry was down there, the girl would be easy prey.

But it was going to be all right, Gash-Eye thought. The unkillable was beginning to stray deeper into the caves, away from them. As long as they kept quiet, it should go away on its own. Gash-Eye looked in the other direction and by the unkillable's fading, departing light, tried to memorize the terrain they'd have to cover, at least the next several paces.

"But we have to kill it," Quarry said.

Furious, Gash-Eye grabbed her and clamped her hand over the girl's mouth, holding her body so close and tight she couldn't make noise by struggling.

Her sibilant whisper had been quiet enough, but it was highlighted by the lack of any other noise. The unkillable jerked to attention, head twitching. But the strange echoes made the whisper's origin impossible to pinpoint, as the sound bounced around the chamber. Gash-Eye stared at the unkillable, willing it to go the other way.

And finally, it did. After a long, twitching uncertainty, the creature decided that the whisperer was somewhere in the opposite direction from Gash-Eye and Quarry, back at some wall her voice had bounced off of. Gash-Eye watched it shuffle away, the illumination dwindling as it got further and as its glow faded, its brain-hunger once more taking hold.

Quarry was straining to break free. Gash-Eye could feel her mouth trying to speak against her palm. Gash-Eye wasn't sure her strength would hold out, so weakened and fever-ravaged was she.

The unkillable had gone far enough that it had rounded a corner and disappeared from view. Gash-Eye decided to risk hissing words into Quarry's ear. Hearing herself speak, the words sounded harder than she'd intended, and she tried to make them gentler but couldn't.

She said, "I know you want to destroy that unkillable. I know you want to destroy them all. I know why; I remember your dream, and maybe I even believe it myself. But I don't have the strength left to fight it, and neither do you. If it meant my death, I wouldn't mind that—I'd give my life to destroy it—many's the time my life's nearly been taken for less. But if I die, there will be no one to take you out of the caves. And I won't die, leaving you here to rot in darkness." Quarry renewed her straining, but could do nothing against Gash-Eye's bulk wrapped around her. Tears fell from Gash-Eye's eyes. She said, "I know you think the world may come to an end if we let even one unkillable go free. And I know you may be right. I would rather lose the world, the whole world, I would rather let the whole world die, than know you were unsafe and yet do nothing. For me the only world that's left is you."

Quarry continued to try to break free, till at last the struggle exhausted her. Still Gash-Eye was reluctant to release the girl.

Eventually, she did. They both lay on their sides in the dark, still. Now that Quarry was docile, Gash-Eye concentrated on remembering that the way back out of the cave complex was behind her, behind her, behind her.

"I'm going after the unkillable," said Quarry, hopelessly, but seriously.

"You'll die. I won't let you."

"Gash-Eye, I think you're sick. I don't think you'll be able to stop me much longer."

"Maybe. But you're about as sick as me." Actually, she was probably a bit less sick, because she'd been clothed more than Gash-Eye had, but Gash-Eye barely thought of that and certainly didn't resent it. "If I won't be able to stop you, you certainly won't be able to stop the unkillable."

Quarry answered in tears. "But we *have* to," she said.

Gash-Eye thought that if they stayed this way much longer, they would wind up dead just as surely as if she'd let Quarry call that unkillable over. Before she could rouse herself, a white light popped into existence far down the passageway.

Quarry went rigid. Gash-Eye gripped her close again.

If Quarry hadn't reacted as well, Gash-Eye would have wondered if the light was real. It wasn't an unkillable light.

It was bright, white, and sudden. It looked to Gash-Eye more like a star than it did anything else. How had a star been shaken loose from the heavens, so that it was floating around here underground? Had the same force or spirit that had set loose the unkillables also shaken stars from the sky?

Whether it was a star or something else, it was definitely heading their way. They had to hide until they figured out whether or not it was trying to kill them. Gash-Eye gave Quarry a light shove in the direction of the pit and hoped she understood. She did. The two of them each rolled to the edge of the pit, and Gash-Eye was about to lower Quarry in, when the light shone right on them, blinding her, and she heard a human exclamation in an unknown language.

When the light glared into her eyes like that, she thought she was being attacked; it physically hurt, after all her time in the darkness with only dim glows and firelight to see by. Aside from sunbeams shining through tree branches, she never thought in terms of beams of light, exactly; she never thought of it as traveling in a straight line; she knew that she should not look directly into, say, the sun, but once she'd looked at the floating star painlessly she had never expected it to all of a sudden become so much stronger. It had never occurred to her that a light could get so much brighter or stronger, depending on the relative angle of its source.

Gash-Eye didn't quite yet understand that the light was a tool for searching things out, basically a more sophisticated version of the lamp she'd invented, using the unkillable's severed head. However, she did realize that someone had just seen her and Quarry, and there was no longer any sense in hiding. She gripped the sharpened stick tightly.

A female shouted something. From the sounds her mouth was able to form, and from the high pitch of her voice, Gash-Eye knew she wasn't a Big-Brow, but the woman was speaking no language Gash-Eye had ever heard. Then she realized that wasn't true—she was speaking the People's tongue! Or trying to, anyhow.

"No scared, be!" she repeated. "Friends, we are!"

That was promising, but Gash-Eye still held tight to the pointed stick.

There was some muttered conversation in what was definitely a foreign language, between the same female, and a male. Gash-Eye still couldn't make out anything but that light, growing brighter as they approached. If the unkillable that had once been Hoof was still close, they could expect it to be attracted by the illumination and come wandering back. "Take care!" Gash-Eye cried. "There are unkillables about!"

"What?" said the unseen woman, alert. "What say you? You say a word new for me. No-dies, you mean?"

No-dies. Gash-Eye supposed that was one way a person who barely knew the People's tongue might try to say "unkillables." "Yes," Gash-Eye called. "At least one no-die. It went off the other way, but you're liable to draw it back with all this light and commotion."

The light stopped advancing while there was another heated, hissed exchange between the unseen man and unseen woman. While they were fighting about whatever they were fighting about, another voice spoke up, this one a man's, and also speaking the People's tongue. Wonderingly, the voice said, "Mother?"

At first Gash-Eye didn't understand at all, she only felt her disorientation grow more extreme.

Again, she heard the Jaw's voice say, "Mother?," more insistently this time.

Gash-Eye was certain this was another cruel trick of the encroaching delirium. It was only in part her fever that made her tremble as she said, "Is that the Jaw? Is that you, my son?"

Still more light slammed without warning into her face—Quarry was so taken by surprise that she screamed. Five more stars even brighter than the first had appeared.

Footsteps raced to her out of the blinding light; Gash-Eye's vision was decaying fast now, but in a moment she saw the dark shape of the Jaw's head bending over her, backlit by the blazing

199

cluster of lost stars behind. "Mother," the Jaw's form said, in the Jaw's voice.

"You've come to trick me," Gash-Eye said. "You're a spirit of the fever, come to trick me with a vision of my dead son."

"I'm not dead yet, Mother. I'm not a spirit, either. Touch me and see."

She did touch him. Then at last the fever unleashed all its strength and clawed her down into a whirlpooling pit of delirium. As she felt all volition and responsibility slip away, and as she saw the Jaw's face recede into the darkness, she felt a mixture of relief and regret.

Sixteen

Veela was furious that Dak refused to administer any drugs to the Neanderthal woman. "She's going to die if we don't help her. Maybe that little girl, too."

"I think the child will probably be fine. As for the Neanderthal, we've dressed her, at least, which should go a long way toward improving her condition. Why would anyone be so foolish as to spend days running around naked down here, anyway? It's damp, and freezing."

"If we could just give her some aspirin."

"And when we run out of aspirin I suppose we can just pay a call at the aspirin factory? I can produce plenty of penicillin and other such simple remedies, but I haven't had time to do so yet and I say we should conserve our limited supplies. I understand that you're excited to interact with your first full-blooded Neanderthal specimen, but there are many thousands more like her in this era."

Veela pointed out the attachment obviously felt by the Jaw for his mother, and suggested that saving her might be a way to insure his aid. Dak considered this, but then decided that it made even better sense to tell the Jaw they would save his mother if and only if he cooperated fully in tracking down the loose zombie. Veela agreed to translate the message, to keep Dak happy, then simply didn't. (Without ever admitting that the translator he'd slapped together was imperfect, Dak had quietly neglected to take it with them when they'd left the ship.)

The reason Dak felt he could with impunity use the life of that physically powerful savage's mother as a pawn, was because he was safely encased in an armored hydraulic frame. The lamps attached to the frame were the stars Gash-Eye had seen. Although Dak's face and chest were exposed, he was guarded by sentacles, eleven robot arms that sprouted from the back of the frame, that could grab and divert any projectile, or anything else that might try to breach their set perimeter. They were easily capable of thwarting bullets, and would have no trouble fending off fists or spears, as Chert had quickly and painfully learned when he'd finally been freed from his bonds. ("Sentacle" was a portmanteau of "sentinel" and "tentacle"—not the happiest coining their inventor's marketing department had ever come up with.)

Keeping the sentacles on high alert was a huge energy-drain. One was supposed to wear the frame with its armor completed by a cuirass fitting over the face and chest, with readouts and a vidscreen on the interior—the sentacles were meant to be used if some part of the armor was missing or badly damaged, and for picking stuff up and moving it around, if need be. But Dak hadn't been able to get any of the cuirasses running. He said none of them functioned—Veela supposed that might be true, but suspected Dak just didn't know how they worked. It wasn't like she did either, though.

There were other armored frames in the ship. Veela had wanted to use four of them, or try to at least—she had a feeling that being hooked up to the exoskeletons might be such an alien experience, it would drive Chert and the Jaw insane.

But Dak had rendered it a moot point. "Absolutely not," he'd said. "Those frames use up a huge amount of our power stores. We have to limit their use to essential personnel only, I'm afraid." So he was the only one wearing a frame.

Now that they were here in the caves, he didn't even want to waste power using the drones he'd finally recovered from storage to find the zombies. After the feverish girl told them that the zombie had run off in the direction of a subterranean lake, Dak thought they should all just hike out there and fan out with their fucking flashlights. But, as Veela vehemently pointed out, the idea was unworkable, even aside from the very high risk of someone

202

getting killed or zombified. The four of them wouldn't be able to cover enough ground, and their lights and the noise of their approach would alert the zombie to their presence.

"But we want the zombie to be alerted to our presence," said Dak. "That way it'll be attracted, and come to us, and we'll be spared the trouble of hunting it."

"Wrong. What we want is for us to know where it is but it not to know where we are. See, if we do it the opposite way, it's liable to eat my brain."

"All right," Dak reluctantly agreed. "Particularly since your friends don't seem to grasp the concept of 'flashlight'."

That was true. Chert and the Jaw were fascinated by their flashlights, and seemed unable to help themselves from staring directly into the bulbs. But they were no good at using them the way they were intended. They were too amazed by the beams of light themselves to pay attention to what they illuminated.

So Dak sent a pair of drones out, one in the direction of this lake, the other to zip through the cave complex, mapping it out for three days' on-foot journey in every direction, doing infrared scans and trying to locate any zombies. The woman and child were bundled up in white thermablankets and attached to the back of Dak's suit, all under the watchful eye of the Jaw. Gash-Eye lay on a stretcher-like platform that unfolded from the armored frame; Quarry was suspended above her by three rigidified sentacles. If they had to pass through any constricted areas the two females would be a problem, but for now it was fine.

Veela watched the Jaw watch the sentacles attach his mother and the kid to the frame. Looking at his face, she felt without exaggeration that she could kill Dak for hoarding the medicine. She touched the Jaw's arm—he didn't acknowledge her, but he didn't shake her off either. He'd told her the names of the newbies. The kid was called something like "Place From Which New Stone Can Be Plentifully Gathered," except it sounded prettier in the People's tongue. His Neanderthal mom's name was something like "Torn Eye." Presumably that had something to do with the scar on her face, even though whatever had happened to her didn't seem to have injured her eye.

They went forth toward the lake, the strangest band ever in the planet's history so far.

Only minutes after the drones had been released, zipping along at a hundred kilometers per hour, the control panel on the arm of Dak's suit started beeping. He raised the forearm and tapped a few of its keys with the fingers of his other hand.

Veela put her hand on the laser-blaster in her hip holster. "Did they find the zombie? Was the girl right that it went to some lake?"

"Yes," said Dak, distractedly. After another moment's study of the readouts, he added, "It seems the water is an effective barrier. Since they don't need to breathe, I was worried it might simply walk into the water and float. Or sink to the bottom, or swim, for all we know. Might have made reaching it more difficult."

Well, shit. That was something it hadn't even occurred to Veela to worry about. "I'm glad that's not the case," she said. "What about the other drone? Has it reported any sightings of any other zombies? Anything to suggest there's more than just the one?" By now the lighting-fast drone with its sensor array should have been able to do as much exploration as twenty spelunkers over the course of a month.

Dak studied the readouts a moment longer. "No," he finally said.

Veela was sure it was only her imagination, the effect of accumulating dislike, suspicion, and frustration. But she thought she heard disappointment in Dak's voice.

Chert trudged along. Never had he been so deep in a cave before, so far beyond all possibility of sunlight, but, numbed and despondent as he was, he had no will left even to feel uneasy. Not even the miraculous bauble Veela had so casually handed him, the miniature, portable sun that was cool to the touch, not even that could interest him after a while.

Since childhood he had been the strongest, smartest, and surest of his age. When this calamity had begun, it had not occurred to him that along with the end of the world had come the end of his competence. It had taken him all these days to understand that the gifts in which he had prided himself in that lost world would not transfer into this one. Gash-Eye had survived when he'd been sure she hadn't—not that he would have cared about her for herself, but the Big-Brow slave had also managed to preserve Quarry, the only other remnant of the People. (Chert didn't realize that she'd also killed a good many of them.) Veela, that woman he'd been so contemptuous of, had proven to be the mistress of powers far outstripping any magic he'd ever dared imagine; she couldn't make a spear, but she was an adept doer of deeds and wielder of tools beyond the pale of dreams. To hear her and the Jaw talk, the key to it all was this "math." To him, no matter how he concentrated, it still sounded like mere prattle; but now it was prattle that filled him, Chert the fearless, with fear.

He quickened his pace until he came alongside the Jaw, then put his hand on his son's arm the way he'd seen the woman Veela do. Without looking at him the Jaw shook it off angrily.

Chert didn't try to put it back. He even walked a half-pace behind the Jaw. With something like humility, he said, "I thought Gash-Eye was dead."

The Jaw snorted. He tightened his grip on his mother's pointed stick, which he'd taken. "The same way you thought Veela was with us, when the undead deer attacked."

"No. That time, I simply wanted get you to safety."

The Jaw shook his head. "I think nothing in my whole life makes me feel stupider than that I believed you."

Chert looked at his son. The Jaw was ever so slightly taller than him. He hadn't noticed till now, but it was true.

He said, "I was telling what I thought was the truth when I said your mother was dead. But if I'd known it was a lie, I would have said it anyway, to get you away from those undead, or no-dies, or zombies, or whatever they are. I would have sacrificed not only Gash-Eye but any other member of the People, to save you."

"Ah. Thank you. And I suppose when you were betraying Veela and leaving her to be torn apart by no-dies, you were also doing me a favor."

Chert's face twisted with the effort of trying to find the right thing to say. "Do you want the woman? I won't stand in the way. Even if I could, I wouldn't press my claim to share her, that was only a.... She's a powerful woman, and would be a great asset in the hunt, I'd be happy to have her with us."

The Jaw blew air out his mouth in exasperation. He stopped, turned, and pushed his father away. Chert could have held his ground, but he allowed himself to be sent a few steps back anyhow. Veela stopped to see what was going on. A moment later Dak noticed everyone else had stopped and he did as well.

"You listen," said the Jaw. "Veela says she doesn't want you killed. I don't know why—maybe she thinks you could be of some use. But know that it's only by her pleasure that you and I are both still alive, because otherwise I would kill you or die trying. All my life I've been the most favored son among the People, when it interested you to make me so. All other times I was a slave as abject as my mother, nothing but a tool to seal in her torment. You shared with me just enough glory to teach me to feel shame, and so divided me from Gash-Eye; but either you couldn't make me a real member of the band, or else you didn't care to, so my pride served me nothing. Now the People are dead and I'm thankful. Before I kill this last no-die I'll bless it for that one good deed its kind have done. And if you speak to me again, Chert, Quarry will be the only full-blooded member of the People left."

The Jaw turned and stalked away. He even went past Dak, and Veela ran after him, shouting for him not to go too far alone.

Soon the little group started moving again. Chert noticed that Veela kept looking over her shoulder at him, as if to make sure he was still following them and hadn't just stopped, or wandered off. Dimly, he wondered what he must look like for her to be so worried. He didn't bother making eye contact with her, he simply trudged along, brooding; he couldn't see any reason why he should ever leave this cave again.

His gaze drifted up to the back of the strange and unbelievable shell covering Dak, like the shell that protected an insect but infinitely harder. No matter what size he was, the little man always needed his protective coverings. Chert's eyes narrowed. If there was one thing he could still be sure of, he reflected, it was that he'd sworn to kill that little man.

As they approached the lakeshore, Dak seemed amused as well as annoyed by Veela's increasing nervousness. "I know exactly where the zombie is," he told her, tapping the readouts on his arm panel, which nobody but him had seen, because the drones' data was streaming back only to the hydraulic frame's computer. "It's remaining basically stationary. I'll let you know when we're closing in, there's no danger."

Veela thought that was an easy thing to say for a guy wearing a tank.

Dak's sentacles grabbed two rocks in passing and began to juggle them. Veela stared. "Isn't it a huge energy-drain to use those things like that?"

"I do have to practice, Veela. Should anything happen, I need to be certain I can manipulate these tools with complete control." After a moment he had the sentacles quietly place the stones on the cave floor again. All the while they continued to walk.

Both of them wore visors. The transparent screens covered their faces and displayed readouts before their pupils, so that when Chert or the Jaw faced the two time-travelers, they saw the readouts in reverse. Veela had hers down and set for night vision, though she shone a flashlight before them for the sake of the two guys. She'd considered grabbing a pair of visors for Chert and the Jaw, but she knew those things would freak the guys out. She paused, using her glance controls to search for any anomalies ahead.

And she could see it, in the distance. A human-shaped heat source, but the wrong temperature for a human—way too cool. With the glance controls she had the visor run a few more diagnostics. Yep, that was definitely a zombie. The last fucking zombie—at least, it had better be. She pulled her laser-blaster out, clicked off the safety, and pointed it at the zombie's head—the visor's targeting app locked in. "Gotcha, cocksucker," she said.

"Hang on, Veela," said Dak. "Don't be hasty."

"Go fuck yourself," she said, and pulled the trigger.

Nothing happened.

She pulled it again, and again nothing happened. Again and again and again, and still nothing.

"What the fuck," she gasped.

"I had a feeling you might be hasty. So I ordered your laser's CPU not to fire without authorization from me."

"Dak, oh my God, if this is to conserve energy...."

The zombie had heard them, either their voices or their brainsong, or both. In her visor she could see it quivering to life, and slowly moving their way. Dak strode to meet it, confident in his armor. Veela scrambled along beside him, pleading: "Fuck the batteries, Dak! Who cares if we wind up having to hunt pigs with spears the rest of our lives? Can't you see that our one and only fucking purpose is to kill these fucking zombies that we brought back with us in the first place?!"

"Veela, please. I could survive here without you, except that I confess to a psychological need for a contemporary, someone at least theoretically capable of the breadth of vision one should expect from someone of our century. Can't you see that this zombie is the very apex of human scientific thought?"

"It's the apex because it's the last thing we invented, and it was the last thing we invented because it killed us."

"Well, actually, time travel was the last. But Veela, even you must be awestruck that, with the zombie, we humans have *created immortality*. The bulk of the work is done—all that remains are the kinks."

"No, Dak, you can't keep this thing and study it. You'll fuck up and it'll get loose."

"*I* will not 'fuck up'!" he said, affronted. "By studying the process of cthuloid fluid generation, I can perfect the serum and

208

live forever, or at least until you and I destroy the universe—and who knows, perhaps I'll even figure out a way to avoid that."

"What are you going to do to cause the cthuloid fluid generation? Feed it the brains of Stone Age people?"

"Well, yes. They certainly are plentiful enough."

"And when are you going to start this brilliant experiment?"

"I have the frame's computer set up to begin right away. I think I may be on the verge of figuring out what the original gengineers did wrong; one cthuloid spurt could be all I need. Of course, it could take a thousand, one never knows."

"Jesus—it wasn't just that you were distracted by building the perimeter wall—you wanted all those people to get zombified, didn't you? So you'd have more subjects!"

"Don't be ridiculous. Though it is true that I judged my priority to be containment. Since, yes, I did know that I would eventually require subjects, anyhow."

"Did you know there was a zombie mouse in the hold? Did you plan for it all starting again, just under more controlled circumstances? You never had any intention of destroying all the zombies, did you? The whole farce of making the contagion look like an accident was only to placate me, to keep me docile, because you need me to translate...."

"Well, actually, I'm perfectly capable of devising translation software that can...."

"*You need me to translate to your test subjects*, so you can manipulate them better! That's the only reason you've been bothering with me at all, was so I could be your fucking kapo!"

"This is a dangerous world, Veela, and our power stores will run out. There's no time to lose in finding a path to immortality."

Veela grabbed the suit, held it as tightly as she could and dug in her heels. The suit continued to walk as if she weren't there at all. The soles of her shoes scraped the rock floor. In her visor she saw they were about to meet the zombie. She screamed in rage.

Dak sighed. "I should have rescued someone else," he said.

"You sure should've, you bastard," she said, and leaped for

his exposed face and chest. The sentacles easily fended her off, picking her up and tossing her into the gloom.

"Veela!" shouted the Jaw, who had been bewildered and terrified by the confrontation between her and Dak. In an instant, he figured out exactly how to use the flashlight—he ran it back and forth, scanning the cave, till he found her prone form on the rock floor—then he kept it trained on her as he ran to her side.

Behind him he heard Chert shout in amazement. Once he'd reached Veela and confirmed she was still alive, he turned to see what was going on. Dak was grappling easily with a no-die. Though the thing writhed and hissed, the new body Dak wore held it with no effort, far enough from Dak's face that the thing could do no harm. That was incredible, but the Jaw turned his attention back to Veela.

She was dazed, but breathing, and stirring. The Jaw lifted her head and rested it upon his knees. "Hush … hush...." he murmured, stroking her hair, keeping one ear out in case that no-die got loose from Dak.

Veela was struggling to say something. Finally, she managed: "Dak—he feeds the brains of your friends to the no-die … he feeds it your friends...."

She had to repeat it again before the Jaw understood. Then he looked back, at Dak and the no-die, and Quarry and Gash-Eye bundled on Dak's back. "Mother!" he roared, and sprang to his feet. "Mother!" he roared again.

Gash-Eye was at the bottom of a shaking dark electric cloud. Though she couldn't be called happy—her delirium was filled with terrors and sickness—she was nevertheless on some level grateful for being warm and at rest.

From somewhere she heard the Jaw screaming "Mother! Mother!," and opened her eyes.

She didn't know where she was. Above her was a white something, a white bundle. Now she remembered having seen

Quarry wrapped up in such a bundle, though she didn't know how Quarry could be floating above her.

Again she heard the Jaw scream. Though she couldn't know it, the Jaw's words were directed to his father: "He's going to give them to the no-die! Quarry and Gash-Eye!"

Quarry.

Dak spent a few moments planning out how he would move things around. Four of his sentacles were focused on keeping the zombie at a safe distance, and four were on the lookout for attacks by the primitives and the linguist. That left only the three already holding her free for picking up the primitive child, lifting her overhead, and feeding her brain to the zombie. He quickly figured out the energy-optimal choreography for those actions.

He scanned through a gamut of readings on the zombie, displayed on his visor. Once he fed the girl's brain to the zombie, he could expect the cthuloid production to generate a huge spike in the zombie's strength and energy. But that shouldn't endanger him; the frame was so incredibly dense and strong that nothing biological could hope to move it, unless it had the body mass of about a dozen elephants—and *nothing* on this world could hope to tear it open. Still, to be safe he increased the power level being diverted to the sentacles holding the zombie.

Less than four feet away the black zombie's wide eyes stared in his direction, blinded by the floodlights; it gnashed and snapped its jaws at Dak's face behind the thin visor, instinctively smelling the skull-muffled song of his brain. Dak eyed the creature impassively—the armor frame protected him more than adequately, and the zombie was merely a natural phenomenon. Or an unnatural one, depending on one's definition.

Using the glance controls, Dak had the sentacles lift the girl and begin unwrapping the thermalblanket. She was on top, so for the first experiment he would use her. Besides, Dak thought he might get richer and more productive results with a Cro-Magnon brain, than with a Neanderthal one.

Gash-Eye heard still more screams, and forced herself to wake up. Or to wake up as much as she could, anyway. Suddenly the bundle above her, the one that she thought was Quarry, was rising. Or she thought it was rising; her vision was funny, it was hard to be sure of anything.

She heard that strange woman who had been with her son try to scream and fail; or maybe she did scream something, and Gash-Eye couldn't understand it.

She felt that the Jaw was somewhere and that he had, somehow, told her that Quarry was going to be fed to one of those things that the strange woman had called no-dies. And there above her the bundle that might be Quarry was being lifted away from her, by something.

Gash-Eye had no strength to move with, but she moved anyway, and quickly. She found herself tied up in some sort of hide, and when she looked down she saw that it was bright white like whatever Quarry was wrapped up in. It was impossible to tear, but Gash-Eye wriggled till she was able to work her arms a bit loose, then thrashed free. It turned out to be one large sheet of skin, or of something.

She threw it off and stood up; she didn't understand that she was on a raised platform, nor did she quite register just how impossibly regular and flat the floor beneath her was. There was a big hard thing right in front of her, and on the other side of it were the weirdly bright, white light sources she was seeing by. Quarry was being lifted up and over the something in front of her by some sort of creatures: snakes made of some sort of opaque crystal, to judge by the way they glinted in the weird light.

With a roar of rage and effort she snatched the Quarry-bundle from the crystal snakes. She didn't have the strength to keep hold of the girl and keep her balance; so all she could do was drop the bundle back the way she'd come, with a silent prayer that it would land safely. Once the bundle was gone she saw that on the other side of the thing she was clambering over was an unkillable.

212

That was the unkillable that was trying to eat Quarry's brain. There was no time to search for a rock, or any weapon at all. With another roar, she threw herself at the creature.

Echoing through the darkness she heard Chert's voice, crying, "Gash-Eye!" Though confused, she still knew she had a fever, and that that voice couldn't be real. Dimly, she thought Chert was an odd choice for the trickster fever spirits to impersonate. But she was too busy to ponder that mystery.

Dak had the terrifying, disorienting impression that things were happening too fast for even the machines to keep up, but of course that was nonsense; he just hadn't properly foreseen what programming would be necessary. That was almost as upsetting, though.

He hadn't foreseen any need to put the sentacles transporting the Cro-Magnon girl on high alert, so he'd decided to conserve a bit of energy there, since so much was being diverted to the sentacles binding the zombie, and those guarding against Veela and the two primitive men. The Neanderthal subject had been able to snatch the Cro-Magnon subject away before Dak could even begin to adjust the settings. He would have to extend the sentacles and have them go retrieve the girl, but for the moment he was still stunned by the next development, the Neanderthal subject's brazen interference with the zombie. For a few seconds he was at a loss as to why the sentacles had let her jump onto the thing, then realized he had set his protective perimeter too close. If the Neanderthal had tried to jump between him and the zombie, the sentacles would have rebuffed her. But hanging off the back of the creature as she was, the sentacles didn't register her as a threat to him. He hadn't programmed them to protect the zombie, as well as himself.

His eyes were involuntarily blinking so rapidly that it interfered with the glance controls. He was about to switch over to the manual console on his arm panel, when a wild scream and a flash of motion on his right distracted him. The second after it was over he realized what had happened—the older primitive male had tried to attack him and been swatted away by a sentacle.

Dak was shaking and breathing fast. It disturbed and confused him that he should be so rattled—after all, he knew perfectly well that he was safe here in the armor.

Regardless of his physical security, he was going to have to neutralize these distractions if he wanted to get any work done. He used the manual arm controls to set all the sentacles to the very highest alert. It took him a few tries, because his fingers were inexplicably shaking.

Gash-Eye hung off the back of the unkillable, her left arm around its neck in a chokehold, her right fist clubbing down upon the crown of its head. Holding it by the neck prevented it from being able to reach her with its biting jaws. She knew that if the crystal snakes stopped holding the unkillable in place, it would easily buck her off and eat her brain. Every time her fist came down on its head she could feel its weak skull give a little, but she soon realized she wasn't going to be able to break the bone with her bare hands. As for the unkillable, it seemed not to notice she was hitting it at all, only to be crazy with hunger for this new food source on its back.

Something flew at them and was knocked away hard by a crystal snake. Gash-Eye wasn't sure, but she thought the thing had looked like Chert. Impossible. She was still delirious.

Whatever it had been, and whether it had been real at all, it startled Gash-Eye so much that she nearly lost her grip on the unkillable's neck. She could feel her mind and her body slipping away. If she was going to destroy this thing, she had better do it right now.

She nearly fell off the thing's back as she changed her grip—now both hands were curved tightly underneath its jaw. She planted the soles of her feet on its back and pushed with them, pulling the head toward her. The unkillable's back arched weirdly and she heard its bones snapping, but the head stayed on, as aggressive as ever.

She remembered how she had torn the head off one of these things before and told herself she could do it again. But that had been an eternity ago, she'd been vastly stronger then. Now she was more likely to tear herself apart than she was the unkillable.

One last supreme effort. She strained back. There were tearing noises, but they sounded strange and she couldn't be sure they were real. Everything was dark. She was falling backwards, but she still had something in her hands—she didn't know if she was falling in the outside world, or falling only in her spirit … or maybe it was both....

Sorry, Hoof....

The Jaw saw Chert leap at the once-tiny man in his shell; the Jaw even heard him scream his mother's name. One of those magic stone vines knocked him aside. Chert went flying, and by the eerie cold light the Jaw saw him land hard on a rock outcropping.

The Jaw was no coward, but he could see he was going to need a weapon. He ran back to where he'd dropped Gash-Eye's pointed stick and retrieved it. Veela was on her hands and knees, and getting to her feet. She was all right. He didn't even have time to be happy about that before spinning around to run back the way he'd come.

As he was running back he saw his mother in the white glare, feet planted upon the zombie's back as she ripped its head off with her bare hands. The sight made him slow down. Then his mother went flying backwards with the head in her hands—she'd been pushing off with her feet, and once the head was detached there was nothing supporting her anymore. She landed with a loud slapping crash on her back, the head rolling out of her hand. The Jaw picked up his pace again.

His first thought was to tend to Gash-Eye, but as he was racing to her side he nearly stepped on the still-chattering head. He stopped and stared down furiously at the repugnant thing. Even in death, or what should have been death, it would have bitten him on the foot and turned him into yet another thing like it. The Jaw raised the stick overhead and drove it into the zombie's skull. It passed through with a popping sound. The Jaw stabbed it again and again, twisting and shaking the stick until finally the head stirred no more.

Then he hurried to Gash-Eye's side and knelt beside her. "Gash-Eye!" he said. "Gash-Eye. Mother."

She didn't answer. Her chest wasn't moving.

The Jaw put his hand under her nose to feel for breath; he put his ear on her naked chest to listen for her heart.

He sat up, tilted back his head, and howled.

Still dazed, Veela was hurrying to the scene of the carnage when she heard an awful noise. That was the Jaw, she realized. He was kneeling over his mother. She must be dead.

It looked like the zombie was more or less dead, too—at least, its severed head lay motionless on the floor, while its twitching body dangled from Dak's sentacles. The body would live on a few hours, but without a mouth to bite with and thus pass on the zombie plague, it should be only minimally dangerous. The worst it might do was kill somebody.

She saw that Chert was lying at a distance from the others, in an odd position. She couldn't tell whether he was still alive or not.

On her way to the Jaw and his mother, she picked up the heaviest stone she could manage. Grunting, she carried it over to the head. It was badly mangled and seemed pretty plainly dead. Nevertheless, Veela dropped the rock on top of it, dancing out of the way of its splatter as best she could.

She went to the Jaw, and could tell by the same signs as he that the woman was dead. She put a light hand on his shoulder, but didn't say anything.

Only then did she turn to Dak. Time to find out why he'd allowed his experiment to go awry, and why he wasn't doing anything now.

Something was clearly wrong. For one thing, it wasn't merely that Dak was doing nothing—his armored frame was completely immobile, and the sentacles were frozen in mid-writhe.

For another, he seemed to be struggling, and even sweating

uncharacteristically, she saw as she cautiously edged closer. His visor was completely clear, there were no readings being displayed on the other side of the transparent panel. He looked at her through it as she approached.

"Okay," she said. "What the fuck, Dak?"

"The math was wrong!" he said. "The equations said there was power to spare, but there wasn't! When I relayed that burst to strengthen the sentacles, more power than necessary must have been expelled. I must have shorted out the frame, or used up all its available power. But I can't be sure, because I can't turn the computer on to check!"

"Dak. Was the math wrong, or were you wrong about the math?"

"All right, I was wrong. Does that satisfy you, to know that I can be wrong as well? But now what are we going to do?!"

Already Veela regretted having been snarky with him, as the full weight of his plight sank in. "Shit, Dak," she said. "How are we going to get you out of that thing?" Never, never, never would they be able to carry it out of the caves, much less cut him out of it even if they did.

Dak said, "You're going to have to go back to the ship. There's still a few portable power packs. Bring one back to replace the one I've used."

"Wait. Did that thing use up a whole power pack today?!"

"There's still plenty of power in the ship itself! It has vast reserves, compared to those portable packs! Anyway, I'll use much less power when I walk out, because I won't need to have the sentacles on as high an alert, now that we've killed the zombie."

We? "Excuse me, Dak, but I am not walking all the way back to the ship and back down into these dark dangerous caves so that you can stroll out in that armored frame. If I get the power pack for you, it'll only be so that we can turn that thing on, order it to open up, get you out, then remove the power pack and abandon this fucking energy-suck."

For a second it looked like he was going to have the gall to argue. But he said, "All right. Fine. Agreed."

But Veela had thought of something obvious. Dak had already proven himself treacherous, to a homicidal degree. Right now, he was helpless. But if they plugged in a new power pack, he would once again become the single most powerful creature on the planet, at least till the new pack wore down, and they would have only his word that he would obediently get out of the frame and turn it off.

But what was the alternative? To leave him here to die of thirst, encased in this tight shell, in the dark once the frame's emergency lights went out in a couple of hours?

She supposed that absent-minded klutziness of his wasn't completely an act, after all. Certainly, he would not have intentionally trapped himself in that thing, just to fool her.

"I just wish I could trust you, Dak," she said.

He stared at her, seeming honestly aggrieved and confused. "What do you mean?" he said. "Of course you can trust me!"

Meanwhile, Chert waited till the Jaw's howling for Gash-Eye subsided. Then, feeling his time was short, he said in a weak voice, "Jaw. My son. Come here."

The Jaw heard. He looked across the short distance at his father. "Come here, my son."

The Jaw relented. As he grew closer, he saw that his father's ribs were plainly broken. Blood trickled from his mouth, and each breath and especially each word was clearly painful. The Jaw knelt beside him to hear what he would say.

With effort, Chert put his hand on the Jaw's arm. "I should have made them give you a proper name," he said.

The Jaw didn't say anything.

"I was wrong about everything," Chert said. He patted the Jaw's arm. "I was wrong about everything." He died.

The Jaw stared down at Chert. His father was dead. The Jaw's breathing came faster and faster. His hand tightened on his mother's sharpened stick.

He stood and turned. "Little man!" he shouted.

The little man was still in his shell. He and Veela were talking about something. They both turned to look when he shouted.

The Jaw walked towards them, with the stick. "Little man, my father owes you a death!"

Veela put herself in front of him. "Wait!...." she said, but he shoved her aside.

He raised the pointed stick. Only now did the little man comprehend, and his eyes widened in terror. The Jaw didn't care—he didn't feel satisfaction, or anything else. He didn't care what the little man felt.

"This is for my father!" he said, and thrust the pointed stick through the opening in the frame and through the little man's throat. He twisted it and listened as the little man's life gurgled and whistled out, then yanked it free again.

Behind him, Veela had given a little cry of shock. Now he turned to face her, defiantly.

She blinked at him a while. Gradually her body relaxed. So maybe it had not been the most civilized solution, she said to herself. But it had probably been the most sensible. Besides, stuff like that happened not infrequently in this world—best to get used to it.

And, of course, it was nothing compared to the horrors she and Dak had brought. So who was she to get high and mighty?

Seventeen

They went back to the ship, Veela, the Jaw, and Quarry. It was parked on the top of the hill, above the cave mouth. They didn't use the ship much—not even the interior lights were left on—Veela figured that if they continued to conserve power this way, the ship might remain functional for a few hundred years. That lifespan would quickly shorten if they took it for a bunch of joyrides.

Usually, only the bare minimum of power needed to operate the code lock was used. Veela taught the Jaw how to tap in the code to open the main hatch. She taught Quarry, too, after debating with herself whether or not the girl was too young to have free access to the ship's interior—there were too many dangerous things roaming this Earth for Veela to deny her such an impregnable shelter. Veela still had no idea that, by her reckoning, the Jaw was only just turning sixteen.

It was almost a week since they'd burned the remains of all the zombie corpses they could find in the caves, and left Dak eternally trapped there in his strange artifact. And left Gash-Eye and Chert, too; at first the Jaw had insisted they take them out, but he couldn't carry them both on his own, and Veela and Quarry could barely help.

Veela had persuaded the Jaw that if they didn't get Quarry out of the caves as soon as possible, she would probably die of a fever. Even so, the Jaw had insisted on digging his parents a shallow grave in a patch of gravel he'd found, barely enough to cover the corpses. They'd been buried together, for the sake of speed and efficiency. Veela had learned enough about their horrific relationship to wonder how they would have felt about that.

Veela stood outside the ship looking out over the little valley. In the distance she could see the white perimeter wall. Eventually they would fly to the other side of it—one quick trip wouldn't dent the reserves too badly.

It was a gorgeous world. A hard and dangerous one, though—Veela planned to introduce agriculture, as well as a few other amenities that would probably blow the Jaw's and Quarry's minds, but she was under no illusions that she was going to get the kind of lifespan she'd always been taught to expect. Then again, it didn't look like she was going to be killed by a zombie, either.

Why wasn't she more freaked out, she wondered? Not so much about the move to a new time—in many ways she preferred this Earth to her old one, and she supposed she liked the Jaw as well as she had liked anyone she'd left behind. More, she wondered why it didn't bother her more that the entire universe was doomed to come to an end the very instant she and Dak jumped back in time. She didn't think it was mere selfishness, a matter of her not caring about a catastrophe so far removed from her in the future, one that wouldn't affect her personally—it wasn't entirely that, anyway. Even if she personally wouldn't have to experience it, she didn't like the idea of all Creation coming to a premature end.

And it wasn't that she didn't believe Dak, even though it did hearten her somewhat that he'd screwed up his math at the end there, and hence must not have been infallible. Even with that, the question still remained: why was there no record of anybody besides themselves traveling back from the future, if there was any more future to travel back from?

Maybe it was partly that she'd grown up thinking of the world as being close to destruction. All her life, since well before the zombie plague, it had been the common consensus that humans were on the verge of making themselves extinct. Maybe living with that notion so long had been good practice for this.

But also, regardless of what her reason told her, she obviously didn't believe in the inevitability of destiny, not deep-down.

Otherwise, never would she have busted her hump trying to wipe out those zombies before they triggered a paleolithic apocalypse; she would have rested secure in the knowledge that the problem would take care of itself, since civilization had to arise so as to one day destroy itself and the universe in her home time.

(For the first time, the uncomfortable idea occurred to her that perhaps the only way to preserve the universe from destruction by herself and Dak would, in fact, have been to let the zombies nip humanity in the bud here and now, and that by preventing that she had set the stage for the catastrophe her escape would one day trigger.)

Anyway—not only had she grown up accustomed to the idea of imminent human extinction, but now, for the first time in her life, she felt like there was something she could do to try to make a difference. Dak had been certain that his equations proved there was no escape, but Veela was teaching Quarry math now as well, and had taught the Jaw all the basics of arithmetic. Tomorrow she would move him on to algebra, and she was also teaching them both to speak and read her language, meaning that soon they could rummage through the ship's library. The memory banks wouldn't last forever, but they could use some power to run off copies of the most important few thousand volumes on nigh-indestructible plastic pages, making books that would survive fires and floods and last millennia. Hopefully she would manage to give physics a forty-five-thousand-year head start, and let her far-distant descendants worry about temporal paradoxes and all that shit.

And she'd leave behind her an account of the zombie plague and how to avoid it. With luck it wouldn't all get distorted into some weird religion.

She heard the Jaw come up behind her—she turned and smiled at him. She'd offered Quarry and the Jaw their own garments of therma-fix fabric, but the Jaw at least seemed not to understand why he wouldn't want to just keep wearing his little strips of hide. That was all he wore now, wrapped around his waist like a loincloth and leaving his torso bare.

They looked out at the view. Veela realized he was actually looking at the perimeter wall, when he said, in her language, "Fly, other side of."

"Think you we should go beyond the barrier?" she verified, in the People's tongue.

He nodded. Sticking to her language, he said, "People, need. Quarry, mate needs."

Veela was about to say that Quarry was still a bit young for that, but then reflected that, here, she probably wasn't. Or soon wouldn't be, at least. Looking out at the enclosed valley again, she said, in her own language, "It's kind of nice, though, not having to worry about people. On the other hand, I've been hearing some mighty big animals roaring out there every once in a while." She glanced over to see how much of that he'd caught. Not all of it, obviously, but she thought he'd gotten the gist. He had a knack for this stuff, just like she did.

"So," she said, still in her own language, "Quarry needs a mate." She turned to face him. "And you? Do you need a mate, too?"

The Jaw grinned and said, in his language, "Maybe I already have one."

He stepped forward, took her in his arms, pressed his mouth to hers and ran his hands over her strange white garb. Kissing him was nicer than she'd feared—she was glad they'd waited, because she'd had time to get used to his breath. She responded, feeling his big strong hairy body under her palms and against her torso, his arms encompassing her, nothing but that little strip of tanned hide between them.

The Jaw put his tongue in her mouth—she didn't mind that. But then her mouth was so full of it she could hardly breathe, and then he physically picked her up, spun her around, and set her down again, and seemed to want to push her onto her knees as he tried to pull her jumpsuit off so he could take her from behind. "Stop," she said, and tried to break free from him. It was like he didn't hear her. She thrashed more violently, and shouted, "Quit it!"

224

He took a step back. Veela stalked a few paces away and turned to glare at him. He looked stricken. "What?" he said, in her language.

"You have pretty high expectations of a first kiss, don't you?"

He screwed his face up in confusion. "What?"

"Don't be such a fucking caveman!"

He had figured out that "fucking" was basically a meaningless word that could be added anywhere, but "caveman" was new. "'Caveman'?" he said. "What is 'caveman'? What did you call me?"

"It means...." Veela paused, feeling silly and embarrassed. "It means, um, someone who lives in a cave."

The Jaw recoiled. "I live outside," he said. As far as he was concerned, he was never stepping foot in a cave again.

"It means, a person from old times."

"But I'm young," he said, and struck his chest with his fist for emphasis.

"Jesus," she said. "Just forget I said it, okay!"

He stared at her, forlorn, at a loss. When she relented enough to return his gaze, she saw that he was teary-eyed.

"You have rules," he said. "I don't know them. Teach me your rules. Your rules for math. And your rules for all things."

She softened, and reached out to him; she put one arm around his huge shoulders, and one hand on his chest. Even as his eyes grew unfocused with desire he watched her attentively, studying her, waiting for cues.

She drew his face down closer at the same time that she raised hers by standing on her tiptoes. "First rule," she breathed, "is take your time. We have time—lots of time...."

THANK YOU FOR READING

If you enjoyed this book, please consider posting a review at Amazon, Goodreads, or any other online forum. And please consider signing up for the mailing list at www.jboyett.net, and buying thousands of copies to distribute to your friends and family.

ALSO FROM SALTIMBANQUE BOOKS:

IRONHEART, by J. Boyett

Part H. P. Lovecraft and part Alien, Ironheart is the story of what happens when the mining ship Canary comes across a strange derelict on the edge of the galaxy—a derelict occupied by a strange woman, a woman who cannot possibly exist but does....

THE LITTLE MERMAID: A HORROR STORY, by J. Boyett

Brenna has an idyllic life with her heroic, dashing, lifeguard boyfriend Mark. She knows it's only natural that other girls should have crushes on the guy. But there's something different about the young girl he's rescued, who seemed to appear in the sea out of nowhere—a young girl with strange powers, and who will stop at nothing to have Mark for herself.

COLD PLATE SPECIAL, by Rob Widdicombe

Jarvis Henders has finally hit the beige bottom of his beige life, his law-school dreams in shambles, and every bar singing to him to end his latest streak of sobriety. Instead of falling back off the wagon, he decides to go take his life back from the child molester who stole it. But his journey through the looking glass turns into an adventure where he's too busy trying to guess what will come at him next, to dwell on the ghosts of his past.

STEWART AND JEAN, by J. Boyett

A blind date between Stewart and Jean explodes into a confrontation from the past when Jean realizes that theirs is not a random meeting at all, but that Stewart is the brother of the man who once tried to rape her. Or is she the woman who murdered his brother? And will anyone ever know?

I'M YOUR MAN, by F. Sykes

It's New York in the 1990's, and every week for years Fred has cruised Port Authority for hustlers, living a double life, dreaming of the one perfect boy that he can really love. When he meets Adam, he wonders if he's found that perfect boy after all ... and even though Adam proves to be very imperfect, and very real, Fred's dream is strengthened to the point that he finds it difficult to awake.

BENJAMIN GOLDEN DEVILHORNS, by Doug Shields

A collection of stories set in a bizarre, almost believable universe: the lord of cockroaches breathes the same air as a genius teenage girl with a thing for criminals, a ruthless meat tycoon who hasn't figured out that secret gay affairs are best conducted out of town, and a telepathic bowling ball. Yes, the bowling ball breathes.

RICKY, by J. Boyett

Ricky's hoping to begin a new life upon his release from prison; but on his second day out, someone murders his sister. Determined to find her killer, but with no idea how to go about it, Ricky follows a dangerous path, led by clues that may only be in his mind.

BROTHEL, by J. Boyett

What to do for kicks if you live in a sleepy college town, and all you need to pass your courses is basic literacy? Well, you could keep up with all the popular TV shows. Or see how much alcohol you can drink without dying. Or spice things up with the occasional hump behind the bushes. And if that's not enough you could start a business....

THE VICTIM (AND OTHER SHORT PLAYS), by J. Boyett

In *The Victim,* April wants Grace to help her prosecute the guys who raped them years before. The only problem is, Grace doesn't remember things that way.... Also included:

A young man picks up a strange woman in a bar, only to realize she's no stranger after all;

An uptight socialite learns some outrageous truths about her family;

A sister stumbles upon her brother's bizarre sexual rite;

A first date ends in grotesque revelations;

A love potion proves all too effective;

A lesbian wedding is complicated when it turns out one bride's brother used to date the other bride.

ABOUT THE AUTHOR

J. Boyett can be reached at jboyettjboyett@gmail.com, unless you are reading this many years after we went to print and no one uses Gmail anymore, and/or unless J. Boyett has died.

Please check out J. Boyett's films, books, and plays at www.jboyett.net, and sign up for the mailing list.

Made in the USA
Columbia, SC
07 September 2021